Seduced BY EDEN

INTERNATIONAL BESTSELLING AUTHOR

JADE MAY

SEDUCED BY

EDEN

MEMBERS ONLY

ISBN: 978-1-7635917-2-1

Formatting and Chapter Art: Katelyn at Design by Kage
Cover Art: Katelyn at Design by Kage
Editing: Deep Roots Editing, Spice Me Up Editing and Penny Carroll
Proofreading: Stacey's Bookcorner Editing

To those who have bloomed after leaving a toxic friendship.

I see you.

You don't belong in someone else's shadow.

Dear reader,

Thank you so much for choosing my book to read. I hope you enjoy it.

Seduced by Eden is the second book in the *Eden* series, a collection of interconnected standalones. Please be aware that it contains mature and graphic scenes, along with language that is suitable for those who are 18+. It also contains scenes that may be triggering to some readers, including; sick family member, attempted sexual assault (not by MMC), toxic mother, light BDSM, spanking, bondage and blackmail.

Much love,

Jade xx

CHAPTER ONE

Hailee

Heavy rain pounds against the metal roof of the taxi, creating a deafening roar that echoes the nervous anticipation thumping in my chest. I swipe my palm across the fogged cab window and peer out at my destination: Madison Avenue hot spot The Drawing Room. It's not just any restaurant—it's one of the most exclusive dining rooms in New York, known as much for its elite clientele as its innovative menu. No wonder my mother chose this place. It's the kind of restaurant where every detail is meticulously curated, much like the facade she works hard to maintain.

Exhaling loudly, I close my eyes for a moment and remind myself why I'm here. Why I flew more than twenty hours to have dinner with my mother.

For my sister, Beth.

Suck it up, you can do this.

Asking my mother for a favor shouldn't be this hard. Under normal circumstances, it wouldn't seem like a huge ask. What mother wouldn't want to do everything in her power to help save her daughter? To extend her life by giving her the operation she desperately needs?

It's been ten years since I last saw her, and even that doesn't feel like long enough. The memory of our last encounter still stings, and the thought of facing her again makes my stomach twist. As much as I've tried to distance myself from her toxic presence, life has pulled me back into her orbit, and I'm dreading every second of it.

I'd rather stick needles in my eyes than ask my mother for anything. But I will endure this conversation and swallow my pride a thousand times for Beth. I would do anything for her.

I tug down the hem of my red dress with clammy hands, my nerves making the fabric feel tighter than it is. Pulling out my compact mirror, I carefully reapply my scarlet lipstick, knowing she will have something to say about my appearance. She always does. I snap the mirror shut, the sound piercing in the cab.

"Are you going in, miss?" The taxi driver's voice startles me and I catch his eyes in the rearview mirror.

"Yes, thank you," I reply with a forced smile.

I pay him, adding a generous tip for making him wait, and thrust open the car door. Flipping my coat over my head, I step out into the pouring rain and dash toward the restaurant.

I'm not leaving until I secure Beth a new heart. Failure is not an option.

Let's fucking go.

CHAPTER TWO

Dameon

T hick, dark lashes flutter against my face as Rachael pecks my cheek, and I suppress a shudder. I've never understood why women feel compelled to stick those fake lashes to their eyelids. They're a huge pain. They fall off at the most inconvenient times, and they end up everywhere—on my pillow, in my sheets. I even peeled one off my balls once. I wouldn't be surprised if the women who wear them become airborne when caught in a strong gust of wind. I can almost hear a cartoonish swoosh in my head whenever they blink.

"I'm so glad you called," Rachael coos, batting those ridiculously long eyelashes as she slides into the seat opposite me.

"Me too." I fake a smile.

My gaze drifts out the restaurant window as rain pelts the sidewalk. It's an unseasonably wet night for August in Manhattan. People dash through the downpour, clutching their raincoats and umbrellas, struggling to stay dry. The rain hasn't let up in twelve hours, yet nothing brings this city to a standstill. Not even torrential rain. It's the city that never sleeps for a reason.

The sound of Rachael's voice snaps me out of my thoughts, invading my brain like a knife piercing my skull.

"I've been waiting for you to reach out. I knew we would get back together eventually." She places her hand on top of mine.

Fuck's sake.

This woman is delusional if she thinks we're getting back together. Calling her an ex is a stretch and laughable at best. A total of five dates almost eighteen months ago barely counts as dating. It was five nights of mediocre, vanilla sex, nothing more, nothing less. As soon as I realized she was becoming a stage-five clinger, I ended it. I bluntly informed her I wasn't interested and moved on. Considering she's been low-level stalking my ass ever since, the message wasn't received.

The barrage of text messages, emails and phone calls, along with her suddenly appearing at events I was attending, were all red flags of her growing obsession. I should have put a stop to it as soon as I realized what was happening, but her contact wasn't consistent enough to make me feel concerned. It was more annoying than anything else, like a mosquito buzzing around my head in the dead of night. I ignored her futile attempts at getting in touch, thinking she would eventually get the hint. Obviously not.

It's time to put an end to it, once and for all. I slide my hand out from under hers and meet her gaze. I can see in her eyes that she knows what's coming. In an attempt to delay the inevitable, she dives into a spiel about some high-society gossip.

Like I give a fuck.

Expelling a deep breath, I redirect my gaze to the window. Her relentless monologue is testing my patience. At this point, I'm not even registering her words. She can't possibly like me for who I am; she doesn't even know me. That's what pisses me off the most. It's my name and money she's after. A wealthy socialite in search of a perfect marriage match with a billionaire media mogul. Marrying for status and power is her sole purpose in life. I need to be more careful where I stick my dick in future.

Running a frustrated hand down my face, I swirl the scotch in my glass, ready for this dinner to be over. "Listen, Rachael, we need to talk," I say, interrupting her incessant chatter.

A flash of red outside the window catches my eye, momentarily halting my words. A blonde woman in a red dress is stepping out from the backseat of a cab parked in front of the restaurant. With her coat pulled over her head to shield her from the rain, she dashes toward the entrance, bypassing the flustered doorman who was on his way to greet her with an umbrella. The door swings open, and in walks *her*.

She peels off her coat, revealing her face and those captivating green eyes that I know all too well. I draw in a quiet breath. She looks incredible in red; it suits her perfectly. Her flawless, tanned skin glows, and her stilettos make her legs seem impossibly long. It hits me that until now, I've only ever seen her barefoot and naked, or in a simple black gown. I'm well acquainted with what lies beneath that snug dress, and so is my cock.

I resist the urge to adjust myself under the table as she smooths down her skirt and finger-combs her long, white-blonde hair, following the hostess to her table. Her dinner companion hasn't arrived yet, and as she takes her seat, she subtly scopes out the restaurant.

The second her bright emerald eyes lock with mine, they go round in recognition. Her tongue slips out, moistening her sultry red lips. Inwardly I groan, thinking about what that talented tongue can do. Her body was made to serve and be worshipped in return. I can't help but smirk as our last encounter at Eden flashes through my mind.

Her glassy eyes shine bright as she looks up at me from beneath her lashes, pink-stained lips stretched wide around my dick. She's an absolute goddess when she's on her knees for me. I fist her hair firmly and pull her off with a pop. A string of saliva from her lips connects her to my cock.

"God, you take me so well." I gaze down at her adoringly with my grip still firm on her hair, tilting her head back. "You want more?"

She mewls and nods as much as my hold will allow. As soon as I release her, she sucks me down her throat like her life depends on it. A few rough thrusts later, I explode so hard that my vision blurs around the edges. She swallows everything I give her, and as soon as she's finished licking me clean, I lift her up by her arms and lay her face down over my lap. She's got an ass begging to be spanked—soft and round yet toned, and perfect for my palm.

"You ready to come, goddess?"

"Yes, sir."

I restrain her wrists in the center of her lower back, so she won't hurt herself if she moves. I know she won't, though. She's my good little kitten who craves the touch of my firm hand. I bring my palm down hard across her ass, alternating between her cheeks. When a nice red glow has started to appear, I softly caress and massage each one, enjoying the warmth seeping into her skin. I spread her legs slightly and the aroma of her arousal instantly fills the air. Breathing her in, I slide my fingers between her hot slippery folds and softly circle her clit. And when I give it a slight tap, she gasps in pleasurable pain.

"Come for me."

My hand comes down harder than before on her left cheek while simultaneously pinching her clit, and she comes upon impact.

She cries out, thrashing in my hold, riding out her orgasm while I stroke her through it. Once she's stopped writhing, laying limp across my lap, I smooth back her hair and continue to pet her while she enjoys the aftershocks.

"Such a good girl."

"Dameon!" Rachael's screech interrupts my hot-as-fuck memory, causing my lip to curl in annoyance. Her voice instantly softens my cock, like stepping into an ice bath. I allow my eyes to linger on my goddess for a beat longer, dipping my head slightly in acknowledgment. It's barely perceptible, but the last thing I need is to draw Rachael's attention to her and cause a scene. Reluctantly, I drag my eyes back to my date.

Time to get this over with.

CHAPTER THREE

Hailee

My mind is a jumbled mess of swirling thoughts when I step inside the restaurant. The three-Michelin-starred establishment is housed in a beautiful art deco building, its opulence impossible to ignore. I'm absorbing the sheer beauty of the décor when a pair of striking sea-green eyes catch mine. Sitting at one of the tables near the French-style windows is *him*. Of all the places in the world, he has to be *here*. At this very restaurant, at this very moment.

Fuck my life.

It's obvious he finds this chance encounter amusing. His eyes briefly glitter with affection, yet they still hold that conceited edge. And that smirk—holy smokes, that dirty smirk that makes his dimples pop—could make even a nun blush. His gaze roves over my face before dipping to my chest, an intimate appraisal that makes my body hum with recognition. His eyes are mesmerizing, and I could get lost in them for hours. There's no denying the man is drop-dead gorgeous. Every time we've been together at Eden, the chemistry has been intoxicating.

The other goddesses are always insanely jealous when he selects me. He's clearly the standout of Eden's clientele—tall, with broad shoulders, a trim waist, and sculpted abs that lead into a delicious V-line. I'm surprised a fight hasn't broken out over him. Usually he's in a tailored suit, but tonight, from what I can tell, his jeans sit low on his hips and a tight black T-shirt conceals those lickable abs.

I wonder if his date knows about the V-line that leads to absolute heaven.

She's a stunning brunette with curves in all the right places, a stark contrast to my slim and petite frame.

Or is she his wife?

I resist the urge to glance at them again but fail miserably. With nothing else to keep my attention while I wait for my mother to arrive, my eyes are repeatedly drawn to them. Their conversation looks tense, and he visibly stiffens when she places her hand on his arm. Maybe they're just another rich couple who hate each other. Doesn't matter, I shouldn't care anyway. He barely acknowledged me after giving me the once-over. Given our scorching-hot encounters, a smile or even a small wave would have been nice. I'm sure nobody wants to run into their escort in public but it's not like I'm going to walk up to his companion and say, *Hey there, did you know he pays me to kneel at his feet before he fucks my brains out? That I love it when he spanks me?* I pull my phone from my purse to avoid staring at them like a creep. Their relationship is none of my business.

Mindlessly, I scroll through social media while I wait. A smile dances on my lips as I come across a picture of Beth, who's just posted a selfie with the caption, *Missing my sis xx*. She's making a sad pout face, with her index finger trailing down her cheek as if indicating a rolling tear. She looks tired; her cheeks have lost their color, and her eyes seem dull. I hope she's looking after herself while I'm away. Leaving my sister on her own makes me uncomfortable. At sixteen she's capable of taking care of herself for a few days, but still, I worry, especially with her condition. I've been her guardian since she was six years old, and it hasn't been easy to walk that fine line between parent and sister, especially considering I was barely an adult myself when I took her under my wing and moved to Australia.

God, I miss her so much.

The sooner I leave New York and get back home to Sydney, the better. I comment on her post, *Miss you too, poo brain x*. My sister and I are the epitome of maturity and sophistication.

I close the app, check the time on my phone and slip it back into my purse. She's late.

Anxiety and frustration simmer through my veins. *Of course she's making me wait.*

My mother and stepfather are part of the wealthy and powerful New York elite. With their influence alone, they have the power to move Beth to the top of any heart transplant list in the world. Yet every request or favor comes at a cost with them. The only question is how much.

My mother is still beautiful at fifty-five. Tall, British, and blonde, she commands attention wherever she goes. Her flawless look, meticulously crafted by her plastic surgeon, is the main weapon in her arsenal. Over the years, she's undergone at least fifteen surgeries, from nose jobs to breast implants to a designer vagina. I remember her eagerly showing me pictures of her new vagina, saying, "Darling, when you get to my age, your pussy will get loose and saggy too. No man will want you then." However, her smooth, manufactured body conceals a rotten core. Everything she says and does is driven by ulterior motives. She relishes playing the role of the dumb, insecure blonde, projecting an image of innocence, but it's all fabricated. A master manipulator, she demands constant attention and praise, exploiting men and friends alike in her ascent through society, often crushing their souls in the process.

When she hooked up with Mark, I took off with Beth to Australia. I had just turned eighteen and couldn't bear to endure her toxic behavior any longer, fearing it would crush my soul too and corrupt my little sister. Beth was still so young and impressionable; she needed a mother who would prioritize her wellbeing. So, I gathered what little money I had saved, and we left to start our own lives as far from Mother's chaos and drama as we could get. Her parting words, "If you think you can do better, be my guest," were the last I heard from her when she signed over Beth's guardianship. She didn't care that we had left; she was still engulfed in her new romance. In the ten years since, she's never made contact, not even a single text to check in on us. To be fair, neither did we. I wanted a fresh start for us.

So I'm not entirely surprised to see Mark, my stepfather, enter the restaurant alone. I was expecting Mother to waltz through the door in one of her obscenely revealing dresses, her ridiculously huge breasts on show. I should have known that she would send him instead.

He's rather attractive for an older gentleman. He's wearing his trademark gray three-piece suit with a black tie. Come to think of it, I don't think I've seen him wear anything else. Not that we've spent a lot of time together. His salt-and-pepper hair has become more salt than pepper over the years, but it adds to his distinguished look. And his stomach is slightly rounder than the last time I saw him. He catches my eye and nods in greeting before confidently striding to my table, bypassing the hostess.

"Hailee. Good to see you. How are you doing, honey?" He gives me a quick kiss on my cheek and settles into the seat across from me. My nose involuntarily scrunches at his condescending pet name, but I quickly recover before he notices.

"Where's Liz?" I refuse to refer to her as Mom. She doesn't deserve that title.

"Elizabeth is in Monaco with her friends."

I snort, unable to hold back my disbelief. Her daughter reaches out to her for help after ten years, and she can't be bothered to show up. *Typical.*

Mark shoots me a look as he halts the passing waitress to order a scotch on the rocks.

"Sorry. I was expecting to see her since, you know, it's been ten years and all." I resist the urge to roll my eyes. "How have you been?"

From what I've heard, he's no fool. Match made in heaven with my mother, it would seem. He's vicious in business and ruthless in high society. Powerful men like Mark don't like to hear the word "no" in any capacity. They always get what they want, which makes me even more nervous to be sitting here with him. Despite my mother's shortcomings, I can handle her. I know her and her manipulative ways. With Mark, I'm flying blind. I wipe my sweaty hands on my napkin in my lap.

"We're well, thank you. Your mother and I were surprised to get your call. To be honest, we thought you'd never come back."

"Oh, umm... We're not coming back..." I fidget with my napkin under the table and take a deep breath. "Beth needs a heart transplant, and we need your help in moving her up the transplant list. Her heart has deteriorated badly, she basically has no quality of life. That's why I reached out to Liz, to see if she—or you—you both—would be willing to assist."

I'm stumbling over my words, thrown by Mark's presence when I had planned for Mother. They have enough money and power to solve world hunger; a phone call to the transplant board is not exactly a big ask. But Mark's expression remains blank, devoid of sympathy.

"I know why you're here, Hailee. I'm well aware of everything about your lives in Australia. Did you honestly think I wouldn't keep tabs on my wife's kids?" My eyes momentarily widen in surprise. He scoffs. "You're naïve if you thought I wouldn't watch over you. Knowledge is power."

I swallow roughly. Maybe I *am* naïve to think my mother would let us walk out of her life, no strings attached. It never crossed my mind that we were being followed or monitored. However, I'm not so naïve to think he'd make that phone call to the transplant board out of the kindness of his heart. Everything has a price.

"How's Eden treating you?"

I freeze, his sly smile sending a shiver of revulsion down my spine. I swallow back the bile threatening to rise in my throat. Since he's brought it up, there's no need to beat around the bush. So, I bluntly ask the question we've been dancing around.

"What do you want in exchange for the call, Mark?"

If there's one thing I've learned at Eden, it's men. It's opened my eyes to the desires and whims of the rich and powerful. When you have everything you could possibly desire at the snap of your fingers, including women, life becomes predictable and boring. It's all about upping the ante—what more can you risk to chase that sweet release of dopamine and endorphins? It all circles back to sex eventually. So I'm not surprised by the direction this conversation is taking. The notion of "once a whore, always a whore" is difficult to shake in the eyes of men.

I take a deep breath and compose my features into a nonchalant expression, preparing for his inevitable response. Regardless of his demand, I refuse to let him see my discomfort or disgust.

His lips form a shrewd smile. "I assure you, it's not what you're imagining. Well, not exactly." He tilts his head, considering his next words carefully. "You're aware that your mother and I didn't have any children together, and I don't have any offspring from my previous marriages. When the time comes for me to retire, I want to ensure that my empire and considerable wealth are carried forward through the generations. I want to leave a legacy. I want an heir."

Oh God, fuck no!

I suppress the urge to gag. He must notice the queasy look on my face.

"For Christ's sake, not me!" He shakes his head, pinching the bridge of his nose. He has the decency to look a little green at the thought. "Both of you must return to New York and rejoin our family. Then, you'll settle down, marry and start a family of your own. But you'll marry someone of my choosing, someone from a prestigious family. I'll ensure Beth gets her new heart, but in exchange, I want you to marry and provide me with a grandchild."

My relief is short-lived. I'm grateful he's not asking me to reproduce *with* him. But an arranged marriage?

"Do I get any say in who you choose?"

"I will select the best possible candidate for you. I know what it takes to run an empire and the business acumen necessary to pass on to your child."

"But Beth doesn't have the luxury of time; she needs the surgery now."

"Beth can have her surgery as soon as a match becomes available. The only stipulation is that you're married within the next twelve months and actively trying to conceive. But don't even think about fucking me over on this, Hailee. If I even get the slightest hint that you're trying to worm your way out of it, you'll regret it. And I'll ensure Beth suffers the consequences." The cruel twist of his lips slices into my chest, stealing my breath.

I lift the glass of water to my dry lips, swallowing the cool liquid to calm my nerves and curb the fear pulsing through my body. Even if I end up with some asshole for a husband, I can play the part of a wife. Sacrificing my own happiness for Beth's sake is a no-brainer. I have no hesitation in agreeing to the marriage. Beth's life is worth it. But deliberately bringing another life into this twisted, transactional agreement warrants more consideration than I can give at this moment.

"I'm not asking you to do anything different to what you're already doing at Eden. You sell your body to multiple men for short periods of time. I'm asking you to be with one man for an extended period."

And there it is: once a whore, always a whore.

"You know this is insane, right? I'm not cattle to be fucking sold and bred!" I exclaim, my voice thick with fury as my body trembles with anger.

Mark rises from the table abruptly, buttoning his suit jacket.

"That's fine, Hailee. I'm not forcing you; I'm only offering you a chance to give Beth her life back."

"Wait... please, just... wait," I plead, rubbing my forehead.

He slowly sits back down. I take a few deep, cleansing breaths to calm my racing heart.

"I don't suppose you'd do this out of the kindness of your heart, you know, because Beth is your stepdaughter and all?" I ask, my tone dripping with sarcasm. Deep down, I already know the answer.

I sigh in resignation. "I need time to think about it."

"Of course, take the time you need. But don't take too long. Beth is relying on you."

It's a low blow, and he knows it. He's got me exactly where he wants me. I came here tonight to see my mother, and now I'm leaving contemplating *becoming* a mother.

What a prick.

"I've already got interviews lined up this week for potential suitors," Mark says, his tone brisk. "Let me know by tomorrow if I should cancel them. Do you still have my number?"

I nod numbly.

"Great. Let me know your decision in the morning."

He sighs at my lack of response and covers my sweaty hand with his dry palm. "I'm not your enemy, Hailee. Trust me to choose someone suitable. I'm not sentencing you to a life of misery. Your mother and I only want what's best for you and Beth. We want you back in our lives."

Yeah, right.

My mother couldn't be bothered to be here with her husband to ambush me. Apparently, drastically altering the course of my life isn't significant enough to warrant postponing her holiday. Sunning herself in Monaco is obviously more important. And wanting what's best for us? Please. Leveraging Beth's life is a messed-up way of showing it.

"I'll let you know."

Mark stands and tosses a couple of notes onto the table to cover his drink. "I'll await your call, honey." I glare at him, not bothering to hide my revulsion at the name this time. He leans down to kiss my cheek and stalks out of the restaurant with the same easy confidence he entered with, knowing I'll agree to his terms.

I pull out my phone and order a rideshare. The bottle of wine in my hotel's minibar is calling my name. When you're contemplating a decision as monumental as this, copious amounts of alcohol are necessary.

Chapter Four

Hailee

Drip. Drip. Drip.

Slow, steady, and hypnotic, each droplet falls from the faucet to the same leisurely rhythm. Sinking deeper beneath the bath water, I plug the leak with the tip of my freshly painted pink toenail, breaking the trance.

The heat of the water seeps into my cold bones and relaxes my muscles. I've always preferred my baths scalding hot. The hotter, the better. If I can't feel the prickle of burn against my skin, it's not hot enough. As I sip from my nearly empty wine glass, my eyes begin to droop. I don't know why wine makes me so tired, but it does—especially on an empty stomach. Such a shame I didn't get to eat anything tonight. What a waste of a nice restaurant.

I raise the glass to my lips once more and sigh. The idea of switching to vodka flits through my sleepy mind, but the minibar is too far away, and I'm too comfortable in this warm cocoon.

The sudden jarring vibration of my phone against the tiled floor jolts me wide awake. I stretch my arm over the edge of the tub to reach it; the glowing screen displays Beth's name. My wet thumb swipes across the screen, but it refuses to unlock. With a determined sigh, I carefully rise from the water, my legs unsteady beneath me as I lean over to snatch the towel from the wall rack. It's a bit far, and I have to juggle my wine in the same hand as my phone, but damn it, I will reach it. I know I should get out of the bath or put my wine glass down at the very least, but being the stubborn and lazy bitch that I am, I place my foot on the edge of the tub so I can lean over further. I have the towel in my fingers when my foot abruptly slips off the bath ledge. I fall hard back into the bath, arms up to protect my precious cargo, making the water splash over the edge and flooding the floor in the process. Pain shoots through my side as the edge of the bath jabs into my ribs.

Ouch, fuck!

Gasping for air, I drop the towel to the floor and clutch at my aching ribs with my spare hand, struggling to draw in a breath as waves of pain radiate through my body. I think I've been winded, though I'm not entirely sure. This is probably something sports people would know. But I'm no athlete, far from it. In fact, the last time I set foot in a gym was back in high school. I lift my arm and check for damage, wincing as I touch the tender, red skin across my ribs.

Shit, that's going to bruise nicely.

Hopefully I didn't break anything. One of these days my laziness will get me killed. I sink into the warm water once again, this time swiping my phone with my dry hand. Success!

Beth

How'd it go? x

As I'm typing back, a series of texts from Beth flood the screen.

Maybe I should have come with you.

You shouldn't have gone alone.

If Mom says no, it's not the end of the world. We'll find another way.

I don't want you to feel responsible. I love you, and we'll get through this together like we always have.

Beth's always been the type to communicate in rapid-fire bursts rather than craft a single cohesive message. A lump forms in my throat at her last text. When did she become so mature, so wise beyond her years?

She's wrong, though: I am responsible. After all, I was the one who took her out of that toxic environment. Since then, she's been my sole focus—my responsibility to protect, to nurture, to provide for. This is my problem to solve, my cross to bear.

Baths have always been my sanctuary, my favorite place to think. There's something about the warm embrace of the water that relaxes my mind, allowing ideas to bubble to the surface, so I can problem-solve my life as though it's a mathematical equation. If I put my mind to it, I reckon I could work out the scientific calculation for time travel in a bath. My lip twitches at the ridiculous thought.

Okay, time to lay off the wine.

I lean back and methodically sift through my options, dissecting each possibility with the precision of a seasoned analyst. My accounting degree may have instilled in me the skill to make calculated decisions, but it's my ability to detach from emotions that proves invaluable in moments like these. In my experience, making emotional decisions nearly always ends in disaster. Approaching Liz for help was my final resort. Now that line has been crossed, it's a matter of making the deal more favorable.

I mentally compile a list of non-negotiables. Moving back to New York to be part of my mother's life again is a hard no. I didn't uproot my life at eighteen and whisk my sister away only to end up back where I started. Beth's wellbeing is my number one priority. At sixteen she's still impressionable, and still grappling with the trauma of her congenital heart condition. The last thing she needs is a narcissistic and manipulative mother in her life.

Could I marry a stranger, someone not of my choosing? Could I let him touch me, fuck me? For Beth, absolutely. I never had any intentions of marrying anyway. A traditional marriage and kids have never been a dream of mine, so it's no hardship to give that up.

Do I want to be a mom? I realize that I've never really considered whether it's something I desire for myself. It was a role I took on from a young age, one that I embraced without question. Raising Beth was not a conscious decision; it was simply what needed to be done. And yet, Beth turned out to be a decent human being—more than decent. She is kind-hearted, compassionate, intelligent, honest, loyal, and overall, a kick-ass girl. I could do it again. I would embrace any child that came into my life with open arms and an open heart. Even if the sperm donor turned out to be an asshole, I would raise the child on my own, just like I did with Beth.

Is bringing a life into this world to save another ethical? I don't know. But what I do know is that I would love this child fiercely and I would do everything in my power to protect them.

As I steel myself to broach the subject with Mark, I compile a list of stipulations to discuss. Then I finish off my text to Beth.

Me

All sorted. You'll be running marathons in no time ;) x

29

When I peel my eyes open the next morning, my mouth resembles the Sahara Desert and my head pounds relentlessly.

God, wine sucks balls.

With a moan, I roll over, relieved to see I had the foresight to place a bottle of water on the nightstand alongside a couple of painkillers. I pop them in my mouth and gulp down half the water, soothing my parched throat. Picking up my phone, I see it's close to midday, which would explain the bright sun streaming through the cracks of the blinds. A text from my stepfather is already waiting for me.

I groan and swipe it open.

Mark

Call me when you get this.

With a deep breath, I dial the number I haven't dared to call in ten long years. Each digit feels heavy as I press it, a silent countdown to the moment when the trajectory of my life will be irrevocably altered.

He answers on the first ring. "About time you called."

"What's the rush? I said I would call when I had made my decision." My voice is hoarse from sleep.

"There's a charity gala tonight that I want you to attend as my plus one, since your mother isn't here. There will be lots of wealthy men in the room, many potential candidates. I have two men in particular I want to introduce you to, and tonight is the perfect opportunity to show you off."

Great, like a prized cow on the auction block.

"I'm sending you a gown. Please wear it, Hailee."

I can't help but grin. He knows I would show up in my flannel pajamas just to piss him off.

"I haven't agreed yet. I have stipulations to our agreement." I let out a rushed exhale.

"We can discuss it tonight. I'm not an unreasonable man, honey."

I cringe again at that dreadful name. But I know better than to believe in his apparent willingness to bend the rules. Let's see how "reasonable" he is once he hears my terms.

"Do you need someone to do your makeup and whatever else?"

I sigh. "I've got it covered."

"I'll send a car at eight. Text me the address."

"Fine," I mutter and disconnect the call. Flopping back onto the pillows, I close my eyes and contemplate the night ahead.

A loud, insistent pounding on my door startles me. Or is that in my head? The knocking grows louder and more aggressive, each rap echoing through my room.

No, not in my head then.

I stagger toward the door on heavy legs and wipe the sleep from my eyes. What time is it? What day is it?

Jesus, that nap fucked me up.

Whoever is on the other side seriously needs to chill. With a swift motion, I swing the door open to a bellhop holding a large black garment bag and two boxes tightly under his arm, clearly unimpressed. My lips curl up into a saccharine smile. Nothing pisses off angry people more than being extra kind. "Can I help you?" I ask sweetly.

"Miss, I've been knocking on your door for the past five minutes. You have an urgent delivery."

"Apologies, I was in the bathroom. Please do come in." I realize too late that he now thinks I have a serious case of diarrhea. I hold the door open wide, allowing him to pass with a huff. He places the garment bag on my bed and the boxes on the small table, his annoyance palpable.

Catching sight of myself in the mirror, I stifle a laugh. It's painfully obvious that I wasn't in the bathroom—crease lines from the pillow are still etched into my face and my hair is a tangled mess.

"Thank you, and apologies for keeping you waiting once again." I hand him a generous tip. He inclines his head in thanks and strides out of my room.

That guy is loving life.

With a curious gaze, I fix my attention on the garment bag and boxes, anticipation fluttering in my chest. My teeth sink into my lower lip as I wonder what my stepfather has selected for me—or more accurately, what his assistant has chosen on his behalf.

Opening the boxes first, a sense of relief washes over me as I find a pair of shoes and a matching handbag. At least he remembered the essentials. As I delicately unwrap the tissue paper surrounding the shoes, my breath catches in my throat. They're nothing short of breathtaking—crystal-covered pointy-toe pumps with a four-inch heel from Jimmy Choo. I've had my eye on these bad boys for a while. With trembling fingers, I run my hand over the sparkling crystals, marveling at their exquisite beauty. It's the quintessential Cinderella slipper, fit for a princess. And if memory serves me right, the crystals are none other than Swarovski. With bated breath, I flip over the heel to check the size. *Perfect.* I let out a girly squeal. The small clutch matches the shoes, and I think I've died and gone to fashion heaven.

I eagerly unzip the garment bag and pull out a floor-length white gown, the silky fabric shimmering in the light. At first glance, it's beautiful, but as I hold it up, a sinking feeling settles in the pit of my stomach. With a low-cut neckline and backless design, this gown is designed to showcase every curve and contour of my body. I'm going to be on show tonight, just as I feared.

CHAPTER FIVE

Hailee

"**C**an you please stop fidgeting? You look beautiful, honey," Mark whispers in my ear. *Yuck.* Suppressing a shudder, I discreetly adjust the bodice of my dress once again, attempting to cover more of my cleavage.

"You couldn't have picked a black dress, could you?" I retort, rolling my eyes. Glancing around the ballroom, all the other women are dressed in elegant black gowns, while the men are in sharp tuxedos—my stepfather included. Evidently there's a dress code, a fact that Mark was well aware of when he sent me a *white* dress. I stand out, well, to be blunt, like a dog's balls. His disapproving gaze flickers to me before he shakes hands with a passing gentleman. My arm is looped through his elbow, and I'm thankful the champagne has been freely flowing as he leads me around the gala. The air is heavy with expensive perfumes and colognes, and the ballroom is alive with the sounds of soft music and lively chatter. Small tables are draped in crisp white linen and adorned with elaborate floral arrangements. Above, soaring stained-glass domes add a dramatic flair, while chandeliers twinkle like stars in the night sky. In my revealing white dress I feel even more like an outsider in this world of wealth and privilege.

As Mark weaves through the crowded ballroom, it becomes abundantly obvious that he's a man in demand. Every few steps, he stops to introduce me to yet another person, each interaction accompanied by a flurry of handshakes, nods, and polite smiles. People clamor for a slice of his time, eager to be noticed and acknowledged. We've only been here thirty minutes, and I'm already over this pony show.

"This dress is more my mother's style than mine," I grumble under my breath.

"Stop your pouting and smile," he chides. "Men want to see what they're getting before committing. Try before you buy, if you will." He smiles as if the most sexist words didn't just roll off his tongue. My lips purse and I swallow a harsh retort. *Whatever*. I'm used to being objectified at Eden. This is no different. Instead of being on stage naked and kneeling with my head bowed, I'm parading around in a dress that leaves little to the imagination. Actually, I would prefer to be naked at Eden, where I'm the one in control, comfortable in my own skin as I perform on stage. There, I am empowered, confident in my ability to command attention. But here, in this gilded ballroom, the control firmly rests in the palm of my stepfather's hand. I am little more than a pawn in his game, forced to play by his rules and conform to his expectations.

"I want to talk about my conditions." I come to an abrupt halt, unhooking my arm from his.

He nods, scanning the bustling ballroom for a quiet spot to talk. Lightly grasping my elbow, he steers me toward the edge of the room.

"Of course, honey, please proceed."

"First, we will not be moving back to New York. I will live wherever my husband wants to live, and Beth will stay with me. That is not negotiable." My gaze locks onto his, unwavering and self-assured. Silence stretches between us for a few tense moments as I hold his stare, refusing to yield to his attempt at intimidation. His eyes bore into mine, a silent challenge hanging in the air. Just as my false bravado starts to crumble, he presses his lips together in a firm line, conceding. It's a small victory, but I'll take it.

"Fine. Your next condition?"

I clear my throat. "After I have a child, I reserve the right to leave and divorce the father if I wish. I will not be stuck in a marriage with an abusive asshole and put my child at risk."

He shakes his head. "No. Divorce will not be an option within the first ten years. This will be written into the contract with your prospective husband and something that I have no doubt he will insist upon. It's to protect him, so you don't get knocked up and do a runner." He crosses his arms over his chest and scowls. He knows that's exactly what I would have done.

Ten years feels like an eternity, but I can sense from the resolve in his eyes that there's no room for negotiation on this point.

I swallow roughly.

"Hailee, I won't choose someone who could be a danger to you," he sighs.

"But you can't guarantee that. You don't know how someone behaves behind closed doors."

He lets out an exasperated breath, his patience wearing thin. "Anything else?"

"What happens if I can't get pregnant?" I worry my lip between my teeth.

"As long as there is medical evidence to support your infertility from a doctor of my choosing, and every option has been exhausted, including IVF, then I will consider your end of the deal upheld," he says carefully. "I don't need to remind you of what will happen if you try to pull the wool over my eyes. I can and will destroy both of your lives."

I stiffen.

"Are we done now?"

My throat has closed over, so I simply nod instead.

"Great, let me introduce you to the lead candidate. There are two you'll meet tonight." He beams, and my head spins at how quickly his demeanor has changed. My stepfather is a grade-A psycho. It's a chilling display of his unsettling ability to switch between charm and manipulation with ease.

Leading me across the ballroom with his hand lingering on the small of my exposed back sends a chill down my spine. Every nerve in my body protests his contact, recoiling from the unwanted intimacy. In a feeble attempt to create some distance, I hook my arm through his elbow once more.

"Hello, Douglas, how are you?" Mark's smile is warm as we approach an elderly gentleman, extending his hand in a friendly greeting. My jaw nearly hits the floor in shock.

This is the lead candidate? THIS guy?

"I would like to introduce you to my beautiful stepdaughter, Hailee Mann. She's lovely, isn't she?" Mark's voice is filled with pride as he presents me.

I lightly grip Douglas's outstretched hand, careful not to apply too much pressure, unlike the bone-crushing handshake Mark just gave him. What was he thinking? He could have seriously hurt the old man. Douglas, who appears to be pushing eighty with thinning white hair on his head but an incredible amount of hair sprouting from his nostrils and ears, leers at me with unsettling focus. His gaze roams up and down my body, settling on my breasts that are threatening to burst out of my dress.

"Nice to meet you, sir," I manage, forcing the words past the lump in my throat.

"The pleasure is all mine, sweetness." He doesn't raise his eyes from my chest.

Gross.

I shoot a glance at my stepfather, but he only narrows his eyes in warning. What's his problem? It's not like Douglas even noticed; his eyes are still glued to my tits. Can this guy even get it up without a little blue pill? Well, at least I don't have to worry about the ten-year clause now. He looks like he's ready to drop dead at any given moment. But then again, that's the thing with these old bastards. You always think they're going to die, then they end up outliving you.

I attempt to retract my hand from his grasp, but he holds it tight and flips it over to kiss the back of my hand. His tongue sneaks out and licks my skin, leaving a wet trail like a slug. I hide my grimace behind a polite smile, desperately resisting the urge to recoil. When he finally releases me, there's an obvious wet patch of saliva on the back of my hand. It takes all my self-control not to lean over and wipe it on his tuxedo jacket.

"Would you excuse me, gentlemen? I'll be back in just a moment." I force a bright smile.

"Take your time, honey. We've got business to discuss." My stepfather waves me off, dismissing me.

"Of course." I incline my head with a gentle smile. Turning on my heel, I weave my way through the sea of guests toward the bathroom. Each step feels like a spotlight shining on me. I hate that I'm drawing the attention of everyone around me.

Damn this stupid dress!

I push my shoulders back and hold my head high. When I reach the bathroom, I lock the door behind me and soap up my hands, washing them twice, then sanitize them. Looking in the mirror, I let my facade drop for the first time since I arrived. My cheeks ache from the constant strain of smiling, and I release a deep sigh, reminding myself why I'm doing this. This isn't about me; it's about Beth. One candidate down, only one more to go. I wait a few moments longer, enjoying the peace and quiet before I have to slip on my mask and return to the cattle auction.

Chapter Six

Dameon

"**D**id you hear what happened to Sheppard Media? They're announcing their insolvency next week..."

I tune out the conversation around me and sweep my eyes over the crowd, looking for my goddess in white. She reappears from the bathroom, and my eyes are instantly drawn to her, bright like a light cutting through the sea of inky black. Every man in this room has her in his sights, some with clear interest in their eyes, others with mild amusement. Doesn't help that she's dressed in a white gown that's teetering on the edge of obscene. If she was looking to make a statement, she has. I suppress a groan when she turns around. *That dress.* Her back is exposed right down to the top of her perky ass. My fingers itch to trail down her spine and watch the goosebumps break out in their wake.

Seeing her with Mark Strickland twice in twenty-four hours has me more than intrigued. What's an escort from Sydney doing in New York with one of the most ruthless businessmen in the city? She must have been bought and paid for.

"Anyone know her story?" I lift my chin in her direction, interrupting the conversation around me.

"Who, the white swan?" Jacob responds with a sly grin, his eyes lingering on her.

"Like you didn't know who he was referring to." Dylan rolls his eyes. "She's gotta be Mark's date."

"Nope." Jacob grins. "That, dear friends, is my future wife."

Dylan laughs out loud, and my fist unexpectedly clenches around the glass of bourbon in my hand.

I narrow my eyes at him. "Explain," I demand, my tone sharper than intended.

"Her name is Hailee Mann. She just happens to be Mark's stepdaughter. And"—he pauses dramatically, relishing the moment—"she's up for sale." His grin widens, and all I want to do is wipe it off his face.

"And what? You're considering 'buying' her?" Dylan asks incredulously.

"Fuck yeah, I am. Have you seen her? And get this, she actually *is* a hooker. She works as a goddess at Eden in Sydney. I heard she sucks dick like a pro too."

My jaw clenches at his crude tone and disrespectful words. But he's not wrong. She's brought me to my knees in ecstasy many times with her exceptional oral skills. She's a master of her craft—her lips, tongue, throat, teeth, and hands all work harmoniously to suck the cum straight out of my balls. I can tell she genuinely enjoys it, reveling in the power trip of making men lose their minds.

"Eden... Is that the kinky brothel I heard about?" Dylan asks.

"What do you mean, she's 'for sale?'" I ignore Dylan's question and keep my voice flat and even this time.

"Mark wants to marry her off so she can push out a couple of brats to take over his throne. He's presenting her tonight, introducing her to potential suitors. A debutante, if you will."

"And you want to get married?" Dylan scoffs.

"Fuck no, but you'd be stupid not to put your hat in the ring. Getting access to Mark's empire when he retires is worth it alone. Plus, pumping her full of cum every night wouldn't exactly be a hardship. If I get bored of her, I can always get a side-piece."

I really want to punch this guy in the face. Jacob is young, decent-looking, and uber-wealthy. I can see why Mark would consider him for Hailee. I roll her name around in my head for the first time. We've never exchanged names or any personal details at Eden. She's always been "goddess" or "kitten" to me. But Hailee... it suits her.

"Too bad you can't make a bid," Jacob gloats at me. My teeth clench, suppressing a growl.

"Why can't he?" Dylan asks, frowning.

"Mark attempted a hostile takeover of Hayes & Hayward Media a few years back, but it fell through. Let's just say, Mark didn't handle the failure well. Dameon would have no chance in hell," he snorts.

Unfortunately, he's right again. Mark and I aren't exactly enemies, but I also wouldn't piss on him if he was on fire. Besides, while I enjoy Hailee's company, marriage isn't my style. Still, it might be fun to make an insane offer just to see if he bites. Mark's a cunning businessman, and I doubt he'd consider Hailee's wishes if the price were right. Or... I could outmaneuver him and claim her for myself, fucking up his plans. Revenge served icy cold. I sip my bourbon and size up the competition. Dylan's out of the running, being married and all. Jacob poses a threat, and then there's Douglas Lawry, who was speaking to her earlier. He's buried more wives than Henry VIII. I scan the room, eyeing up potential adversaries.

"Want to make a bet? Let's make this interesting," I propose to Jacob. "If I win her, your penthouse in Paris is mine." I raise an eyebrow in challenge. "And if you win, my Milan villa is all yours."

"Oh, you're on." He smiles confidently, like he's got this in the bag already. I grasp his outstretched hand. Dylan simply watches, shaking his head at our stupidity.

Let the games begin.

CHAPTER SEVEN

My stilettos are exquisite yet excruciating, like a beautiful torture. But as my mother always said, "Beauty is pain, suck it up." I sway gently, seeking relief for my throbbing feet. Thank goodness for the support of this wall against my back. Mark has granted me a short reprieve from socializing, so I've retreated to a quiet corner where I can indulge in some people-watching while nibbling on canapés. I glance at the measly bite-sized food in my napkin and sigh. I would kill for a slice of pizza right about now. Popping the last one in my mouth, I scrunch up the napkin in my hand.

"Here, let me take that for you."

Caught off guard with a mouth full of food, I inhale sharply when I see it's him. A crumb slips down the wrong pipe and I begin to choke, gasping loudly for air as panic sets in. My attempts to dislodge the crumb result in a cacophony of hacking and wheezing, causing quite the scene. To my deep embarrassment, I can't stop the dry heaves as I scramble to suck in air into my burning lungs. He steps forward, patting me firmly on the back and offering a glass of water that seemingly materializes out of thin air. I take a sip and the fire raging in my throat subsides. Though concern flickers in his eyes, I detect a hint of amusement, adding to my mortification.

"Are you okay? Lucky you don't sound like that when you're choking on my cock," he deadpans.

I burst out laughing, still coughing, the heat rising to my cheeks. Blushing isn't something I do often, if ever. But this? This takes the cake. I'm beyond horrified he almost saw me throw up a canapé.

I wipe at the tears in my eyes and steady my breath before croaking out, "What are you doing here?" My voice sounds raspy, so I take another mouthful of water. Finally, I have the chance to take in his appearance. My goodness, this man is sin personified in his tailored tuxedo. I would totally bend over and give him a freebie right here, right now. If I were wearing panties, they would be ruined.

He smirks. "Twice in twenty-four hours, lucky me." He gently peels open my palm and removes the scrunched napkin, replacing it with a sleek black card. My brows knit together. "I should be asking what brings you to this event. It's not your typical scene. But then again, high society thrives on gossip."

I start to speak but falter, unsure of how to respond.

"I have a proposition for you. One that you'll definitely want to hear." His voice is a delicious rumble, and I feel it all over my body. He closes my fingers around the black card in my palm.

"What—"

"Hailee, are you alright? We heard you from the other side of the ballroom."

I wince as my stepfather approaches, another man trailing behind him.

"I'm fine, thank you, Mark." I wave him off, trying to downplay the embarrassing gaffe. Then my stepfather notices I'm not alone and his face transforms; this must be the ruthlessness everyone talks about, because his game face is downright scary.

"Dameon." Mark spits out the name with disdain, but Dameon is unfazed. He just smiles, as if he's enjoying some inside joke, his gorgeous dimples on display.

"Hello, Mark. Good to see you again. I was just catching up with an old friend." Dameon flashes that dazzling smile my way.

I raise my eyebrows. My stepfather and his companion know we're not old friends, that we don't move in the same circles. Dameon's not-so-subtle implication that we've fucked is unmistakable. To what purpose, who knows? But he's certainly succeeding in getting under my stepfather's skin. I can almost see the steam coming out of his ears.

Dameon turns to me. "It was lovely seeing you again, Hailee." Taking my hand, which is still clutching his card, he presses his lips gently to the back of it. Unlike slimy Douglas. With a subtle wink, he releases my hand, and without another word or glance at Mark or his companion, he leaves. My eyes track him through the crowd until he disappears beyond the exit.

"Hailee," my stepfather snaps, pulling me out of my trance.

"Excuse me?"

"I would like to introduce you to Jacob," he says pointedly, taking the water glass from my hand.

"Oh, sorry about that. Hello, Jacob, lovely to meet you." I plaster on an apologetic smile. He shakes my hand, flashing a grin with perfect, straight white teeth. He's young and attractive, but he doesn't come close to the god that just left us.

"Ignore Dameon, he has that choking effect on a lot of women," Jacob jokes. "They'd do anything to get away from him."

I laugh politely at his quip, but it's not funny. At all.

Jacob launches into a spiel about his father's oil company and his recent takeover, mentioning his desire to settle down. It's obvious he's a total playboy, or as I prefer to call it, fuck boy. I nod along, feigning interest, but my burning curiosity about the card in my hand is hard to ignore. If only Jacob would piss off.

After what feels like an eternity, he moves on, promising to see me again soon. The moment he's gone, I rush to the bathroom as fast as I can without actually running and lock the door behind me. I inspect the card, running my finger over its glossy black finish and embossed silver lettering that reads: *Dameon Hayward, CEO, Hayes & Hayward Media.*

So, Dameon Hayward, what proposition do you have for me?

My eyes flutter open, taking in my surroundings. Soft light seeps through the blinds, casting a gentle glow over the small hotel room. It's way too early for me to be awake, especially after struggling to fall asleep until well past 2 a.m. My mind was relentless, refusing to quiet down even after a scalding hot bath.

A notification blinks bright on my phone on the nightstand. Instinct tells me it's from my stepfather, and a sense of foreboding creeps into the pit of my stomach. I push it aside for the moment and roll over, stretching out my back, calves, and the arches of my feet. As much as I love those Jimmy Choos, they have wreaked havoc on my body.

I grab my phone, dismiss the notification and shoot a message to Beth, just to check in. Then I open a social media app and let my mind drift. It's become a habit now, endlessly scrolling without really absorbing anything. Another notification from my stepfather interrupts my browsing. He's persistent, I'll give him that; it's not even nine in the morning. I roll my eyes and flick away the notification once more. He can wait.

The more I think about last night and the men my stepfather introduced me to, the angrier I become. The thought of being tethered to Do Not Resuscitate Douglas or Fuck Boy Jacob for a decade is infuriating. It's a steep price to pay for one lousy phone call to the transplant board. Fuck him. And fuck my mother for allowing it. Actually, I wouldn't be surprised if this was all her idea.

I drop my phone onto the mattress with a heavy sigh. The shiny black business card on the nightstand catches my eye, and I feel a surge of curiosity. I know next to nothing about Dameon Hayward. Yet, I know every inch of his decadent body, the sound he emits when aroused, the way he shuts his eyes in pleasure when he comes, and the earthy taste of his release on my tongue. Is that enough to trust him? Hell, no. But before I entangle myself with a stranger for a decade, I'm intrigued to hear what he has to say. I snatch up the card, type his number into my phone and send him a text.

Me

> I'm happy to report I survived the attack of the canapé.

Dameon

> Good to hear. Would hate for anything to mar that beautiful throat of yours, except, perhaps, for my cock.

I giggle at his swift reply. That dirty bastard. But I love it. I could continue this banter all day, but unfortunately, I have a Machiavellian stepfather breathing down my neck.

I smile at his *Godfather* reference. It's my all-time favorite movie—not that he would know that. But nevertheless, point one to Mr. Hayward. I "like" his message and jump into the shower.

An hour later, as I step out of the rideshare on to Lafayette Street, the enticing aroma of butter and pastries wafts through the air, making my mouth water. The NoHo brasserie is buzzing, but it's not overwhelmingly noisy, just right for a conversation. Spotting Dameon near the back of the café, I make my way toward him. The thought of indulging in Lafayette's lemon ricotta pancakes makes my stomach growl.

When Dameon catches sight of me, he devours my outfit from head to toe with an appreciative gaze. I've opted for a floral summer dress, paired with ballet flats, and left my hair loose, still drying at the ends after my shower. My makeup is non-existent—I wanted to keep my face clean and fresh. After all, this man has seen me naked more times than I can count, in all sorts of unflattering positions. Trying to impress him with contouring and styled hair seems unnecessary at this point.

Dameon is dressed casually in slouchy faded jeans that probably cost more than my entire outfit, a simple white T-shirt and sneakers. He looks so *normal*, not like a multi-billionaire media tycoon. During the ride to Lafayette's, I did a quick search on him and found numerous articles about Hayes & Hayward Media, including one particularly intriguing piece about a failed hostile takeover attempt by my stepfather's company a few years ago. That explains their tense interaction last night.

"Hello, Mr. Hayward." A genuine smile stretches across my lips.

"Hello, Ms. Mann." He dips his head in greeting, and those dimples make an appearance. You'd think dimples would give him a boyish charm, but no. He's all man, and those dimples are sexy as hell. He gestures to the seat across from him.

"Thank you," I respond, pulling out the chair. "Three times in forty-eight hours, we're going for a new record." I wink.

"Indeed, we are. You look gorgeous, by the way, even better than last night. Although I must say, I prefer you naked."

"Ah, I would have to agree with you there." His striking eyes heat at my admission.

The waiter interrupts our conversation to take our order. Dameon briskly orders for both of us: lemon ricotta pancakes for me and the brisket burger for him, along with a selection of pastries to share. Point two to Mr. Hayward. I'm not fond of men ordering for me—not just because I find it chauvinistic, but because they never order enough, and what they do order is usually rabbit food. A light salad is not a meal.

"I'm on the edge of my seat," I say when the waiter disappears. "What's this offer that's too good to refuse? Nice *Godfather* reference, by the way. It's a classic."

"You've seen it?" he asks, mildly surprised. "Most of the women I date have never watched it."

"Really? Then that was risky, mentioning a dead horse head. I might have thought you were a serial killer."

"True. Worth the risk, though." He shrugs nonchalantly.

"Hang on, is that what we're doing here? Is this a date?" I say, pointing back and forth between us.

"Not quite. I'm here to offer you a long-term position." He crosses his arms over his chest, and I'm momentarily distracted by his bulging biceps.

Forcing my eyes back to his, I ask, "Okay, I'll bite... What type of position?"

"I want you to be my full-time submissive, to live with me, and be at my beck and call. To serve me for twelve months. Honestly, I'm tired of going to Eden. And going through the process of NDAs for a one-night stand is more hassle than it's worth. I'm over it. I want something long-term with someone I have amazing chemistry with. There's no denying I find you attractive, physically. And our sexual chemistry has always been explosive. I'm proposing that you agree to be mine to fuck senseless for a year. And, of course, I'll make it worth your while."

I inhale deeply, letting the air fill my lungs before slowly exhaling, giving myself time to absorb his words.

"I'm offering twelve million dollars: one million a month. That's a lot more than you would make at Eden. Plus..." He pauses, his gaze piercing mine, ensuring I grasp the weight of his next words. "Plus, whatever Mark is holding over your head. There's no way a woman like you agrees to marry someone not of her choosing without being coerced. So, what is it?"

"Wait, a woman like me?"

"A strong, independent woman who bows down to no man unless it's her choice."

Taken aback by his unexpected compliment, I clear my throat before responding. If there's even a chance he has the power to get Beth what she needs, then this offer is too good to pass up.

"My sister has a severe congenital heart condition and needs a heart transplant. She needs the surgery sooner rather than later, as she's only going to get worse. I want her moved to the top of the list."

"Is that it?" he asks, shocked.

"Yep."

"Let me get this straight: you were willing to marry a complete stranger and start a family with him, all for the sake of a simple phone call?" he asks incredulously. I can sense his anger on my behalf, which is touching. But his judgmental tone also puts me on the defensive.

"My stepfather backed me into a corner. I had no other options. Beth needs that surgery, and I'll do whatever it takes to make sure she gets it. But I don't have the same influence or resources as you and my stepfather. I'm not part of your world. I'm just trying to make the best of a bad situation."

"I'm not here to judge. I just think it's fucked up for your family to put you in this position. That's all." He raises his hands in a placating gesture.

"Tell me about it," I sigh, feeling some tension ease out of my shoulders. "So, just to make sure I completely understand: I spend a year with you as your submissive, and then we both go our separate ways, no strings attached. No marriage, no kids, no commitment. And I get twelve million dollars and a new heart for Beth?"

"That's correct."

"What's the catch? There's always a catch."

"There's no catch, I promise. But I'm gonna be honest with you: Your stepfather does play a role in this. I've heard he's desperate for a grandchild to be his heir. Stealing you from right under his nose and destroying his well-laid-out plan, is, well, it's rather amusing to me."

"Okaaay." Understanding dawns on me. "So, this is like a big 'fuck you' to him, revenge for his attempt at taking over your company?"

"Something like that." He smiles darkly.

How can I refuse? One year of submitting to this perfect alpha male specimen and breaking free from Mark's controlling grip, versus a decade trapped with someone like Douglas. Not to mention steering clear of my mother's toxic influence. Um, where do I sign up?

My panties are already damp and my core throbs at the prospect of spending the next twelve months with Dameon. But I have to approach this with a clear head. It's a job, and although it's one I know I'll love, I must keep reminding myself of that. Otherwise, I risk sliding down that slippery slope into the murky waters of feelings, where a whole lot of hurt awaits.

The gentlemen at Eden often pretend to be dominant, but few truly embody the innate authority that Dameon possesses. None have ever fully satisfied my desires like he has, even though our encounters have been limited to the confines of Eden. Outside of that world, he remains a mystery to me. Yet, if I were a betting woman, I would wager that he's every bit the alpha male beyond Eden's walls.

This job is risky for precisely that reason. In Eden, everything is short-term—there's no space for love, intimacy, or even friendship to develop. Keeping this relationship strictly professional and transactional will be a challenge. One night? No problem. But a whole year? That's a different story.

"What do you say? Be mine for a year?" He smiles broadly with those gorgeous dimples.

"Absolutely, it's a deal." We shake hands, and the energy that vibrates between us is almost tangible.

"We're going to have a lot of fun together," he murmurs, his voice deep and thick with promise. I bite my bottom lip to stifle a groan, but he leans closer, gently freeing it with his thumb. His touch is soft as he strokes my lip, and I can't resist. With a teasing glance, I wet the tip of his thumb with my tongue before taking it fully into my mouth, locking eyes with his sea-green ones. I wrap my tongue around his thumb and suck gently, his eyes fluttering closed in pleasure. Showing mercy, I release his thumb with a playful pop. Dameon leans back, composing himself, and shoots me a warning glance. I can't help but smile, secretly pleased to have such a potent effect on him as well.

Dameon clears his throat, transitioning seamlessly into business mode. "In anticipation of your agreement," he begins, "I had my lawyer draft the contract and NDA last night. Take your time to review them carefully and sign both documents. I'm available to answer any questions you might have. But I'll be flying back to Sydney tomorrow. I'd appreciate it if you'd join me."

"Perfect, I'll be there." I can't wait to get home to Beth. Despite being away for only six days, it feels like forever. He hands over the documents, and I carefully tuck them into my handbag.

When our plates arrive, I eagerly dig into my pancakes, enjoying the flavors of lemon and ricotta exploding across my tongue. A satisfied moan slips from my lips, probably a little too loud to be socially acceptable, but I couldn't care less. These pancakes are to die for. I catch Dameon discreetly adjusting himself under the table, and I suppress a giggle.

"You'll pay for that little stunt."

"Promises, promises."

Walking out of the restaurant, my stomach and heart are full. Hope blooms in my chest for the first time since my arrival in New York. I don't need to examine the contract to know I'll accept his offer.

I slide into the back seat of a yellow cab and retrieve my phone from my handbag. I've been around rich and powerful men long enough to know that you don't put all your eggs in one basket. It's risky not to have a backup plan ready to deploy if the deal with Dameon falls through. Time to check the text messages from my stepfather that have been waiting for me since this morning.

Mark

> I've made my decision on the candidate. Call me.

Jeez, would it kill him to say "Good morning"? Or "How are you?" Or even "Thank you for coming with me last night"?

Mark

> I would appreciate it if Sleeping Beauty graced me with her presence when she wakes up. Come to my office when you get this.

I roll my eyes at his feeble attempt at fatherly sarcasm and instruct the driver to head to the address he sent. As the taxi pulls away, I sink back into my seat, nerves knotting in my gut. What if I'm making a mistake?

Arriving at his office building in the financial district, I find myself drenched in a cold sweat. Unease bubbles inside me like molten lava, threatening to erupt and spill over. Playing this dangerous game with my stepfather is reckless, and I nearly reconsider, tempted to turn back. My summery dress clings to my skin, and tremors run through my body as adrenaline surges through my veins.

With false bravado, I stride into the grand foyer of his towering skyscraper. I'm literally walking into the lion's den waving a juicy piece of steak, expecting not to be eaten. Sending a text to my stepfather backing out of our agreement and seeking refuge in Sydney under Dameon's protection would be the simplest option. Yet, something holds me back. I need to cover all bases, prepare for all eventualities.

"Hi, I'm Hailee. I'm here to see Mark Strickland," I tell the woman stationed at the reception desk.

"Do you have an appointment?" she asks, not bothering to look up from her computer screen.

"Um. I don't—" I begin, but she cuts me off.

"I'm sorry, miss, you'll need an appointment to see Mr. Strickland," she says, dismissing me.

Rude.

"But I'm—"

"Mr. Strickland doesn't just see anyone who walks in off the street." She eventually tears her gaze away from her screen to scold me.

I roll my eyes, pull out my phone and type a quick message. She raises an eyebrow as I hit send.

Me: Your guard dog won't let me up.

Within seconds, her desk phone rings. I struggle to suppress a smug smile as her expression drops in recognition.

She hangs up, looking flustered. "I'm sorry, Ms. Mann, I didn't recognize you. His office is on the sixtieth floor. Please, go on up," she stammers, and I almost feel sorry for her.

When I step into Mark's office, I'm not surprised at how flashy it is. Floor-to-ceiling glass windows frame a breathtaking panorama of the Manhattan skyline and a magnificent mahogany desk dominates the center of the room. It's been stained and polished to a gorgeous reddish brown. Behind it sits the man himself, exuding an air of authority like a king reigning over his empire.

I roll my shoulders back and straighten my spine, meeting his gaze head on as I swallow the knot in my throat. Time to play with fire and see if I get burned.

"Mark, I have a counter proposition for you."

CHAPTER EIGHT

She's late.

I flip my wrist to check the time. Hailee was supposed to arrive thirty minutes ago. She has ten minutes to get her ass here before I tan it red, making the long flight very uncomfortable for her.

"Sir, we're scheduled to depart in ten minutes," my pilot reminds me.

"I'm aware," I grit out.

The pilot wisely steps back, resuming his pre-flight checks. Punctuality was a lesson instilled in me by my father from an early age—a virtue I expect from everyone. Either arrive early or on time. Arriving late and making others wait implies that you prioritize your time above theirs. Sending a car for her would have been my preference, but she insisted on meeting me here. A mistake I won't make again.

A taxi approaches and pulls up alongside the plane. I check my watch again; she made it with just one minute to spare.

She doesn't realize how close she came to standing for the next eighteen hours.

I watch through the plane window as Hailee hurriedly exits the vehicle, retrieving a small suitcase from the trunk before briskly striding toward the plane with her luggage rolling behind her. A flight attendant stationed on the tarmac greets her and takes her belongings. Hailee pauses to take in the size of the aircraft, her jaw slackening slightly.

My private jet is huge, rivaling the scale of commercial airliners. Living in Sydney means long-haul travel is an evil necessity. If I need to spend an outrageous amount of time in the air, I want to be comfortable and have all the luxuries I would at home. But beyond the comfort, it grants me the privacy, efficiency, and flexibility I demand.

If she's impressed by the sheer size of the plane, wait until she sees the interior. It's set up like an upscale apartment, complete with a master bedroom and a spacious ensuite, a full dining room and kitchen, and a suite for the crew. I've nicknamed it my "flying penthouse." Given how much it cost, it damn well better drop a few jaws.

Hailee finally ascends the stairs, the flight attendant trailing behind to secure the aircraft door. As she steps into the main cabin, her eyes widen.

"You're late," I remark as I rise from my seat to greet her.

"I'm sorry, Dameon, the traffic was horrendous!" She's flustered, and her cheeks are red from exertion, yet her wide eyes continue to appraise the interior.

"I guess I should have asked for more money, huh?" she jokes, puffing lightly.

"Speaking of... Have you signed the documents yet?"

"Not yet," she responds with a sweet smile.

I raise an eyebrow in question.

"Don't stress. I have eighteen hours to look through them and sign. It will be done before we land, I promise." Bouncing on the balls of her feet, she raises her hand in a scout's honor sign.

She's absolutely adorable, my every desire wrapped in one perfect small package. She's wearing tight jeans that hug her ass and a white crop top that exposes her tanned midriff, effortlessly pulling off cute and sexy at the same time. Though she looks phenomenal in jeans, this will be the last time she wears pants again in my presence.

"Come, take a seat." I lead her over to two plush leather couches facing each other with a small table in between, where my laptop is resting. We strap in and the plane starts rolling down the tarmac. I click my laptop out of sleep mode and begin to respond to emails, but the white-blonde goddess across from me continually steals my attention.

The realization that she's agreed to my offer sets my heart racing. Now that she's here, I want to own her. I know she submits beautifully, and there's nothing I want more than to have her at my mercy for a whole year. I want to dominate her body and infiltrate her mind, to be the last person she thinks of before falling asleep and the first thing on her mind upon waking. I've lost count of how many blow jobs I've received in my lifetime, but nothing compares to her hot little mouth wrapped around my cock and her big emerald eyes looking up at me, eager to please. The thought leaves me hard as a rock. Luckily, I'm wearing sweats.

"Would you like a drink, sir?" My flight attendant Chelsea leans in with a coy smile, her cleavage on full display. I hadn't noticed her approach, my mind consumed with owning my beautiful sub.

"Scotch, neat," I reply.

"Of course, sir," she purrs, lightly touching my shoulder. "Miss, can I offer you a glass of champagne?" The smile Chelsea directs at Hailee is as fake as her tits, and she doesn't make any effort to conceal it either. But if Hailee is bothered by her tone, she doesn't show it.

"That would be lovely, thank you," Hailee replies graciously. So far she's only been polite, warm, and bubbly around me. I'm curious to push her buttons, to discover what it will take to see her inner bitch emerge. I know it's there, lurking beneath the surface. But there will be a time for that, later... after she signs.

"Actually, no alcohol for my companion," I interject. "She has some important documents to sign first."

"Of course, sir." Chelsea smiles before departing.

I arch an eyebrow. "I believe you have some homework to do."

Hailee rolls her eyes at me, and I cannot wait to put an end to that habit. I'm almost thrilled at the prospect. In fact, I can't recall the last time I felt a buzz or excitement about a woman in my life. I watch as Hailee pulls out the documents from her handbag and lays them out flat on the table before her.

Handing her a pen, I grin. "In case you didn't bring one." Her unamused glare almost makes me chuckle. "Actually, it's a good thing you haven't signed yet. I've had the contract updated." I slide over the new paperwork. "If you have any questions, you know what to do."

Still grinning like a fool, I return my focus to my laptop.

*W*hat a smartass.

As if I wouldn't bring a pen with me to sign a contract. Skimming through the first page, I'm met with a bunch of legal jargon outlining the involved parties and *blah, blah, blah*. I flip to the end: it's a whopping forty-five pages long. I let out a long exhale, wishing I had that champagne right about now.

The extravagant jet interior pulls my attention from the paperwork. It's one thing to know that someone is a billionaire but experiencing it firsthand is a whole new level. The plane is extraordinary, unlike anything I've ever laid eyes on, even in movies. It's beyond my wildest imagination. I struggle to comprehend the kind of wealth required to own something like this—it's in an entirely different ballpark to my mother's. Yet, the plane isn't the only extraordinary thing here. Dameon is lounging before me in gray sweatpants, paired with sneakers and a tight black T-shirt. My brain short-circuits from the visual stimulation. He seems to grow hotter every time I see him.

I sneak another glance, finding him diligently typing on his keyboard, a look of concentration etched on his perfectly sculpted face. His sharp jawline is prominent, as if his teeth are clenched, and when he runs a hand through his hair, he tugs slightly on the long ends. He's clearly frustrated. And I bet I could make him feel better.

"Focus, Hailee," he says without taking his eyes off the screen.

Damn it, when did he start reading minds?

I fake a pout, mumbling "party pooper" under my breath. From the corner of my eye, I catch a twitch at the edge of his lips. And just like that, my panties become a little bit wetter.

With a sigh I flip back to page two and begin reviewing the compensation details. True to his word, everything is listed as discussed. One million US dollars will be deposited into my nominated bank account at the end of each month. I skim the rest, searching for the section regarding Beth, anticipating some kind of stipulation about his promised phone call to the transplant board. But what I find brings tears to my eyes.

Special Clause: Dameon Hayward (the Dominant) guarantees that Beth Mann (the Patient) will receive a heart transplant as soon as a match becomes available. The Dominant will exert every effort to secure the operation, including but not limited to: contacting the transplant board, ensuring the Patient is prioritized on the waiting list by any means necessary; engaging the best surgeons and medical professionals for the Patient's care; covering all costs associated with the operation; providing a dedicated full-time nurse for the Patient's recovery; arranging suitable living accommodations; and supplying all

necessary personnel, such as a chef, housekeeper, guardian, nurse, educator, rehabilitation trainers, and facilities to assist in the Patient's recovery.

Emotion wells up in my throat, making it difficult to swallow. I can't bring myself to look at him right now; I'll break down into a blubbering mess. This gesture surpasses anything I could have imagined. The fact that he's willing to go above and beyond for Beth because she's important to me is incredibly touching.

But it's not merely about what he's offering; it goes deeper than that. It's about having someone to share the heavy burden of caring for someone who's ill. To have someone take control and manage all the logistics. The relief is like diving into the cool ocean on a scorching summer day. The realization that I no longer have to face this alone, that he has my back, is overwhelming. I have a sinking feeling that striking that backup deal with Mark is going to haunt me.

I subtly dab my eyes and sniffle, hoping he doesn't notice me falling apart in front of him. But I sense his gaze watching me intently. He's always been attuned to my emotional wellbeing when we've been together at Eden. I suppose that's why he's such a good dom.

"Thank you," I whisper hoarsely, keeping my head down, eyes glued to the page.

"You're welcome, Hailee." His deep, smooth cadence is a balm to my soul.

I clear my throat and move on to the contract termination clause.

At the conclusion of this twelve-month agreement, both the Dominant and the Submissive will part ways, releasing each other of all prior commitments. Either party reserves the right to terminate the agreement early for any reason. Upon termination of the contract, no further compensation will be provided, except as outlined in the Special Clause.

I whip my head up, finding his attention still firmly locked on me.

"Are you serious? I can leave at any time, and you'll still provide everything that you've stipulated in this contract for Beth?" I ask, astounded.

"That's correct."

"But, why? What would stop me from leaving as soon as Beth has her new heart?"

"Nothing... But you won't," he states confidently.

Leaning forward, he peers deep into my eyes. "Because I know you, Hailee. I know your deepest, darkest desires. And when you finally commit to throwing yourself into this lifestyle rather than just playing a role, when you let go and accept that your body and mind want to follow me instinctively, you'll come to realize your full potential. And then, you won't want to leave."

I'm stunned into silence, wholly confused by this man's generosity, yet deep down, I know he's right. Keeping my walls up around him is going to be near impossible, but I don't have a choice. This is an agreement, clearly stating that the Dominant and the Submissive will part ways after twelve months, releasing each other of all prior commitments. This has to remain a job, a role I play. Otherwise, Beth won't be the only one mending a broken heart.

I lower my eyes from his all-knowing, piercing stare back to the page, flipping over until I find the good part... the deliciously salacious part.

The roles and expectations of the Submissive (Hailee Mann) and the Dominant (Dameon Hayward) are outlined below.
The Submissive is tasked with satisfying the Dominant's needs and desires whenever possible, with the expectation of pleasing him. To fulfill this, the Submissive will willingly offer the use of her body, vaginally, anally, and orally.
The Dominant assumes the responsibility of utilizing the Submissive's body for the fulfillment and enhancement of both of their sexual needs. To achieve this, he possesses unrestricted access to the Submissive's body at any time, in any place, and in the presence of anyone he deems appropriate.
The primary duty of the Submissive is to please. This entails attending the Dominant's physical and emotional needs; acting as his sexual plaything; providing physical comfort; demonstrating obedience; maintaining honesty and loyalty; and fulfilling any desires of the Dominant.
Respect must be shown at all times. Disrespect is considered a serious offense and will result in punishment. Respect is demonstrated

through speech, timeliness, willingness to kneel and serve (when able), providing thorough responses, obedience, and unwavering honesty. The Submissive must address the Dominant as "Sir" or "Master" at all times, including in public. In situations where privacy is limited, the Submissive may address the Dominant by his given name.
The Submissive must conform to the Dominant's preferences regarding attire. Contraception use is mandatory for the duration of the agreement with the Dominant and will be overseen by a physician chosen by the Dominant. The Submissive will only achieve orgasm with the explicit permission of the Dominant...

Holy. Shit.

The contract goes on and on, detailing punishments, hard and soft limits, and safety measures, including the safe word "red." I should feel overwhelmed by the exhaustive list of rules and requirements. But at this moment, my body is pulsing with an urgent need that eclipses everything else. I squirm in my seat, heat and dampness building in my jeans. The urge to slide my hand under the table and apply pressure to my clit grows stronger by the second. The relentless throbbing is almost unbearable. I wonder if I can...

"Don't even think about it."

My breath catches when I meet his stormy sea-green gaze.

"Rest assured, I will tend to my pretty pussy soon enough, kitten. She's mine to touch, lick, and stroke. No one else will lay a finger on what's mine, including you. Do you understand?"

I nod, struggling to suppress a whimper.

"Fill in your limits and sign," he commands.

I fly through the remaining paperwork, replicating my limits from Eden—which pretty much includes everything except bloodplay—scribble my signature, and slide it over to Dameon. He briefly scans it, grunts his agreement, and countersigns. Abruptly he stands and moves to one of the cream sofas in the center of the plane.

He reclines and spreads his legs wide. Then he snaps his fingers and points to the floor between his legs. My knees weaken when I stand, and every step toward him feels unsteady. When I reach him, I immediately drop between his legs.

He leans in close, lifting my chin with two fingers, his breath warm against my lips. "Eyes on me at all times," he murmurs. His eyes dart back and forth between my eyes and lips. "I own you, goddess, for a year. Your body and your mind. You don't do anything without permission, including breathing."

My breath hitches as he crushes his lips against mine, his grip on my hair guiding my head to his desired angle. His tongue sweeps past my lips, and I moan at the heady taste of whiskey lingering on his tongue. His scent slams into me, a mix of cologne and something uniquely him, and I'm completely lost in the taste, scent, and feel of him. He invades my senses, taking control of my entire being. When he pulls back, I gasp for air, as if it could somehow clear him from my head.

"Fuck. You taste good."

Mmm, my sentiments exactly, Mr. Hayward.

"Stand and strip."

I gratefully accept Dameon's offered hand, rising from my knees and kicking off my flats, then shimmy my tight jeans down over my ass. Removing these skin-tight jeans usually involves contorting my body into ridiculous positions while huffing and puffing a few choice swear words. There's nothing remotely sexy about it. And as expected, they get stuck halfway down my thighs.

"Erm... can I get a little help here, sir?"

Dameon chuckles. "And that's exactly why you won't be wearing pants from now on. I want quick and discreet access to my cunt at all times."

Oof, this man certainly has a way with words.

"Hold onto my shoulders."

I grasp his shoulders with both hands, the muscles bunching beneath my touch. Clutching my waist, he draws me closer, and manages to peel the jeans down my thighs a few more inches until they get stuck again. With a series of rough tugs, he forces the material down, causing me to burst out laughing, cutting the intense sexual tension.

"I'm going to burn these fuckers. They'll never see the light of day again," he mutters under his breath. I burst into laughter once more, and his gorgeous smile makes an appearance, setting off those beautiful dimples. I decide to make it my personal mission to make him smile as often as possible over the next year.

"I like your laugh. It's cute and contagious... like you." Dameon's still grinning as he lifts each foot, pulling off my jeans. He tosses them aside, grips my waist and dives face-first into my crotch, running his nose and up and down my slit over my drenched panties.

He inhales deeply. "Mmm, you smell incredible. Take these off."

I step back and pull down my panties, then peel off my white crop top, leaving me bare as the day I was born. Dameon examines my body, his gaze traveling from the top of my head to the tips of my pink-painted toes. His eyes narrow when they settle on my ribs.

"Who did this to you?" His voice carries a gruff edge.

"What are you talking about?"

"This." He lifts my arm and ghosts his fingertips over my bruised ribs. His touch is feather-light, making my skin prickle.

"Oh... that. It's nothing. I did it myself." I wave off his concern.

"Explain." His tone remains deep and husky.

"I fell over in the bath. It was stupid, really," I admit rather sheepishly. Considering he looks ready to commit murder, I'm not about to mention that I do stupid shit like that all the time.

"You will take more care in the future. I'm the only one allowed to mark this beautiful skin. Neglecting yourself and your body counts as disrespect, and you will be punished for it. Am I clear?"

"Yes, sir." The words fly out of my mouth without thought, and I resist the urge to salute him.

"Good girl," he replies, smirking. He pats his thigh. "Sit, kitten, let me take care of that needy pussy for you."

I position myself in his lap, relishing the sensation of his clothes against my hypersensitive naked skin. He adjusts me so my back is against his chest and spreads my legs over his parted ones, leaving my pussy fully exposed. His fingertips trail down my throat, lightly stroking my chest and tracing circles around each nipple, coaxing them into tight buds. Moving lower, he eventually arrives at my slick folds and grunts when he feels how wet I've become. With deliberate slowness, he glides his fingers up and down my slit, gathering my wetness before zeroing in on my clit. His touch is gentle, unhurried. So, I lean back against him, resting my head on his shoulder, and close my eyes as he leisurely pleasures me at his own pace.

Up and down.

Up and down.

I release a contented sigh, enjoying the comforting sensation that slowly stokes the flames of my arousal.

"Let's go over some house rules, goddess," he whispers against the shell of my ear.

"Every morning, you'll wake me with your hot little mouth on my cock. You'll remain naked at all times in my house, including in front of my household staff. They've all signed NDAs and are aware of my proclivities. You'll stay naked even when we have guests over, unless I state otherwise. During the day, when I'm not at home, you're free to choose your outfit as long as it doesn't include pants, shorts, a bra or panties." He pauses for a moment. "Except when you want to exercise.

"You'll greet me at the door on your knees in the traditional submissive position," he continues to softly whisper in my ear, his hot breath tickling my skin. His pace and pressure on my slit haven't changed, but his words alone have brought me closer to the edge.

"Look at you, kitten, you've drenched my sweats. Do you like my house rules? Does it turn you on, hmm?"

I moan and arch my back, chasing the friction I need to drop off that cliff into ecstasy.

"Do you need to come?"

"Yesss!" I hiss.

He turns my chin toward him and smashes his lips firmly against mine, kissing me passionately, a battle of lips, teeth, and tongue. He ramps up the pace with his fingers, sending me into a frenzy before giving my pussy a sharp, short slap.

"You can come."

I gasp as my orgasm rolls through my body like an earthquake, leaving me shivering in its wake.

"Good girl," he murmurs with obvious approval.

I slump back against him, taking a few deep breaths to calm my hammering heart. He brings his fingers, still glistening with my essence, to his mouth and savors my taste.

"Mmm, fucking delicious. But I need more." Rising from the sofa, he carries me bridal style to the dining room.

"Time for my snack." He winks as he crosses the threshold.

I huff a laugh, enjoying this unexpectedly corny side to him. He gently lays me out on the dining table, the polished dark wood biting cold against my back, making me shiver again. He sits in a high-back chair and grips my ankles, dragging me toward him and pushing open my legs until his face is right on top of my core. He lazily draws his tongue up my slit and moans.

"You're gonna come two more times for me," he commands.

I shake my head. "I can't, I'm too sensitive."

"That wasn't a request. I'll take it slowly, but you will give me two more." His hard eyes on mine make my core clench. Dameon gets back to work, and just like before, he's in no rush, savoring me like a fine wine. His eyes are closed, and he's lost in the moment, lost in my taste. He's enjoying pleasuring me, and it makes it so much hotter. Dameon has always been amazing at eating pussy; it's his specialty, and something I've always craved during our time together at Eden. Eating pussy is a lot like eating ribs: if it's not all over your face and fingers, you're not doing it right. And Dameon doesn't hold back. He's a man on a mission and won't stop until I'm screaming his name, and he's covered in my juices.

I relax against the table with my hands raised over my head, enjoying the sensation of his thick tongue exploring the contours of my pussy. So far, he's astutely avoided my clit, as he leisurely traces the outline, drawing each lip into his mouth for a sensual suck. His tongue delves between my folds, circling my entrance before briefly plunging inside and then withdrawing.

When he lifts his head from between my legs, he growls, "Incredible." Not wanting to miss the show, I raise myself onto my elbows to watch him. He presses a small silver button on the table and dives back to my pussy, spreading my thighs wide in a tight grip to ensure I'm fully exposed once again. He thrusts two fingers inside me, and my body easily accepts them with no resistance. He works me expertly, drawing out every bit of pleasure with his tongue while his fingers move inside me, causing my legs to shake.

A moment later, a female voice clears her throat. "Excuse me, sir. Did you need something?"

I'm shocked to find Chelsea standing to his left. I didn't even notice her arrival. Dameon hasn't stopped his wicked tongue, and Chelsea's eyes are firmly planted on my pussy, watching him eat me out. Her lips part and her pupils dilate.

Without missing a beat, and without removing his face from between my legs, he speaks, his voice a little muffled. "Please bring Hailee something to eat."

"And what about you, sir, can I get you anything?" She swallows and licks her dry lips.

"This is all I need."

Chelsea lingers by his side, her eyes briefly meeting mine before returning to Dameon's skillful ministrations. His talented tongue and the presence of a witness send me spiraling out of control. I collapse against the hard table, my body arching in response to the overwhelming stimulation.

"Is there something you need, Chelsea?"

"No, sir," she breathes, yet she remains unmoving despite being dismissed.

"Would you like a taste of my kitten?"

Dameon's face remains buried in my pussy throughout the interaction. And Chelsea hasn't taken her eyes off the scene unfolding before her, utterly captivated.

"Yes, sir," she whispers, her voice barely audible over my moans. His domination, the control he has over this room and everyone in it, combined with her presence, is driving me to the edge at lightning speed.

"Kitten, let go."

He sucks my clit into his mouth hard and I explode, my core tightening around his fingers, flooding his mouth as stars burst behind my eyelids.

"Good girl." He taps my outer thigh in approval.

"You may have a taste, Chelsea."

Panting hard, I lift myself back up onto my elbows and watch as she brings her face close to his. For a brief moment, I think she's about to kiss him, but at the last minute, her tongue peeks out from behind her full lips, and she licks my juices off his lips, chin, then around his cheeks, until he's thoroughly clean.

"How does she taste?"

"Mmm... exquisite," she sighs, licking her lips.

"I might let you taste it from the source next time—if my kitten wants it."

My clit pulses hard at the thought. That was fucking hot.

"I would like that very much, sir." She bows her head before exiting the dining room. I collapse back onto the table, my mind reeling.

"On your hands and knees, kitten, and back that gorgeous ass onto my face. You owe me one more."

I'm a boneless, sweaty mess, but I obey and roll over, arching my back so that my pussy is at the right level for him. He slaps my ass hard, and I yelp in surprise.

"Shh, that was a light tap. Come on, one more time for me before Chelsea gets back," he demands.

He spreads my cheeks and trails his tongue up my crack, teasing my back entrance in a way that makes me lose my mind in pleasure. He runs the tip of his tongue around the rim over and over again, and when he finally pushes inside, he reaches underneath and flicks my clit with his finger.

I'm utterly drained, completely spent, yet I feel that familiar pull in my abdomen building toward another earth-shattering release. It's hurtling toward me at such a speed that it scares me. I can't control it; I'm completely at the mercy of the man who is playing my body like a violin. The climax hits me so hard it's almost painful. My eyes squeeze shut and I scream out his name, completely lost in the moment.

"Fuck me, that was incredible. You're incredible," he breathes out softly. He gathers me in his arms, placing me on his lap and giving my knees reprieve from the hard table. He soothes back the sweaty hair on my forehead and drops a kiss. It's intimate and gentle, exactly what I need in this moment. I curl into his chest as he tenderly rubs my back.

"Chelsea will be back in a minute with your food. Take a seat so she can serve you."

I slide out of his lap, moving to the other side of the table. Exhaustion washes over me as I flop onto the chair.

Chelsea returns, wheeling a silver cart with an array of decadent food, along with a bottle of Dom Pérignon chilling on ice. She places a platter of cheese, fruit, and nuts on the table. I bite the inside of my cheek to conceal my smirk; I was laid bare on this table only a few short moments ago. Chelsea pours each of us a glass of champagne and turns to leave, but not before looking me dead in the eye, astutely avoiding my nakedness. An unspoken conversation flies between us. There's no need for words.

You lucky bitch. Enjoy it.

Oh, I intend to.

She offers me a slight smile and slips out of the dining room without even a glance at Dameon. I chuckle at our strange encounter. It seems we've reached some sort of truce. An agreement, if you will.

"What was that about?" Dameon's head is lowered, fingers tapping away at his phone.

Geez, this man doesn't miss a thing.

"Nothing much." I shrug.

He looks up, raising an eyebrow.

"Apparently, Chelsea and I are now friends," I explain, widening my eyes.

He shakes his head, a smile playing on his lips.

I take a sip of fizz and sink into the plush high-back chair. My face is still flushed and I'm sweating like a pig, but I could easily get used to this high-flying lifestyle with its multiple orgasms and French champagne.

I make a small plate of food, piling it high with cheese, crackers, and strawberries. Honestly, what's the point of these tiny-ass plates? You can only fit two, maybe three pieces at most.

Dameon snorts, eyeing my towering plate.

"What? She should have brought bigger plates," I defend.

"You love your food, don't you?"

"I'm not exactly a salad girl."

"Duly noted. I'll keep that in mind for the future." The corner of his lips tilts up.

Gosh, I want to taste those lips, just like Chelsea did. I tear my eyes away from his mouth and focus on my food, savoring the burst of flavor on my tongue as I bite into a strawberry.

"Can I ask you something, sir?" I say.

I look up to find his eyes still locked on me, watching me eat.

"Go ahead," he gestures with his hand.

"When will you contact the transplant board?"

"I already did this morning. Beth has been moved to the top of the list. You should receive an email with confirmation shortly. She'll receive a new heart as soon as there's a compatible match."

Relief floods my body, and I sag back into my chair. The fact that he took care of this before I even stepped foot on his plane or signed the agreement is not lost on me.

"Thank you," I whisper, emotion thick in my voice.

"You're welcome." He dips his head and picks up his phone, returning to his work.

I swallow roughly as the deal with Mark flits through my mind. Guilt begins to creep in and I finish the rest of my plate in silence, contemplating the kind of man Dameon is.

He's successful, wealthy, attractive, kind, and eats pussy like a champ. How is he still single? I don't really buy his excuse that he can't find a woman who likes to be dominated and shares his kinks. Undoubtedly, it makes finding the right person harder, but with more than six million people in Sydney and eight million in New York, it's hardly impossible. Convenience and privacy surely can't be the only reasons he visits Eden.

"You're staring, Hailee," he remarks without lifting his head from his phone.

Shit.

"What are you thinking about?"

"Nothing." I look away, but his inquisitive gaze bores into my face.

"This is your first and final warning. I've asked you two questions in the last fifteen minutes, and both times you've responded with 'nothing.' I'll let it go this time, but you're to answer my questions with full honesty and be open with me at all times. Next time will result in punishment."

Whoa, there's no hiding anything from him.

"Yes, sir."

"Good girl. Why don't you take the master suite to rest while I finish up work?"

That's not a bad idea. Three amazing orgasms, two glasses of Dom Pérignon, and a full stomach later, I'm wiped, physically and mentally. I rise from my chair, feeling his eyes on my naked form, and make my way to the back of the plane in search of the bedroom.

The constant hum of the engines keeps me in a serene state of sleep, the white noise lulling me into slumber. I stretch and roll over, surrendering to being awake. That was the best nap I've ever had. Hours of uninterrupted sleep on a mattress as soft as the clouds we're flying above. I look around the suite and shake my head. Beth would lose her mind over this bedroom. With a flick of the covers, I tumble out and search for my suitcase in the wardrobe, but it's nowhere to be found. Instead, I find a cute sundress and wedged heels, but no bra or panties. After indulging in a long, luxurious shower stocked with all the high-quality products a girl could ask for, I dress and step out of the master bedroom, in search of the master himself.

I find Dameon reclined on a sofa in the main cabin, drinking a coffee and engrossed in his tablet. I approach from behind and see he's perusing the world news, headlines flashing across the screen. Running my hand over his shoulder as I pass, I greet him with a bright smile.

"Good morning, sir."

"Good morning, gorgeous. Did you sleep well?" His eyes light up as he takes me in.

"Amazingly. What time is it, anyway?"

"We're landing in a couple of hours," he replies, flipping his wrist to check the time. "You pretty much slept the entire flight."

"Really? I must have needed it." I stifle a yawn.

"Three orgasms will do that to you. Lift your dress and present yourself. Let's see if you've complied with my dress code." His lips curve up.

I offer a sultry smile and gracefully kneel on the couch, my back facing him. I lift my dress, letting it drape over the arch of my spine, and part my knees, gripping the back of the couch for support. This position grants him an unobstructed view of my pussy. Glancing over my shoulder, I see his eyes darken as he devours every detail of my exposed core. He doesn't rush, he simply takes another sip of his coffee and enjoys the view.

"You can sit now," he finally commands.

I lower myself onto the couch and pull down my dress.

"Have some breakfast." He gestures to the spread on the coffee table in front of me.

I pile my plate high with food again, this time using a large dinner plate. I can't help but smirk at the upgrade.

"I've been meaning to ask you something," I begin. "Is it possible for Beth to move in with us? I don't want to be separated from her." This question has been weighing heavily on my mind since I read the contract yesterday. I know she'll have a guardian, a nurse, and all the necessary staff, but I hate the idea of us being apart.

"Don't worry, Beth will move into the same building as us. We'll be in the penthouse, and she'll be on the level below. I own the entire building, so you'll be able to visit her anytime. She can't live with us, though, as you'll be naked and on your knees most of the time." His beautiful sea-green eyes sparkle.

Alrighty, then. I didn't think of that, but fuck if that doesn't make me hot.

Satisfied that Beth will be nearby, I let the matter drop. Besides, I wouldn't expose her to the kinky fuckery that Dameon and I will be indulging in.

"You both have three days to pack and get organized; movers will be arriving at your home on Monday."

"Yes, sir," I mock salute him. He shakes his head, amused by my antics.

He really doesn't know what he's signed up for.

The remainder of the flight passes quickly, and before I know it, we're descending the front stairs onto the tarmac. Waiting for us are two sleek black Range Rovers, their drivers standing at attention, hands clasped behind their backs. Dameon guides me toward one of the cars, and when we reach it, he spins me around, cradles my head in his hands and plants a gentle kiss on my forehead.

"My driver will take you home," he says. "I'll see you in three days. Be good." He winks, giving my ass a playful pat as I step into the car.

"Never." I grin, blowing him a kiss before the door closes.

Chapter Ten

Hailee

"Honey, I'm home!" I sing out, dragging my luggage behind me as I toe the front door shut. Our quaint townhouse in Sydney's inner city has been our home for the past decade. Built in the early 1900s, it's a unique blend of timeless elegance and modern chic, thanks to the extensive renovations carried out by the owners. Despite its updated features, it still has character and a certain lived-in, rustic charm. *I'm going to miss this place.*

I've decided to hold onto the lease while we live in Dameon's building. Sydney's rental market is ridiculously expensive, but with a monthly income of a million dollars, I can certainly afford to keep it empty for twelve months. This house holds so many memories—it was a soft place to land when we first arrived in Australia and I'm not quite ready to give it up.

"Beth?" I shout, dropping my handbag and suitcase in the living room.

"Yeah, yeah, I'm here. You woke me up." Beth shuffles in, rubbing the sleep from her eyes, yawning. Her black leggings

99

and slouchy T-shirt accentuate her petite frame, but her pale complexion and the dark circles under her eyes make my heart hurt. She's looked better.

"Sorry." I cringe. "Come here, my Betty Boo." I pull her in for a big hug and plant a kiss on the top of her head. "I missed you."

"Relax. It's been six days," she mumbles into my chest. "And I hate when you call me that."

"Okay, poo brain. But I can't help that I miss your face."

She wraps her arms around me and, noticing how she subtly breathes me in, I squeeze her tighter.

"I missed you too," she sighs, pulling out of my embrace and eyeing my dress. "That's cute, where did you get it from? And more importantly, can I borrow it?"

"Boy, do I have news for you!" I widen my eyes dramatically. "And yes, you can wear it. But let me shower and unpack first, and then I'll fill you in over margaritas and tacos." Even though I just had breakfast, it's already late afternoon in Sydney, and I assume Beth hasn't organized dinner for herself yet.

"Good, I'm starving," she says through another yawn.

I head upstairs to my bedroom and unpack, throwing everything into the drawers haphazardly. We're going to be packing over the next couple of days, so there's no point in putting things away properly. I take the speediest shower on record and dress in something comfy: leggings, and a tank top.

A quick check of the cupboards confirms my suspicion: no ingredients to make tacos in sight. But a short walk to the supermarket around the corner solves that problem. I'll miss this neighborhood. Living near all these conveniences—supermarket, post office, doctor, dentist, pharmacy, cafés—has been wonderful. Despite owning a car, I hardly use it, preferring to walk, especially when everything is just a stone's throw away.

After putting away the groceries, I begin slicing the limes to make margaritas. Drinking while cooking is a must in my book. I whip up a virgin one for Beth and a double-strength for myself—because, why the hell not? We're celebrating.

"Mmm, can I try yours?" Beth strolls into the kitchen as I finish pouring the mixtures into margarita glasses, garnishing them with a lime slice on the salted rim.

"Sorry, kiddo, you know the deal. No alcohol until you're eighteen."

"Ugh, fine," she grumbles, rolling her eyes and settling on a stool at the kitchen bench.

"Cheers." I clink my glass with hers and take a sip, licking the salt off my lips. *Not bad.*

"Guess what?"

"What?" She looks at me expectantly and I can tell she's a little afraid to hear the answer.

"You're getting a new heart."

"Fuck off, no way!" Beth's smile is radiant, warming my heart in the best possible way.

"Uh-huh."

"I can't believe Mom came through," she says, shaking her head.

"Well, not exactly," I hedge. Beth deserves the truth, but I'll do everything I can to shield her from the pain of knowing that her mother doesn't give a shit about her.

"What do you mean?"

"I found another way." I grab my phone from the counter and open the email from the transplant board verifying Beth's new status as urgent. Just as Dameon promised, she's now a priority for surgery as soon as a suitable match is found. Passing my phone to Beth, I turn my attention to chopping tomatoes, lettuce, and onions for the tacos, keeping a close eye on her reaction as she reads the email. She must read it over a dozen times, because it's not that long.

"I can't believe it," she whispers. Tears well in her eyes, but her smile lights up her whole face, despite her gaunt look.

Oh, my Betty Boo.

"How?"

"I've accepted a twelve-month contract, a job for one of my clients at Eden."

"Really? Are you sure about this?"

"Positive. Plus, we get to move into a posh new apartment in Bondi near the beach, and you get your own place with a chef, cleaner, and even a tutor. How cool is that?"

"No way!" Beth narrows her eyes at me. "This sounds almost too good to be true." Even at sixteen, she clearly understands the concept that there is no such thing as a free lunch.

"Don't worry, I've got this."

"Well... Okay... Fuck, I can't believe it!" Her worry fades quickly into excitement.

"We have to pack over the weekend. We're moving on Monday."

"You said it's just for twelve months, right? So, what are we doing with all our furniture and stuff?"

"I was thinking of keeping this place, so we can come back after the contract finishes. Or we could move somewhere else, wherever you want to go. I just want you fully recovered and healed so you can finish high school and start life afresh at uni."

"Hell yeah!" Her excitement is contagious, and I can't help but be swept up in it too.

"Here, help me cut up the rest of the veggies." I slide over the chopping board and hand her the knife. "Soft or hard-shell tacos?"

"Por qué no los dos?" she says, mimicking the cute kid from the Old El Paso commercial.

God, Beth is such a weirdo. And I love her for it.

"I don't see why we have to do this ourselves. Isn't he super rich?" Beth whines.

"He's sending movers, but we still need to be packed and ready to go tomorrow morning. Stop being a lazy shit."

Beth and I spent Saturday hanging out and pampering each other. We made face masks and gave each other manicures and pedicures. It was nice to spend time at home, just the two of us. But I made Beth promise me that if we bummed around yesterday, we'd pack today.

"Do you really want a stranger going through your stuff anyway?" I reason.

"No, I suppose not," she grumbles.

"Besides, you don't have much to pack."

"What are you talking about? I've got clothes, shoes, bags, toiletries, makeup, plus all my schoolwork and books—that's heaps to pack! And you literally just said we had to empty out the pantry and fridge too. This is going to take forever."

"Maybe we should've started yesterday, like I wanted to," I say, a tad smug.

"Did you forget I have a heart condition? Exertion isn't good for me."

I roll my eyes. I've got no one to blame for her laziness but myself. She likes to push the boundaries with what she can get away with, using her illness as an excuse. Exercise is good for her, but it's been a constant battle to get her to do even the lightest cardio.

"You're not doing any heavy lifting. You'll be fine," I reassure her, flipping through one of our photo albums. I'm trying to treat her like every other teenager. But it's difficult when my instincts are to wrap her in cotton wool and protect her from the world.

She hums her dissatisfaction.

"Hey, check this out." I stop at a photo of us when Beth was six and I was eighteen. It was shortly after we arrived in Australia, and I took her to get ice cream at Bronte Beach. In the picture both of us have huge grins on our faces, and our ice cream cones are melting down our hands. My arm is around her shoulders, squeezing her tightly into my side. I remember asking a random stranger to take the photo for us.

"I remember that," she says, looking over my shoulder at the photo.

"Really? You were only six. But it feels like it was just yesterday for me," I say fondly.

"We look happy."

"We were. Honestly, I had no clue what I was doing raising a kid, but I figured it out along the way." I shrug.

"I know I don't say this enough, but thank you for taking me with you. I don't remember much about Mom, but it must have been rough. I know it couldn't have been easy for you with a sick little kid holding you down." She blows out a breath and runs a hand through her ponytail. "I can't wait to start the next chapter of my life—with a new heart and without this hanging over our heads."

I wrap my arms around her, pulling her close. "I know, and I'll always have your back, no matter how old you are."

We pull apart and I smile softly. "Let's get back to work. This house isn't going to pack itself." Carefully, I place the photo album in the "take" pile and head to the kitchen to clear out the cupboards.

Three hours later, I stand in the entryway and release an exhausted sigh at all the stuff we've put aside to pack. I reach for my car keys. "I'm going to grab more boxes." Thankfully we're not packing up the entire house, furniture and all. I shudder at the thought. It's enough to make me swear off moving forever.

"Great, I'm going for a nap then," Beth announces, already heading upstairs to her bedroom. I guarantee that I won't see her again until I've finished all the packing.

CHAPTER ELEVEN

Hailee

"Holy shit balls," Beth gasps.

"You can say that again," I murmur, leaning over Beth to take in the beautiful building through the car window. The six-story structure looks like a modern version of those white cave houses you see on the Greek island of Santorini. And to top it off, directly across the street lies Bondi Beach. Imagining waking up to that breathtaking blue horizon, where the sea meets the sky, has me feeling positively giddy.

Our SUV pulls into the curved driveaway and Dameon swings my door open with a flourish. "Hey, welcome to my humble abode." He stretches his arms out wide in a grand gesture.

"There's nothing humble about this place, sir," I snort, accepting his offered hand. He's dressed casually in board shorts and a snug tank top, which showcases his remarkable shoulders and biceps. The laid-back beach lifestyle really suits him.

"In fact, there's nothing humble about you," I tease, eyeing the outline of his impressive package in those shorts.

"Gross, is that a sex thing? It's a sex thing, isn't it." Beth steps out of the car behind me, fake gagging.

"And you must be Beth. I've heard a lot about you. I'm Dameon." He extends his hand with a chuckle and shoots her a charming wink. Beth's cheeks flush beet red, a reaction I've never seen from her before. She shakes his hand awkwardly, avoiding eye contact.

Stifling my laugh, I take pity on her. "Come on, let's check out our new digs for the next year," I say, pulling her into my side for a hug.

"Ladies, if you'll follow me." The moment he turns away, Beth looks at me and mouths, *He's fucking hot.*

No shit, I mouth back, widening my eyes.

We step into the foyer, where cream tiling and luxurious marble reflect the soft palette of the beach across the street, saturating the space with warmth.

"I'd like to introduce you to Kevin. He's my building manager, and if there's anything you need, please just let him know." Dameon gestures to a short, stocky man in his sixties, who emerges from behind the concierge desk.

I shake his hand and Beth gives a small wave. "Nice to meet you, Kevin."

"Please, call me Kev."

His kind brown eyes crinkle at the edges, and I instantly take a liking to him.

"You got it, Kev." I give a playful wink and his large, bulbous nose burns bright red. There's a lot of blushing going on this morning.

"Kevin's aware you're both my distinguished guests, and he's here to help make your stay more comfortable," Dameon says.

"Thank you, I appreciate it. I promise we won't cause any trouble or make your life hell... Well, not much, anyway," I joke.

"Honestly, it will be a pleasure to assist you in anything you need," Kevin responds earnestly.

Okay, I'm officially sweet on Kev. It's funny how some people you meet in life just emit a trustworthy aura that you instantly connect with. Kev is one of those people.

"Let's head up, and I'll show you Beth's apartment," Dameon calls, leading the way toward the elevators. We follow behind, bidding Kev goodbye with a wave. "There are two elevators: one for the residences, the other private, with only one stop—the penthouse."

We step into the residents' elevator and exit on the fifth floor. "Welcome to your new home, Beth." Dameon unlocks the first door on our left, pushing it open. Beth enters first, gasping dramatically.

"Holy fucking shit."

"Beth, language!" I chide, though I couldn't care less about her choice of words. But since we're in company, I figure I should at least appear to play the role of the responsible older sister and guardian.

She's not wrong, though, this place is epic. The sleek interior in a muted palette is all quiet luxury and lived-in comfort.

Beth spins around, taking in the open-plan living and dining areas. "Can you believe this?"

"Do you like it?" I ask.

"What kind of question is that? This place is insane. And I get to stay here on my own?" she asks hopefully, but with a hint of healthy skepticism. Ever since I mentioned she would have her own place I could sense her excitement. I know she craves privacy and independence, something her illness has deprived her of. This is the perfect opportunity for her to flex those independent muscles.

"Not exactly," Dameon interjects. "Allow me to introduce you to Martha. She'll be your guardian and housekeeper."

I hadn't even noticed the elderly woman standing there, too caught up in this gorgeous place and Beth's excitement.

"Hi, Martha, wonderful to meet you," I say, extending my hand. She smiles, grasping my palm gently.

"Martha was actually my nanny when I was growing up; I trust her implicitly," Dameon says. "And she's Kevin's wife. Honestly, I'd be lost without them. When I moved to Australia, I made sure to bring them both with me."

Ah, that makes sense. They both exude that same calm, genuine, and friendly energy. I can see they would make a lovely couple.

Beth gives Martha a shy smile and a soft hello.

"Lovely to meet you both." Martha's voice is serene, like a warm hug.

"You're going to be on your best behavior for Martha, right?" I say, giving Beth a gentle nudge.

"Yes, Mom," she says, rolling her eyes.

Dameon clears his throat, stepping forward. "Alright, now that introductions are done, I'm sure you'll want to check out your room and get settled in, Beth. Kevin will bring up your stuff shortly, and Martha will help you unpack."

"Hell yeah!"

Before she has a chance to dart off and explore, I pull her into a hug and whisper in her ear. "I'm only upstairs if you need me, okay? I'll be back down in an hour to check on you." I don't want her to think I'm abandoning her. We've never lived apart. My trip to New York was the first time we've been separated.

"Can you please stop worrying? Seriously, I'm good. Better than good, actually. This place is unreal." I release her from the hug, meet her eyes and find sincerity shining back at me. After a moment's pause, I relent.

"Alright, I'll be back in an hour."

With another eye roll, she dashes off in search of her bedroom, without looking back.

"I know this must be hard for you," Martha murmurs, "but rest assured, she's in good hands, dear. I'll take care of her as if she were my own."

I scrutinize Martha just as I did Beth, searching for any hint of insincerity. "Thank you, Martha. I really appreciate it."

"Martha has been briefed on Beth's health situation, and she'll notify you immediately if anything changes," Dameon adds.

Right. Trust. It's been Beth and I against the world for a very long time. While it's a relief to share the burden with someone, it's also difficult to relinquish control.

Thanking Martha once more, I trail behind Dameon as we leave the apartment and take the elevator to the penthouse.

"I want you to know, I trust Martha with my life. I wouldn't hire just anyone to look after Beth." He dips his head, searching for my eyes.

"I know." I offer a small, grateful smile as I gently squeeze his arm.

The lift door opens, revealing the view of a lifetime: Bondi's spectacular ocean stretching endlessly into the distance. While Beth's apartment mirrors the vibrant energy of the beach by day, Dameon's penthouse appears to reflect the allure of Bondi at night—the sand shimmering under soft moonlight; the waves gently caressing the shore. No detail has been spared in creating the striking space. Yet, it's the breathtaking view that draws my attention.

My heart races and I swallow hard, fighting back the bitter bile of guilt that threatens to rise, bringing with it a wave of sudden nausea.

This is truly beautiful. I don't deserve any of it.

Walking through the apartment on autopilot, I'm drawn toward the open sliding glass doors leading to the outdoor area. The balcony is surprisingly large and the edge disappears into an infinity pool. I can easily see myself lounging out here in a bikini, getting lost in the view. Beth would totally freak out over this pool. Though the sun's rays beat down from above, a gentle breeze sweeps through, keeping the temperature pleasantly cool.

I shield my eyes from the brightness and squint at the ocean shimmering before me. Being near water is almost a spiritual experience for me. The gentle rhythm of the ocean draws me in, seducing me into a state of tranquil calm and heightened awareness. If only I could bottle up that sensation and carry it with me, I would. Perhaps that's why I find solace in baths; they offer a similar experience, albeit on a smaller scale.

Strong, muscular arms circle my waist from behind, and I melt into Dameon's embrace. His warmth seeps into my back, hotter than the sun above, and the scent of his skin mixes with the salty sea breeze, creating a provocative fusion that I inhale deeply into my lungs.

"What are you thinking about?" he whispers, his breath caressing the shell of my ear.

"The ocean. How peaceful it is here. Do you ever tire of the view?"

"Never," he murmurs softly. I feel his gaze on me, and somehow, I doubt he's referring to the coastline. My heart flutters, but I quickly remind myself that any sweet sentiments that fall from his lips aren't real. Still, it doesn't stop the sliver of hope blossoming in my chest at the thought, that maybe, just maybe... he meant it. That's the thing about hope; once you've had a taste, you crave more, regardless of how dangerous it might be.

He nuzzles my neck, placing tender kisses along my jawline before forcefully tilting my head back to claim my lips. His tongue massages against mine in firm strokes, and I'm lost in his taste and heat. I arch into him like a needy cat, my ass seeking out his rock-hard cock. As I press against him, his guttural groan sends heat coursing through my veins. I move against him, desperate for more, but it's not enough.

"I need you inside me, like right now," I demand.

"Needy kitten, are we?"

"Please..." The ocean, the sun, and the sea air combined with Dameon's heat and scent overload my senses. My skin is on fire. I'm burning from the inside out, and only he can douse this infernal heat. There's only so much flirting and sexual tension a girl can endure. I'm not above begging to get what I want, to satiate this ache in my core.

"Another house rule for you: you don't top from the bottom. You need my cock, you ask nicely." I hear the shuffle of his shorts being pushed down before he lifts my sundress. He kicks out my feet wider and runs his cock up and down my slit, spreading my wetness. With a sigh of relief, I bend over the glass barrier in front of me, arching my back to give him better access. As soon as he slides home, inch by inch, we both pause. It's pure bliss. He fills me up, stretching me almost to the point of pain. Dameon's not a small man and taking him in one go is a challenge. Usually, he takes his time, stretching me with his fingers, making sure I'm well-prepped. But this time I wanted him inside me as quickly as possible.

"You feel incredible. Hot, wet, and... tight," he grits out through clenched teeth. I push back but struggle to take all of him.

"Only one more inch. You can take it."

"Yesss," I hiss when he's fully seated inside me.

"That's it. Fuck... Look at that pretty pussy stretching open for me," he growls, running his palm down my spine. Now that he's balls deep, he grips my hips hard and drives into me. I cling to the barrier with both hands as he pummels into me. With the ocean ahead and Dameon behind, I plummet into ecstasy a lot quicker than I'd care to admit. Dameon tumbles after me, his heavy breaths on the back of my neck. We remain connected, staring out at the horizon, enjoying the view and the intimate moment. After a few minutes he pulls out, and we both groan at the loss of connection. His cum drips out of me, coating my inner thighs. I can sense he's enjoying the view, and it's not the one in front of us. His fingers brushing against my sensitive slit startles me as he collects his cum and brings it to my lips.

"Open."

I push up from the partition and turn around to meet his eyes, parting my lips and swirling my tongue around his fingers, tasting our combined juices.

"Mmm. Perfection." He kisses me thoroughly, enjoying the taste of us on my tongue. "Go see your sister and unpack. Your things will be here shortly." He gives my ass a playful tap.

"Where are you going?"

"Work. I'll see you tonight. Make yourself at home; I want you to be comfortable here." He cradles my head in his hands, his eyes shining bright.

Honestly, this place feels more homely than our own ever did. I have no qualms about settling in. "I will," I assure him.

"Good. Welcome home, goddess." He flashes those gorgeous dimples, and I wonder how I got so fucking lucky.

Dameon

I'm going to be late, sorry. Have dinner without me and we'll officially start tomorrow.

Well, shit...

I had hoped he'd be on his way back by now. I'm itching to sit down and have a conversation with him, to get a sense of what to expect. How will our nightly routine unfold? Will this become the norm—him working late, while I wait in limbo? With nothing better to do, I run a bath to wash away the grime from unpacking.

After checking in on Beth earlier, I made the most of being alone to explore every inch of his home. Invasive and creepy? Probably... But the urge to snoop was too hard to resist. I craved any morsel of information that might offer a glimpse into the man I'll be serving for the next twelve months.

When I eventually made my way upstairs and reached his bedroom door, I hesitated, lingering on the threshold. There's something taboo about entering someone else's private sanctuary without their permission. I would hate it if someone went rifling through my personal space. Yet, my curiosity got the better of me, and after a brief pause, I stepped inside.

I took my time exploring, rummaging through the contents of the nightstands, the walk-in closet, and the bathroom, but found nothing of real interest. It was mildly disappointing, to be honest. I'm not entirely sure what I had hoped to uncover—something, *anything*, that would shed some light on the enigma that is Dameon Hayward. Instead, all I garnered was his expectation that I would share his room rather than use the spare bedroom (since my luggage had been delivered here), and his over-the-top orderliness. I briefly entertained the idea of messing up the meticulously arranged suits in his wardrobe just to see if he would notice they weren't two inches apart anymore.

Stepping into the scalding embrace of the bathwater, I sigh as the heat prickles against my skin. Eyes closed, I draw in a few deep breaths, allowing the steam to fill my lungs and transport me to my usual place of calm and serenity. Then I grab my phone and hit the Play button on my familiar playlist, the pop ballads providing a soothing backdrop to my thoughts as I scroll through my notifications.

One particular email catches my attention—from a Dr. Isla Romey, Dameon's physician. She wants my consent to access my medical records from my gynecologist for a review of my birth control regimen. Birth control is a routine requirement for all goddesses, but I totally understand why Dameon would want his own doctor to double-check. With a quick response, I send back my approval and set my phone aside on the tiled floor.

With Taylor Swift belting out her heartache into the thick steam of the bathroom air, I reach for the box of pad Thai beside my phone. Twirling the noodles around my fork, I find myself wondering whether this is just a preview of the next twelve months. In truth, it's not much different from a typical night at home, except I'm getting paid big bucks to chill in this fancy bathtub. I swallow down the guilt that threatens to rise back up.

Two hours later, I emerge from the bath and lounge on Dameon's bed with my Kindle, but I can't shake off the uneasiness. It feels odd being in someone's bed for the first time... without them. I'm unsure of what to do with myself. What if I've wrongly assumed that I'm wanted here in his bed? Should I play it safe and move into the spare room? And what do I wear? Sure, the contract said he wants me naked, but since we haven't officially started yet...

I slip out of my negligée and ease myself under the covers.

Fuck, this is awkward.

Just as I'm about to reach for my negligée again, the bedroom door swings open.

"Hey! You didn't have to wait up for me." He flashes that heart-stopping smile, complete with those captivating dimples.

"That's okay, I didn't mind." Internally I breathe a sigh of relief that he's not kicking me out of his bed.

"You all unpacked and settled?" he asks, already in the process of shedding his tie and unbuttoning his shirt.

"Yep, all sorted."

"Great. I'm gonna jump in the shower real quick." He peels off his shirt and heads into the bathroom, dressed in only his suit pants, a sight I could easily get used to seeing every night.

When the sound of the shower fills the room, I gnaw at my thumbnail. Should I join him? But then again, he did say we'd start tomorrow. If he wanted me to join him, he would have asked, right?

Argh!

Fuck it, I'm going in. If he doesn't want me there, he can ask me to leave. With a determined huff, I throw off the covers and pad to the bathroom. As I push open the door, the steam from the shower carries the rich sandalwood scent of his body wash, hitting me squarely in the face. I pause, taking in the sight before me—the water cascading down his muscular back, his toned ass on full display through the glass shower screen. I resist the urge to wipe the drool from the corner of my mouth.

He turns around, his lips tilting up when he catches me staring. With a playful challenge in his gaze, he continues to soap up his body, tempting me.

Trust me, I don't need any encouragement.

His eyes roam over my naked body, and he tightens his fist on his hard cock, lazily stroking it from base to tip. I wet my lips instinctively, and his eyes zero in on the movement. He grows even harder before my eyes, and I need no further invitation.

I sway my hips toward him, and his hungry eyes devour every inch of my body. Stepping into the billowing steam of the shower, I'm met with a firm grip on my jaw as he attacks my lips with his own. The force of the kiss presses me back against the cool tiles, and I gasp in surprise.

He skillfully slips his tongue inside, setting off a wildfire of sensation. The kiss feels endless, and I'm lost in the heat of his body, intoxicated by the scent of his body wash and the taste of his lips. In this moment, nothing else exists but the feel of his lips consuming mine.

He pulls away abruptly and lifts me, my legs instinctively wrapping around his waist. With a swift movement, he maneuvers us to the other side of the shower, stepping under the cascading water and soaking me in the process. I must look like a drowned rat, but that thought disappears the instant he presses my back against the tiled wall, shielding me from the spray with his body. When I look up into his stormy green eyes, I'm lost in their depths and sudden intensity.

He ravishes my mouth and slides into me effortlessly, as if he knows my body better than I do—a beacon finding its way home in the dark. Despite his tight fit, I'm able to take him in one thrust.

He pounds into me with relentless passion, gripping my thighs tightly to support my weight. Pinning me against the tiled wall, he hits all those spots inside me that make my eyes cross.

"Fuck." I gasp for breath, the steam thick in my lungs. This is far more intimate than our quickie earlier, way too intimate. I break eye contact first, biting down on his shoulder to stifle the overwhelming connection. His groan is deliciously filthy, and I want to hear it again.

He slows his pace, punctuating each thrust with a force that threatens to unravel me completely.

"I'm gonna come," I manage to choke out as my walls begin to collapse around him.

"That's it, soak my cock, goddess. I want to feel your hot cunt squeezing the cum right out of my balls," he breathes, pushing me back against the wall as I wrap my legs around him again once more. He grips my throat and squeezes. With his eyes locked on mine, I teeter on the edge of release, my body trembling until at last, I detonate, my mouth wide open on a silent scream.

"That's my girl," he murmurs, his own release echoing mine as he fills me completely. With my face buried in his shoulder, I sink my teeth into his flesh once again, drawing another throaty groan from him.

After a few deep breaths, I'm able to speak. "Wow, that was…"

"Fucking incredible," he finishes my sentence, pulling out gently and lowering me until my feet reach the tiled floor. I wince as my locked-up muscles protest the movement.

"Turn around," he instructs, grabbing the loofah and body wash. With tender care, he washes and massages every inch of my sore muscles, peppering my clean skin with soft kisses. Each brush of his lips reshapes my view of what the next twelve months might hold.

If that was any indication, I'm going to need to start a regular stretching routine.

Like, as soon as possible.

My eyes fly open the next morning with my bladder screaming at me for relief. I flip off the sheet, almost getting tangled in it, and rush to the bathroom. Then I take my time washing my face and brushing my teeth, making sure to gargle with mouthwash for that extra fresh sensation. I tie my hair up in a messy bun with the hairband perpetually looped around my wrist and prepare to commence my morning "job."

Emerging from the bathroom, the sight before me stops me in my tracks. Dameon lies sprawled on his back, fast asleep, his naked form bathed in the soft morning light filtering through the blinds. The white sheet barely covers his package, drawing my gaze like a magnet. I lean against the doorframe and take a moment to admire this perfect male specimen. His chest rises and falls in a steady rhythm, and soft snores escape his parted lips. With one arm thrown above his head and his face turned slightly into the pillow, he looks utterly peaceful. His sandy blond hair is tousled, but that doesn't detract from his perfection; it only adds to it. The defined muscles of his chest and abs call out to be explored, preferably with my tongue. It's surreal to think that I'll have the pleasure of being with this man for the next twelve months. I'm one lucky bitch.

I climb onto the bed with caution, moving on my hands and knees, careful not to jolt him awake. Pulling down the sheet, I find him semi-hard, even in his sleep. I position myself between his legs, carefully pick up his cock and plant a kiss on the tip. It pulses in response. With my minty-fresh tongue, I give the head a teasing lick, and I'm rewarded with a spurt of precum and a moan. Taking him fully into my mouth until he reaches the back of my throat, I hum, the vibrations causing him to harden further.

"Fuuuck, that feels good," he moans, his voice husky from sleep. I slide off his dick with a pop.

"Good morning," I say with a smirk.

"Mmm, it sure is, goddess." He smiles sleepily, stretching out. With an arm behind his head, he closes his eyes and fists my bun with the other hand, guiding me back onto his cock. Hint taken—no more talking. Seems someone isn't a morning person. I can make him one, though. I almost snicker at the thought. I suck him down hard and don't relent, using my hands, tongue, and lips to give him one hell of a blow job—one he won't soon forget. I don't stop until I'm rewarded with his release, swallowing it down.

Dameon blinks his eyes until they're wide open. "That was *the* best way to wake up. What on earth did you put on my dick? It was ice cold yet burning at the same time," he marvels.

"Mouthwash."

"Mouthwash?" he repeats slowly, as though trying to wrap his head around the concept.

"Yeah, did you like it?"

"Fuck yeah." Our eyes lock, and the air thickens with tension. "Thank you," he adds quietly, his eyes softening.

"Just doing my duty." I shrug, trying to lighten the mood and break the intimate moment. I'm joking, but also, I'm kind of not. It's a reminder that this is just a job, nothing more. For both of us.

His eyes narrow playfully. "Come here." He quickly grabs my arm, flipping us over and pinning me beneath him. A surprised squeal escapes my lips as he lands on top, and I burst into laughter when he starts tickling my ribs.

"Just doing your duty? I bet your cunt is dripping for me, kitten. You get off from having my dick in your hot little mouth, don't you?"

When I can no longer breathe through the laughter, I concede, "Fine, yes, you win. I love having your cock in my mouth, sir."

His hand cups my core, squeezing, and I gasp at the sensation of his warm palm against my slick folds.

"It's a shame I don't have time to take care of my pussy right now. You'll just have to wait until tonight. Only if you're a good girl today."

I feign shock, mouthing, *Good, me?* and pointing at myself.

He runs a hand through his messy hair. "Don't act cute with me, you're not fooling anyone with that innocent act. Come on, get up. I'll introduce you to the staff before I head to the office." He slips into a pair of boxers and pulls me to my feet. "Let's go," he says, smacking me on the ass as he leads me down the staircase.

Two women are bustling about the kitchen, and suddenly, I feel acutely aware of my nakedness. One of them, an elderly woman rummaging through the fridge, is dressed in crisp chef whites. She bears a striking resemblance to Martha; she could almost pass for her sister. Given Dameon's penchant for keeping it in the family, it wouldn't surprise me if they were related.

The other woman, considerably younger, is dressed in snug black slacks and a fitted white shirt that's molded to her curves. It's so tight it's practically painted on. She's strikingly beautiful, with flowing black hair and wide doe-like eyes, and she's rigorously polishing the stone benchtop, making her large breasts bounce. Self-conscious, I almost reach to cover myself, when Dameon clears his throat. Both women turn around, and I push my shoulders back, making sure to look each of them square in the eye. I refuse to feel ashamed.

Their reactions couldn't be more different: the older woman smiles, her expression seemingly pleased by my presence, while the younger one's eyes trail down Dameon's bare chest before fixing on me with a sneer. An actual sneer—I didn't realize people still did that. She wrinkles her nose like she's just stepped in dog shit and gives my naked body a disdainful once-over.

"This is Eloise, my talented chef," Dameon says, gesturing to the poised woman in chef whites. "She ensures I'm well-fed every day, too well if you ask me."

"Psh, if anything, you need more fattening up," she retorts, lips pursed. "Hello, dear. It's a pleasure to meet you. If there's anything specific you'd like to eat, don't hesitate to let me know." To her credit, her eyes never shift below my chin.

"Thank you, that's very kind of you."

"And this is Maddy, my housekeeper. She keeps everything in order and spotless."

I bet she does.

And I bet she doesn't mind polishing his knob, either. There's no way they haven't fucked. Not when she prances around with that ridiculously tight shirt with her bra peeking out, a full face of makeup, and blown-out hair. No one goes to that much effort for their job. Not even me, and my role is literally to seduce men.

"Nice to meet you, Maddy." I fake a smile.

"It's Madeline. Only those close to me call me Maddy."

Oh, they've definitely hooked up.

"For goodness' sake, Maddy, would it kill you to be nice?" Eloise rolls her eyes. "Once you've finished with the stone bench, the oven needs cleaning."

"Since when do you tell me what to do? I don't work for you, or *her*, for that matter."

"No, but you work for me," Dameon warns. "Be nice, Maddy," he adds, dismissing her like an annoying fly.

Dameon laces his fingers through mine and leads me back to the bedroom. I'm itching to ask him about Maddy and the status of their relationship. On one hand, it's none of my business. But if I'm living here for the next twelve months, I need to know what I'm dealing with. I have a right to know the score. But I also don't want him thinking I can't handle a little cattiness or that I care if he's fucking someone else.

Shit, this is a mind fuck.

I swallow the burning question on the tip of my tongue, and it goes down like acid.

"I'm going to jump in the shower and head to work. I'll see you tonight." He plants a quick peck on my lips and disappears into the bathroom.

What the hell am I supposed to do all day?

Ouch. Fuck.

I gently massage aloe vera gel into my chest, welcoming the soothing coolness seeping into my burning skin. Glancing over my shoulder into the mirror, I grimace at the sight of my bright red back.

Crap.

I can't reach my back, so I slather on another thick layer of gel across my chest and shoulders instead. My skin sizzles and prickles as the gel works its magic. This is ridiculous. I look like a lobster. I wouldn't be surprised if it starts blistering. Serves me right for being lazy and not going back to grab the sunscreen.

After Dameon headed off to work, I decided to give the penthouse a wide berth, especially with bitch face Maddy lurking about. I didn't want to interrupt Beth while she was kicking off her homeschooling today, either. So, I roamed around Bondi, taking in the sights and sounds. Bondi has such a unique vibe—it's got an international flair, with loads of tourists and backpackers, but there's also a tight-knit local community. You can spot the locals easily, especially the women in their Lululemon leggings, inflated tits and lips. My mother would feel right at home here. After signing up for a Pilates class—apparently it's quite the thing to do in Bondi, with more studios than organic juice bars—I took a leisurely stroll along the beach.

Walking along the shoreline, feeling the warm sand between my toes while the sun blazed overhead, was pure bliss. I stripped down to my bikini and threw on a hat and sunglasses, but a quick rummage of my bag revealed that in my excitement, I had forgotten the damn sunscreen. The thought of going back to fetch it felt like too much effort.

I always knew my laziness would get me killed one day, but I didn't think I would be going out with heat stroke at the start of spring. When I got back to the empty penthouse, a glance in the mirror confirmed my fear—that I had fucked up. Downing a bottle of water, I collapsed into bed, exhausted from the sweltering heat. When I woke up in the afternoon, it was worse. Much worse. My skin, at first a mild pink, now blazed a furious red.

Fifteen minutes ago, Dameon texted that he was on his way home. Now I'm standing in front of the mirror, feeling sorry for myself, and praying that aloe vera works miracles. My skin is like the surface of the sun, and I could almost cry from the pain. Giving myself a quick once-over, I can't help but half laugh and half cry at the sorry sight. Wiping under my eyes, I sniffle and head downstairs to wait for him.

Chapter Thirteen

Dameon

My driver pulls up in front of my building, and I exhale loudly into the still air of the car. It's been a clusterfuck of a day, but the thought of returning to my goddess, patiently waiting on her knees for me, has made it that much more bearable.

Kevin opens my door with his usual greeting. "Evening, sir."

"Kevin," I acknowledge with a nod. "How was her day?"

"She spent most of it at the beach. She seemed to enjoy it, sir," he reports as we stride through the foyer toward my private elevator. I loosen my tie and undo the top button of my shirt.

"Thank you," I reply, stepping into the elevator and pressing the button for the penthouse. "Have a good night."

"You too, sir."

The tension eases from my shoulders the closer I get to Hailee. Stepping into the penthouse, I'm greeted by a sight of pure beauty—one that I could easily get used to seeing every day. She kneels before me, naked, assuming the traditional submissive posture of Eden. With her back straight, knees slightly parted, hands resting on her thighs, and head bowed, her white-blonde hair falls gracefully around her face.

"Hi, gorgeous." My fingers gently trace the soft strands of her hair.

"Good evening, sir. Did you have a good day?" Her voice is strained, off somehow. Instantly, I tense. Something isn't right. My mind races through a million different scenarios.

What happened? Has someone hurt her? Is she unhappy? Does she want to leave?

I lift her chin with two fingers, searching her face for answers. She manages a smile through watery eyes, and my heart fucking shatters at the sight. My eyes drift down her body, and then I see it.

"What the fuck happened to your skin, Hailee?" I can't contain my shock at seeing her once flawless tanned skin now beet red.

"It's nothing, sir. Just a little sunburn." She tries to laugh it off, but her attempt falls flat with a sniffle. It's far from just a little sunburn; her skin is inflamed and painfully red. Placing my hand on her shoulder, I feel the heat radiating from her, almost burning my palm. This is first-degree sunburn at the very least.

"Stand, gorgeous," I command, offering her my hand. As she rises from her knees, I notice the wince that crosses her face. "Let's go." I dump my laptop bag in the lounge before leading her upstairs to our bedroom.

"Lie on the bed."

She complies without a word. I shed my jacket and toss my tie over a nearby chair, roll up my sleeves and enter the bathroom to run a tepid bath. Once it's filled to the right level, I return to the bedroom and scoop up my kitten, carrying her bridal style to the tub.

Her eyes track my movements like a deer caught in the headlights. I don't like seeing her docile like this. I want my sassy ball of sunshine back. Carefully I lower her into the cool bath, and she hisses when the water touches her overheated skin. Once she's comfortably settled, I head downstairs and return with a bottle of water and ibuprofen for the pain. She must be in a world of hurt.

"Drink this," I instruct, handing her the bottle and the tablets. She takes a sip and swallows them down, handing the bottle back to me.

"Thank you," she says sheepishly.

"Nope. All of it." She hesitates for a moment before bringing the bottle back to her lips.

Good girl.

It takes her a few minutes, but she finishes it all before I take the empty bottle from her.

"Now, tell me what happened," I say, softening my voice. I've been barking orders at her since I got home, and she's responded well without putting up much of a fight. Even though I'm fuming, there's a time and place for punishment.

"Not much to tell, really. I went for a walk along the beach, and I forgot the sunscreen, that's all."

"How long were you in the sun for?"

"Only a couple of hours."

That's not very long, but still, she should know better. The Australian sun is brutal, even in early spring.

"I had my hat and sunglasses, though," she adds.

"Hailee, look at me," I say firmly. She's been pointedly avoiding my gaze, studying the bathwater the entire time. She raises her head, and I capture her beautiful green eyes that always make me lose my breath.

"Your body belongs to me for the next twelve months. You will look after *my* property while under my care. Only *I* get to mark your beautiful skin as I see fit, not you. Got it?"

"Yes, sir. Are you going to punish me?"

"You bet your ass, I am. As soon as you're healed, I guarantee that fine ass of yours will be as red as your shoulders when I'm through with it."

Her lips curl up in a small smile, and she looks away. I know she's just as excited about the prospect of her punishment as I am.

I strip off my pants and shirt, leaving my boxers, and spread a towel on her side of the bed. Gently I lift her from the bathtub, and she winces from the contact of my arms on her irritated skin. Laying her out on the towel, I roll her onto her stomach and pick up the bottle of aloe vera she was using, smoothing it into her back until it evaporates. Moving onto her front, I rub the gel into her chest and shoulders. At least she remembered a hat, so her beautiful face was saved from being scorched.

"Did you have lunch?" I ask.

She shakes her head. My hand itches to take her over my knee and tan her ass red.

"Breakfast, at least?"

She nods. "I'm sorry, sir. I feel so stupid. This wasn't how our first official night was supposed to go." Her chin trembles and she sniffs. She's in pain and hasn't eaten since breakfast; no wonder she's emotional. Rising from the bed, I kiss her forehead, the only spot not red.

"You're just racking up the punishments on day one, aren't you? At this rate, you'll need a cushion to sit down for the rest of the year." I wink, earning a small laugh from her. I press my lips to her forehead again. "I'll be back."

In the kitchen I heat up the dinner Eloise prepared—chicken cordon bleu and sautéed vegetables. Carrying it on a tray, I return to the bedroom and lay it out on the bed. I cut up her chicken and offer her a bite. The aroma of buttery goodness wafts up, making her stomach rumble. Loudly.

"I can feed myself," she sulks. "I may be burned to a crisp, but I can still use my arms."

"I know. Open," I command.

Her lips obediently part as I bring the fork to her mouth. She takes a bite, chewing slowly, and closes her eyes, savoring the flavor before swallowing. The sight of her throat moving and her little sighs of pleasure ignite something primal within me. Feeding her feels unexpectedly intimate, yet erotic at the same time. I never would have imagined it could be such a turn-on. My cock strains against my boxers, the glistening tip peeking out. Hailee's gaze lingers on it, her tongue darting out to moisten her lips.

"There will be plenty of time for you to taste my cock later... when you're not in pain," I reassure her, though it takes every ounce of self-control to will my cock back down.

"Tell me, how did you end up in Sydney?" I shift the conversation to distract myself from the way her lips wrap around the fork.

"It's a long story, but the short version is that my mother is a complete nightmare. She's toxic, narcissistic... a horrible human being. I had to get Beth away from her. So, when I turned eighteen, I became her official guardian and we moved as far away as possible, to the other side of the world."

I wince. "Unfortunately, I've come across a few women like your mother myself. It must have been tough for you growing up."

"It was. But I've dealt with it. I go to therapy to work through it and make sure I don't turn out like her. I'm convinced everyone should see a counselor at least once in their lifetime. There are already enough assholes in the world without adding another one."

"True that," I chuckle. "You hail from New York, right? How did you end up with tanned skin and green eyes? You look more European than Big Apple."

"Yep, born and bred in NYC. I'm assuming my father; it's a guessing game, really. My dad's a total mystery; never knew him. Probably some random rich guy that my mom was chasing back then. Mom's British, which explains my sister's fair skin and brown eyes. Her dad was one of my mom's failed marriages." She shrugs, and silence falls between us. Hailee shifts, tucking a strand of hair behind her ear, avoiding my gaze.

"Hey, look at me." I gently lift her chin with my thumb and forefinger to search her eyes. "You're a good sister, Hailee. A good person. And you're nothing like your mother." Her eyes shine bright like fresh blades of grass.

"Thank you," she murmurs softly.

As I finish feeding her most of her dinner, the color returns to her cheeks, and I sense the ibuprofen is taking effect. A comfortable silence envelops us as I tuck into my own meal. In her presence, I find myself relaxing, the tension of the day melting away. Normally, sipping a top-shelf whiskey while sinking into a warm pussy is my go-to stress reliever, but tonight is different. I don't feel the urge, or any longing for it. My focus is entirely on Hailee, ensuring her wellbeing. Right here, right now, the chaos of my day fades into the background, replaced by the calmness of being fully absorbed in her presence.

CHAPTER FOURTEEN

Hailee

I'm officially bored out of my brain. A whole week of swimming and Pilates and lunching with Beth has been wonderful. It's the life of luxury, and I should be lapping it up, making the most of it. Living the dream, as they say. And I have. But I'm also losing my fucking mind. If I don't find something to do with my time during the day while I wait for my master to return home, I will drive myself insane. Plus, staying out of Maddy's way seems to be a good strategy… so far.

"You ready yet?" Dameon's voice echoes from downstairs.

I pull my denim skirt over my bikini bottoms. "Yep, coming!"

This time I make sure to put a bottle of sunscreen in my bag. It's Saturday, and it's our first weekend together. The week has seemingly gone well, and we've settled into a routine. We wake up, I perform my morning "job," he goes to work, and I avoid Maddy by going to the beach or a Pilates class, followed by lunch with Beth. Then in the afternoon, I lounge around by the pool before he comes home. I greet him on my knees and serve him dinner; we talk, laugh, and share stories late into the evening, and finally, end the night with phenomenal, mind-blowing sex. See, routine. And I'm loving it. Except, I'm starting to go stir crazy.

"Please tell me you learned your lesson and brought the sunscreen?"

"Of course, sir." I bat my lashes playfully at him as I sashay down the stairs. He shakes his head, but I catch the corner of his lips twitching.

The air is warm but pleasant as we step out of our building and into the sunshine. We wander through the local flea market, strolling hand in hand, checking out stalls stocked with homemade candles, soaps, and chocolates. When we eventually reach the beach, Dameon decides to go for a swim. I settle on my towel and make sure to cover my legs and arms with copious amounts of sunscreen, determined not to repeat my mistake. With my Kindle in hand, I pass the time while I wait for him to return. Twenty minutes later, just when I'm getting to the juicy part of my reverse harem story, he returns, looking like the King of Atlantis himself—dripping wet and panting heavily, with muscles that glisten under the sun's rays. I capture my lower lip with my teeth and freely run my eyes over his sculpted form. With a body like that, Dameon Hayward was born to fuck.

"Keep looking at me like that, kitten, and you'll be on your knees in front of the entire beach. And I don't give a fuck who sees."

Liquid heat pools low in my stomach in response to his threat. But I'm unfazed by the prospect of an audience; in fact, I relish the opportunity to put on a captivating performance just for him. Which he knows all too well.

"Strip. I'll rub sunscreen on your back," Dameon commands.

I push down my skirt and slip my tank top over my head, revealing a pale pink bikini that contrasts beautifully with my sun-kissed skin. I love the way his eyes darken to a turbulent shade of green whenever he admires my figure. Those eyes are my drug of choice. Intoxicating and addictive.

I lay down on my stomach and Dameon pulls the strings of my bikini, pouring sunscreen over my back. As he massages it into my skin, I savor the sensation, relieved that this time I'm not writhing in agony.

The coconut scent of the lotion lingers in the air between us as his firm fingers expertly manipulate the muscles in my shoulders and back. It's pure heaven, an exquisite blend of pleasure and pain, so divine that I can't contain the moan of relief that escapes my lips. With his hard cock digging into my ass, I'm certain I'm making a large wet spot on my bikini bottoms.

"Flip over."

I do as ordered, revealing my bare breasts. Bondi isn't a nudist beach, but no one really bats an eye at a naked breast or an ass cheek. Dameon straddles my hips and squeezes the sunscreen onto my chest, rubbing the thick, white cream into my breasts.

"You're such a pretty whore for me. I can't wait to massage my cum into these gorgeous tits," he mutters under his breath. He continues to squeeze and massage before pinching my nipples. A strangled groan slips past my lips. The beach is jam-packed, and people are everywhere, but there's no being quiet when his skilled hands are playing with my body like this.

"You think you can come?"

"I don't know... I'm close, though," I reply with raw honesty on another breathy moan.

"Keep quiet for me, kitten. Being arrested isn't on the agenda for today." I bite down on my lower lip, stifling any sounds that threaten to escape as he drizzles more lotion across my chest. His hands resume their sensual strokes and massages, before becoming more intense, his fingers gripping and pinching my nipples with a deliciously brutal force.

I clamp down on my bottom lip until a metallic taste trickles into my mouth. The view here on my back is breathtaking: I have a front-row seat to his bare chest and powerful forearms as they skillfully tend to my breasts. I'm on the brink of ecstasy, so tantalizingly close, but I crave that extra spark to send me hurtling over the edge.

"I know exactly what you need, kitten." I swear he's a mind reader. He leans over and quickly sucks a nipple into his mouth, bites down hard and then soothes the abused bud with his tongue. I gasp as the sensation washes over me, precisely what I needed to plunge headfirst into an orgasmic rush. While it may not be earth-shattering, it's a small yet potent release that sends a delicious shiver of pleasure coursing down my spine.

"Hmm, I know my pain slut well." He kisses me passionately, our tongues battling as he licks into my mouth with dominance. Pulling back slightly, his breath is hot against my lips when he whispers the word "perfection." I melt into a puddle right here, in the middle of the beach, suddenly overcome with emotion.

I've never experienced an orgasm solely from my breasts before; this is new and uncharted territory for me. Consider my mind blown. When Dameon shifts away from me and helps me sit up, I quickly survey our surroundings, noticing two young couples staring at us. I don't bother trying to discern their expressions; their faces are shielded by sunglasses and hats. Instead, I'm scanning for any children nearby.

"Don't worry, I already checked," he chuckles. See, mind reader. I just shake my head, amused.

"I'm going for a swim," I announce, craving the refreshing embrace of the ocean to calm my thoughts and restore balance. A reset to get my head back in the game. Dameon ties my bikini top back in place, and I make my way toward the water's edge. I need a moment alone to process what just happened.

It's only been a week, yet I already sense this man will be my downfall.

CHAPTER FIFTEEN

Dameon

"How was the swim?" I ask as she steps into my field of vision above me. I sit up, propping myself on my elbow with my knee bent, watching rivulets of water cascade down her cleavage, tempting me to lick off every salty drop. I'm still as hard as granite from her breathtaking performance earlier.

"Beautiful," she replies, wringing out her hair. I glance down the beach and then back up to her.

"Wait, where did you swim?"

Her brows pinch together. "Just here." She gestures to the ocean directly ahead of us.

"Are you fucking kidding me?" I ask incredulously, fully sitting up. "You went swimming outside the red and yellow flags?"

"Yeah, what's the big deal?"

"Are you serious?" I press.

"What's the problem? You swam there as well," she points out.

"No, I didn't. I walked down to the other side of the beach where the flags are."

She rolls her eyes. "I'm not a child, I wasn't going to drown."

"Says every dumb fuck who thinks they can swim at Bondi Beach," I retort. "Hailee, they've made a whole TV show about saving stupid tourists. The surf is rough; it's unlike any other beach in the world with its unexpected currents and rips. The number of rescues needed on a daily basis is crazy." My eyebrows hit my hairline.

"Okay, okay. No swimming outside the flags. Got it." She raises her palms in a calming gesture.

"Why on earth didn't you just walk down to the flags?" I can't let this slide. She could've drowned.

I see her hesitate for a moment before sighing. "It was all the way on the other side of the beach." She points to the flags as if I haven't already made the same trek today. She grumbles, and it's too cute for words. If this weren't so serious, I'd laugh.

"Let me get this straight. You put your life in danger because you were too lazy to walk, like, eight hundred meters?" I tease.

She mumbles something under her breath that I can't quite catch.

"What was that?" I ask.

"I said, yes, sir."

"You're just racking up the punishments, aren't you? Don't think I've forgotten about being burned to a crisp, either. Or skipping meals," I say, amused. I'm thrilled at the prospect of doling out her first real punishment tonight. She mock pouts, but I know she's craving it as much as I am.

She hovers on the edge between pleasure and pain, a place I savor the most during punishment. Exploring ways to bring her pleasure while denying her the ultimate release she craves is my favorite game. Her cries, filled with wanton desperation, ignite a primal hunger within me. It makes me fucking feral. Her moans, both filthy and beautiful, are only for my ears. No one else will ever hear those sweet sounds again; they belong only to me. The sight before me will be permanently burned into my brain. She kneels in the center of the bed, her arms bound to the headboard, and her ankles secured to a spreader bar, offering me unrestricted access to her pussy and plugged ass.

"Please..." Her plea comes out garbled through the ring gag. I lean in, brushing the hair from her face, revealing eyes that shine bright with submission. Her face glistens with drool and sweat.

"You're doing so well, goddess," I praise.

As my fingers trail over the delicate lips of her swollen cunt, she moans and squirms, desperate for my touch. I chuckle darkly, admiring the deep red hue of her ass, having warmed her up with my palm. I've kept her on the edge for the past forty minutes, and she's soaked, swollen, and I bet, sore as hell.

"You'll receive three lashes from my belt, one for each infraction," I declare, looping my belt and letting it crack against her left cheek with a satisfying snap. The blow is deliberate, precise—a reminder of her transgressions. Only using a quarter of my strength, it was as light as I could make it without making it seem I was going easy on her.

"You will care for your wellbeing and never skip meals," I command, as a faint "Yes, sir" escapes her lips. The belt strikes her right cheek, this time with more force, eliciting a gasp of pleasurable pain.

"You will care for your body, for my sake if not your own. I own this ass, and you will treat it with respect," I assert, watching as she sniffs and nods.

The final lash across her ass is delivered with a force meant to leave a lasting impression. I want her to remember this, forever. "You will never put your life in danger again," I stress. She sobs into the pillow, a chorus of apologies tumbling from her lips in a jumbled mess.

"Shh, it's all over now," I soothe, rubbing her back gently. The three raised stripes on her ass contrast with the rosy blush from the earlier spanking and only serve to enhance her beauty. *That's my girl, so fucking beautiful.*

I start to release her from the restraints: First, the spreader bar between her legs, then her wrists from the headboard and the gag from behind her teeth. I wrap her in a warm blanket, cradling her in my arms. As she sobs, I hold her close, the warmth of her petite body seeping into mine. I rest against the headboard as she curls into my lap, nestled against my chest. It's a natural fit, like second nature, like I've been doing this for years. Despite my own arousal, I remain still, focused solely on comforting her. Tonight is about my goddess, and if she can't find release, neither will I. I continue to soothe and praise her until her hiccups fade away, and she grows quiet.

"How do you feel?" I ask.

"Good. Really good, actually. Thank you," she mumbles, a faint frown marring her beautiful face.

I chuckle. "If you need a punishment, kitten, just ask. There's no shame in asking for what your body needs. I'd rather you do that than be a brat and break the rules."

She smiles shyly, hiding it beneath the blanket.

"Trust me, you don't have to ask me twice to punish your sexy ass," I tease, earning another hidden smile from her.

"Here." I pass her a bottle of water. "Drink," I urge, and she obediently finishes it. Once she's done, I take the empty bottle from her.

"Can I ask you something?" Her curious gaze is fixed on me.

"Sure, but after a bath and after I put lotion on your ass. I don't want you to bruise." I lift her up from the bed and carry her into our bathroom. Okay, maybe that was a little white lie—bathing her and massaging her sore muscles might just be my favorite part of a punishment, or at least a very close second.

After we finish up in the bath, I apply the lotion to her cheeks, taking care not to press too hard. The three welts look good; the skin is intact without any signs of bruising. She'll heal nicely in the next couple of days. I lay down next to her, propped up on my elbow so I can see her expression while she waits for the lotion to dry. "What is it? I know you're dying to ask," I say, chuckling at her fidgeting fingers.

She hesitates for a moment, then blurts, "Why do you need relationships to be transactional?"

What?!

I'm floored. This is what she wants to know? What she wants to discuss at this very moment?

Fuck me.

"Why do you want to know?" I draw out slowly.

"Because I want to understand. I want to get to know you."

Talk about going for the jugular. I was expecting an easy question, not asking me to unload past trauma. I'm tempted to blow her off and change the subject, but when she looks at me like that, raw and sincere, I can't deny her anything.

"Okay." I sigh, reluctant to fall down the rabbit hole and reopen past wounds. I scrub my hand down my face, feeling the memories bearing down on me.

"I met Mia when I was in college. She was intelligent, funny and had this wild streak to her. Nothing and no one could tame her, dampen her fire. We fell hard for each other." I swallow the knot in my throat, and Hailee nods in encouragement.

"We started experimenting together, discovering what we liked sexually and what we didn't. We realized our kinks were a perfect fit: I liked to dominate and be in complete control, whereas she liked to relinquish it in the bedroom. Mia didn't come from a wealthy family, but that didn't bother me. It wasn't even a consideration until I wanted to propose.

"When I mentioned my plans I got a lot of push back from my family, especially from my dad. He didn't want me to marry her, saying she didn't come from 'good stock' and wasn't good enough for me. James, my best mate, didn't like her either, though he wouldn't say why. I figured he kept quiet because he knew how crazy I was about her. And unlike *every* other teenager, I actually listened to my dad and decided to hold off on the proposal." I hesitate, considering how much to share. She's silent, waiting for me to continue. I decide to skip over a few details.

"I'm glad I did listen in the end because she became obsessed with getting married and becoming my wife. Our relationship became strained, and eventually I ended it. She didn't take it well at all—she got really bitter and vindictive. She went to the press, telling them I abused her, that I was into kinky shit, and I coerced her into it. Given who my dad is, it was newsworthy, and our competitors had a field day with the story. Everything we did was one hundred percent consensual. But I had no proof; it was my word against hers."

"God, that pisses me off. Women like her make it hard for other women who have *actually* been assaulted to be heard and believed," Hailee remarks with frustration. I lightly run my fingers up her spine, enjoying the sensation of her soft skin beneath my touch.

"Yeah, well, now every sexual encounter I have is documented. Everyone signs on the dotted line to express their consent, and everyone signs an NDA. I can't go through something like that again. It nearly destroyed me." The weight of the past is still heavy on my shoulders.

"Thank you for sharing with me," she says softly.

"You're welcome," I reply, tucking a piece of hair behind her ear. "Plus, it's only fair if you share your ass with me that I return the favor." I wink at her.

She covers her mouth to stifle a yawn. "Time for sleep," I order, pulling the covers over us as I spoon her from behind. She wiggles her ass into me, which causes her to hiss in pain. I bite the inside of my cheek to smother a laugh. She forgot her ass has just been punished and is still plugged.

"Can you please remove the plug?" She looks back at me over her shoulder with a sweet and innocent expression.

"I'll remove it in the morning. I shouldn't need to remind you, but just in case, no touching my pretty pink pussy until I say otherwise." She groans in frustration.

I don't plan on making her wait long for relief, though. I know she's dying for it. She just doesn't know that yet. With a smirk, my eyes drift shut as we settle in for the night.

Chapter Sixteen

Hailee

"Later, Kev." I give a small wave as I pass the front desk.

"Have a lovely day, ma'am." His eyes crinkle with a gentle smile.

Leaving the apartment building, I'm excited to have a busy day ahead. I've missed Cora; I haven't seen her much since she left Eden. In fact, I haven't been in contact with anyone from Eden since I moved in with Dameon a month ago. Cora's idling out the front in a brand-new black BMW convertible, looking every bit the goddess she is. This lifestyle really suits her.

"Get in, bitch, we've got money to burn!" She slides on her sunglasses. I shake my head and drop onto the soft leather passenger seat.

"Cute outfit, by the way," she comments, eyeing my lacy pink crop top.

"Thanks! Where're we going?"

"I've got the whole day planned. Shopping, followed by lunch at Ivy, and then finishing off with full body massages."

I clap my hands like a little kid, grateful to have my day filled and to be spending it with my friend.

Fifteen minutes later, Cora tosses her car keys to the valet at one of Sydney's most exclusive department stores. We make our way inside, and a line of staff greets us, ready to escort us to a private dressing room. Suddenly I feel underdressed in my tiny crop top, denim skirt, and sandals. I link my arm with Cora's as we follow behind.

"This is a bit over-the-top, isn't it?" I whisper.

"James organized it for us." She rolls her eyes. Enough said. Her husband—Dameon's best friend and co-CEO—is even more controlling than Dameon.

We enter the dressing room, where rack upon rack of clothing stand, ready for us to peruse.

"Would you like assistance in selecting items, or would you prefer privacy?" a staff member asks.

"Privacy would be great, thank you," Cora responds.

"Of course. There's champagne on ice for you both to enjoy, and if you require assistance, please press this button." We both thank her as she leaves us to browse. I flick through the formal gowns, casual wear, lingerie, bikinis, and resort wear on the groaning racks. A realization sparks and I fling open the dressing room door. "Excuse me," I sing out, "have these clothes been pre-selected?"

"Yes, ma'am, Mr. Hayward and Mr. Hayes have chosen everything in this room," the attendant confirms.

"Of course, thank you."

She walks away, leaving us in privacy. I glance over at Cora and snort with laughter.

"Doesn't it bother you that he's so controlling and demanding all the time?" I keep my tone playful, but I genuinely want to know her answer.

"Not at all. I kind of like it... crave it," Cora replies. "I resisted at the start—you know, my own thoughts and feelings about feminism and what's socially acceptable getting in my way. But at the end of the day, it's my choice to submit, and if I change my mind about anything we do, I know he'll agree and support my wishes." She shrugs. "He loves me, he would do anything for me, and in the end, I'm the one who controls our relationship. Plus, I can't deny, his dominance makes me so fucking wet," she adds with a coy smile.

She's lucky to have found James. I remember seeing them together at Eden; they were so sweet, the yin to each other's yang—perfect for each other. When they're together his eyes never stray far from her; he's always captivated by her, seeming to anticipate her needs before she even realizes she has them. My heart aches with want, and I can't help but feel a pang of jealousy.

We hit the rails and begin browsing, but there's not a single pair of pants in sight. I smirk. *Kinky bastards.* The clothes are all from expensive labels, and I start to make a pile. I pull out slinky skirts, tops and cocktail dresses, my fingers grazing the soft, luxurious fabrics. Moving to the accessories table, I pick out shoes and handbags to complete the looks. I bypass the lingerie; it seems kind of pointless when I'm naked all the time anyway. Cora, on the other hand, pulls out a barely-there red bikini.

"Oh, this will be perfect for the boat!" she exclaims.

"What boat?"

"Dameon hasn't told you?"

"Told me what?"

"We're going on a cruise together in a couple of weeks. James and Dameon co-own a yacht and there will be about..." She pauses. "Four couples in total, I think? All clients from Eden. It's kind of a kinky cruise." She raises her shoulders in excitement.

"A what?" I huff a laugh.

"Yeah, kind of like Eden but on the ocean. It'll be so much fun. You should totally get a new bikini too."

I look through the swimsuits that our men selected, and they can barely be called bikinis. All of them are G-strings with tiny scraps of material for the tops. They wouldn't even cover a nipple. But by the sound of this cruise, I think that's the point. I select an emerald-green bikini that matches my eyes and add it the pile.

"Do you want some champagne?" I ask, heading over to the side table where a selection of savory and sweet treats is set up.

"Yes, please."

I pour two glasses as Cora joins me, and we collapse onto the loungers. Handing her a glass, I notice her eyeing me warily.

"You can ask me, you know." I side-eye her.

"I didn't know I was that transparent," she laughs.

We both sip our champagne, falling into a comfortable silence as I wait for Cora to form her question.

"How do you do it?" She nibbles on her bottom lip as she pauses to gather her thoughts. "What I mean is, how can you keep your feelings separate? For me, submitting is deeply entwined with my feelings for James. I don't think I could separate the two."

I sigh. "It's tough, I'm not going to lie. But it's a mutual agreement; we're both getting something out of it, and when the twelve months is up, we'll walk away." I shrug like it's not a big deal.

"But *will* you be able to walk away when time's up? I know you've always had a thing for him."

"I like Dameon a lot. I do. But this is just a job, and if I need to keep reminding myself of that, I will. To be honest, I'm a little envious of your relationship with James. It's clear that he absolutely adores you. And you get to serve him and submit. That's what I want with someone. But men like Dameon don't fall for women like me." It feels good to finally admit the brutal truth, acknowledging the harsh realities that come with the complexities of my job.

"Oh, Hailee. That's not true. James fell for me! We certainly had our difficulties getting to this point, but all that pain and anguish was worth it in the end. It was worth fighting for."

"No offense, but your situation is different. You've only ever had one client at Eden, and that was James. And you had that connection through Leo," I point out. Her eyes soften at the mention of her little boy. "This isn't a fairy tale; this is real life. And hot billionaires who are kinky and like to dominate when they fuck don't end up with hookers. They end up with a socialite from the same elite circle who has no idea what he really needs in bed. I've been down this road before... I know how it ends," I confess.

"I get it... I do." She squeezes my arm gently and looks directly into my eyes. "But you forget that you're an intelligent, kind-hearted, vivacious woman who doesn't let her profession dictate her worthiness. One day the right man will come along who will recognize your worth and see that you're more than just your job. Exactly how you see yourself."

"Maybe," I respond with a grateful smile, though inside, doubt gnaws at me. Cora's perceptive gaze tells me she sees through my smile, that she understands the burden of the taboo that clings to me like a stubborn shadow. *Once a whore, always a whore*—as if a simple label could ever define the entirety of a person. Despite Cora's reassurance, I know that shedding that stigma won't be easy. It's etched into the fabric of society, ingrained in the judgments of others, and sometimes, even in the quiet doubts that lurk within me. Yet, in moments like these, I find a glimmer of hope—a belief that maybe, there's a path forward where the weight of judgment fades, and I'm free to define myself on my own terms.

"Dameon is..." she begins, her voice trailing off as she searches for the right words. "From what James has said, Dameon hasn't had it easy with relationships either. He's only had one serious girlfriend and that was years ago. Apparently, she was a piece of work."

"He told me."

Her eyebrows shoot up in surprise. "Then you know why he is the way he is. He rarely dates, and he won't ever touch a woman without an NDA and a contract. He believes he's only cut out for one type of relationship: transactional." Cora's words carry a weighty truth, that behind the veneer of power and control lies a man shaped by betrayal. "This really needs to be *just* a job."

"It is, I promise," I say with forced confidence, though I'm not sure who I'm trying harder to convince—Cora or myself.

Downing the rest of my champagne in one determined gulp, I push aside the lingering uncertainty. "Let's try these on and get to the restaurant. I'm starving." My growling stomach reminds me of the irony that Dameon's first punishment was partly for skipping lunch. I never miss a meal. The only reason I did that day was because I passed out from heat stroke. Not that I would ever admit that to him.

I strip in the middle of the dressing room and slip on the bikini first. It's totally obscene, and I can't wait for this boat trip. Cora does the same without hesitation. By the time we've finish trying on our selections, we each have a decent-sized pile and the guilt for spending Dameon's money settles in the pit of my stomach. The thought of taking even more from him churns my insides. I haven't touched his black Amex card yet, but it's in for quite the workout today.

We leave the department store with the reassurance our purchases will be delivered the next day and make our way around the corner to the restaurant. The hostess seats us at a table and runs through the specials, including the daily cocktail: an espresso martini. Cora and I exchange a look but our faces are plastered with very different expressions. Mine reflects horror, while hers sparkles with amusement.

"No, thank you," we chorus, bursting into laughter.

"Oh God," I groan. "You have no idea how sorry I am for putting you in that position."

I still feel terrible about the night I got blind drunk on espresso martinis and asked Cora to drive my car home so I could take Beth to the doctor the next morning. Little did I know, Cora was also pretty drunk and a little sick from the cocktails, and she was arrested for drink driving. She was lucky to escape a charge, but James ended up using the incident to discredit her as a mother, because he stupidly thought she was out to destroy him. It all worked out in the end for Cora, but I've never forgiven myself for putting her in that position, even though she has said many times that all is forgiven and forgotten.

"Please, you need to let this go. It's actually kind of funny now," she insists. I vigorously shake my head—I don't think I'll ever be able to laugh about it.

As we order our food and gossip about Eden, the clientele, and the owner Madame Sophia, I can't shake the feeling that I'm being watched. Since we walked through the door, I could feel a pair of eyes trained on me. Now when I scan the restaurant, my gaze locks with a gorgeous brunette. She's not even attempting to hide her stare. I offer her a warm smile in acknowledgment, but she doesn't return it. Turning back to Cora, I lean over the table and whisper, "Is that woman still watching me?"

"Who?" Cora looks up from her plate. "The brunette in white?" she whispers.

"Yeah, she's been watching me since we arrived."

"Wife?"

"Maybe." It's not uncommon to encounter a client's wife in public. Usually, when a partner suspects cheating, she'll hire a private eye to follow him to Eden. Then after some thorough investigating and stalking, she'll make herself known to the goddess. Most of the time it's an honest and friendly conversation. We usually get the blame for the husband's wandering eyes and hands, which is utterly insane. We're not responsible for their philandering ways. But after explaining that we're just doing our job and that most of the time when we're with their husband, we're thinking about what to have for dinner, not plotting to destroy their marriage, they get it. But on the odd occasion, you come across a woman who's slightly unhinged...

"What a weirdo." Cora shakes her head, dismissing the woman's stare.

"So, tell me," she says, distracting me from the eyes piercing into my back. "What's it like with Dameon? Spill, I want to know all the juicy goss." She wiggles her eyebrows up and down, and I can't help but smile. Talking about Dameon is my favorite subject.

"God, he's incredible. Apart from being gorgeous and eating pussy like it's his favorite meal"—Cora blushes hard at this, her cheeks tinting red. It's a mystery to me how she can still blush after working at Eden—"he's thoughtful and compassionate, always putting my needs first." I swallow roughly and repeat my mantra.

This is a job.

This is a job.

This is a job.

Despite my chant, I can't shake the feeling of being adrift, caught between the life I'm living and the life I want.

"And the kinky stuff?" she asks, her eagerness palpable. And who am I to deny her the spicy details?

"Well, he has me naked all the time, even in front of his staff. I have to kneel at the front door like a bitch in heat when he comes home."

"Ohh, I love that! I'm getting ideas here, keep going." Her eyes sparkle with a mischievous glint.

"I suck his dick every morning to wake him up. Breakfast of champions." I wink at her, and she blushes again. "I almost crave it now. I miss his dick in my mouth when he wakes up before me and leaves for work." I frown at how quickly into our arrangement that happened. "The punishments are my favorite though. I feel *sooo* good after a thorough spanking. And he knows it, so it's not really a punishment," I admit with a shrug.

Cora's eyes glow. "Same here. Sometimes I push James's buttons just so I can get a spanking." She smiles wickedly. I knew she would be a brat.

"He also loves to feed me. Depending on his mood, he'll have me sit on his lap while he hand-feeds me. Sometimes it's hot, other times I'm too hungry and just want to eat in peace." I laugh. "But most of all, I love his laugh and smile. And those beautiful dimples. It gives me so much pleasure seeing him relaxed and happy." Cora's slight wince makes me panic at my overshare. I didn't mean to say that; it just slipped out of my mouth without thought.

Fuck.

She takes a sip of her water and changes the subject, showing me mercy.

"So, what do you do with your days when you're not pleasuring your master?" she drawls.

"Not much, actually. To be honest, I'm bored out of my mind. Other than visiting Beth, my days are completely free. I've tried Pilates, but it's not really me. I can't annoy Beth all the time; she has a tutor during the day and needs to concentrate on her studies. I'm not sure what to do. It's only been a month and I'm already going batshit crazy."

"Maybe you could go back to Eden?" she suggests.

"Do you think he would allow it?"

"If you don't ask, you'll never know."

"Mmm, I don't know. Men are possessive bastards; he'll never go for it." It's hard to keep the resignation out of my voice.

"You never know. He's not like most men," she counters optimistically.

And she's right, he's not. He's so much more.

We finish lunch and head to our spa appointment. By the end of the day, I'm fully relaxed and blissed out. This is exactly what I needed. When Cora drops me home, I wave her goodbye and head into the foyer. I'm surprised to see John, the night manager, already on his shift. Which means...

Oh, no.

I quickly fish my phone out of my purse. It's five forty-five and I have three missed calls from Dameon.

Shit.

Chapter Seventeen

Hailee

I type in the code to our private elevator and hit the top floor button. I've never been late before. I place my hands on my stomach to calm the nervous flutters. When I reach the penthouse, Dameon is waiting for me.

"You're late." His jaw flares, and my fingers itch to soothe the strained muscles.

"I'm so sorry, I lost track of time."

"Not good enough. I expect you to be here when I get home."

"I'm really sorry, it won't happen again," I promise, lowering my eyes.

"Go to our room and wait for your punishment," he commands, frustration pouring off him in waves.

"Yes, sir," I respond, pivoting on my heel and hurrying up the stairs. I waste no time in stripping off my clothes and jumping into the shower to rinse off the massage oil. I'm back out in record time, and I wait for him as instructed.

But fifteen minutes turn into thirty, and still, he hasn't arrived. I crawl out of bed and begin to pace, restlessness gnawing at me. It's as if time itself has become a part of the punishment, a test of endurance. I'm becoming more anxious with each passing minute, and my body pulses with apprehension. Just when I begin to feel the rising anxiety clawing up my throat, my phone chimes with a notification. Exhaling with relief, I welcome the distraction, only to find the text message brings little comfort.

Mark

> Hailee, I'm waiting. Do not disappoint me.

Fuck.

I swiftly delete the message and toss my phone onto the nightstand.

Finally, the door cracks open. Dameon strides in and settles on the edge of the bed, gesturing with a snap of his fingers for me to kneel before him. I scramble into position without hesitation.

"Since both you and Cora were late, James and I have decided to punish you together. Come wait for them in the living room."

I have no idea what that means, but I find myself intrigued, and I'm all for it. A shiver of anticipation courses down my spine as I follow him. When Dameon settles into one of the lounge chairs, I obediently take my place at his feet.

"Good girl," he murmurs, his touch gentle as he strokes my hair. Leaning into his caress, I can sense he's not as upset about my tardiness as he appears. Annoyed and disappointed? Maybe. But not truly angry. We share a comfortable silence for a few moments as he idly scrolls through his phone, his fingers still tangling in my hair. When the elevator dings, signaling the arrival of Cora and James, my heart rate quickens.

"It appears our girls have been misbehaving today," James announces, striding into the room with Cora by his side, their hands intertwined. I catch a subtle smile playing on her lips as she takes in the sight of me, naked and kneeling at Dameon's feet. She takes off her robe, handing it to James, leaving her completely bare.

"Apparently, neither of them owns a phone or has access to a clock. Isn't that strange?" Dameon remarks.

"Bizarre," James drawls.

"Girls who are naughty together should be punished together."

"Couldn't agree more."

"Ladies, if you'll follow me." Dameon slides open the balcony doors and leads us out to the patio. "Your hands, please."

I extend my hands, and he wraps them in a red, velvety soft rope before attaching it to a hook hanging from the ceiling. I've never noticed that hook before, despite living here for a month. My hands are stretched above my head, leaving me barely able to stand on my tiptoes.

He does the same to Cora, fastening her on the same hook so that we're facing each other, completely naked with only an inch between our bodies. Our eyes connect, and Cora blushes a deep shade of red. Unable to help myself, I burst into laughter at the predicament we've found ourselves in. Trapped in such close proximity, there's no escaping the intimate experience of witnessing each other's punishment unfold.

"Laugh now, goddess, because you won't be laughing in a minute," Dameon warns.

With a sharp crack, James spanks Cora's ass, and she jolts forward, her naked body brushing against mine. Her nipples rub against my soft breasts, and I fail to suppress a moan.

Dameon spanks my right cheek with just as much force, causing my body to slide against Cora's once again. She bites her bottom lip at the sensation. It's exquisite torture, feeling her body rub against mine while Dameon turns my ass red. Before long, both of us are panting in need, sweat slicking our hair to our temples. Cora breaks first, with a desperate plea.

"James..." she hisses.

I follow closely behind, unable to hold back any longer. "Sir, please, I—"

Dameon interrupts me. "Shh, we know. We've got you." He runs his hand soothingly down my spine.

They work together to untie us and carry us inside, gently placing us on the carpet. Our legs are like jelly, unable to support our weight, and we collapse in a sweaty heap. James and Dameon take seats in opposite lounges, facing each other.

"Come suck my cock, my sweet slut," James calls, prompting Cora to get on her hands and knees and crawl between his legs.

"You too, goddess." I swivel my head back toward Dameon so fast, I almost give myself whiplash.

What?

"You heard me," he responds to my unspoken question. I flash him a sly smile and make my way over to James on my hands and knees. Checking in with Cora first, I glance over for her approval, and she gives me a subtle nod, her cheeks glowing like they're on fire. Turning to James, I await his permission, which he grants with a nod of his own. With that signal, Cora and I shuffle forward on our knees, drawing close together. James frees himself from his suit pants, his long, hard dick standing tall and proud. He's not as big as Dameon, but it's certainly got some girth to it. Cora takes him in her mouth first with a long, deep suck, her tongue slipping out as it swirls around the head. Then she offers me his length, and I eagerly take him down my throat, humming in pleasure as I suck hard. Putting pressure on the vein that runs down his shaft with my tongue, I glance up. James's head is thrown back, his Adam's apple sliding up and down. I release him from my mouth and Cora takes over, bobbing up and down on his dick. I lean down and suck one of his balls into my mouth, massaging it with my tongue before moving to the next one.

James grips the armrests, his fingers digging into the leather. "Fucking hell." His eyes are screwed shut, lost in the pleasure we're giving him.

I let his ball pop from my mouth and smirk at Cora. She runs her lips along one side of his length, so I join her on the other side, both of us licking and sucking his dick. As we reach the head, our tongues twirl around his tip, tangling against each other. Her tongue is warm and soft, and I crave a better taste. We lean in further and kiss with the head of his cock between us. Her lips are as sweet as strawberries, and mixed with the unique taste of James, it's a delicious combination.

"Fuck me, that's hot," Dameon breathes out. I glance over my shoulder, tossing him a wicked smile. His legs are spread wide and his fingers are interlaced behind his head, watching the scene unfold. Catching my eye, he gives me a loaded look.

"You have no fucking idea," James grits out between his clenched teeth, his voice strained. His cock twitches in Cora's hand, so she sucks him down and starts bobbing her head vigorously. The moment I begin to play with his balls, he explodes with a shout. His body tenses with release as he spills his load into Cora's mouth. "Fuuuck," he groans.

She continues to suck him dry until he leans back, spent. Then she tilts her chin up, opening her mouth to show him his seed on her tongue.

"Swallow. Wait... Don't be greedy, my sweet slut. I think you should share it with Hailee." She turns to look at me, unsure.

Never one to shy away from salacious acts, I take control and pry her lips apart with my tongue, tasting her thoroughly and drawing his cum into my mouth.

We make out passionately for a while, exchanging James's release between us. Her lips feel soft against mine, and her gentle moans and silky skin offer a refreshing contrast to Dameon's rugged stubble and growls. When we eventually part, remnants of cum smeared on our lips and chins, Cora's eyes meet mine. I'm certain her expression mirrors my own—a mix of wide-eyed astonishment and disbelief. This is far from how I envisioned our day ending. Cora bursts into giggles, and I find myself joining in. As our laughter eventually fades, I steal another glance at Dameon. His smile is radiant, those irresistible dimples on full display, clearly amused by our shared euphoria.

"Hate to break up the giggle party, but there's another cock that needs sucking," James interjects. I glance at Cora, who responds with a shrug of her shoulders and a dirty smile.

With the grace of panthers, we crawl over to Dameon and gorge on his cock. Our movements, now more confident and practiced, repeat with enthusiasm. Cora lavishes his balls with her tongue while I swallow his length, looking at him from beneath my lashes. His fierce intensity, jaw clenched and twitching under the pressure of pleasure, captivates me, drawing me into the depths of his sea-green eyes. Dameon grips my hair, pulling me off with a slurp. A string of saliva connects us before disappearing.

"Having fun, kitten?"

I smile before collecting the drool on my lips with my tongue. "Yes, sir."

"Then get back on my cock." He forces my head down, and I moan loudly, sucking with a renewed force.

It doesn't take long before he's growling his release, and Cora and I share another cum-covered kiss. Savoring his taste, I search her mouth for his essence, driven by a greedy need. I want every drop inside me, unwilling to share. Not even with Cora. When I pull back, I lick my lips and lean forward to clean Cora's lips and chin before she has a chance. Apparently I'm a greedy slut too. Turning back to Dameon, I swipe my tongue around his head, collecting the last few drops before pressing a kiss to his tip.

"Perfection," he praises with those gorgeous dimples.

With all this pent-up sexual tension, I'm on the brink of exploding. The slightest breeze against my clit will be enough to set me off. I'm unsure whether this marks the end of our double date or if there's more to come, especially considering this is meant to be a punishment. But my question is answered when they start to disrobe. And holy hell, what a show it is. Cora's eyes go wide, like a kid in a candy shop, and I can't help but snort at her expression. Their physiques are impressive; James is broader, while Dameon is leaner and more defined. Beneath their defined torsos, their hard dicks protrude like weapons. It's continually surprising to me that Dameon never needs downtime; he's always ready to dive straight back in. His boundless energy and relentless stamina never cease to leave me in awe.

James and Dameon position us on our hands and knees, facing each other.

"Hold onto each other's arms," James commands, and we reach out, grasping each other's forearms. James moves behind Cora, and I sense Dameon mirroring his actions. I'm already sopping wet, and he slides in effortlessly, all the way to the hilt. He begins to snap his hips against my sore ass with frantic speed, catching me off guard with his sudden ferocity. There's no warm-up; I'm thrown straight in the deep end. I lock eyes with Cora as we pant and struggle to keep from smacking our heads together due to the force of their thrusts. Our tits sway vigorously with each movement, and all we can do is hold on and enjoy the wild ride. Pleasure courses through my veins, bubbling up, ready to erupt at any moment.

"Fuck. You were made to take my cock." Dameon punctuates each word with a hard, deep thrust. He drives forcefully into me before gushing inside me with a low grunt. He immediately reaches under and pinches my clit, triggering my own release. I scrunch my eyes shut and cry out, terrified of the cliff I'm being propelled over.

The four us move in perfect harmony as we navigate the tumultuous sea of ecstasy.

As our climaxes wash over us, we collapse in a tangled heap of limbs, our breaths ragged and labored. The air is heavy with the scent of our desire and the musky aroma of sweat. Completely spent, we lie intertwined, savoring the aftermath of our encounter, knowing that we have journeyed to the very edge of passion and back. And I want to do it all over again.

CHAPTER EIGHTEEN

Hailee

"**G**ood morning, Portia," I greet as I step into the pristine white marble foyer on the fortieth floor of the Hayes & Hayward Media building. Despite my attempt at a natural smile, it feels more like a grimace. I hastily wipe my sweaty palms on my dress before shaking her hand.

"Good morning, dear. You must be Hailee. Cora told me you'd be dropping by this morning." Portia welcomes me with a warm smile. Her white hair is elegantly slicked back into a neat bun, and her impeccably tailored beige pantsuit complements her petite frame. She must be in her sixties, but she exudes an effortless confidence and grace, and it's clear she takes pride in her appearance. Kudos to the men for not hiring the clichéd young tart with tits and ass hanging out as their executive assistant.

"I wanted to surprise Dameon, if that's okay?" I worry my bottom lip between my teeth, nerves fluttering like trapped butterflies in my stomach.

"Of course. You can go on through." She gives me a conspiratorial wink.

"Thank you," I reply with a slight grin.

I wish that were the only reason I'm here.

With renewed purpose, I stride down the hallway, each step echoing the thunderous rhythm of my heart. My hand trembles slightly as I lightly knock on Dameon's office door.

"Come in." His clear command rings through the frosted glass. I push it open, and his face lights up when he sees me, the warmth in his expression making me feel even more like a piece of shit.

"Hey, thought I'd drop by and surprise you. Plus, I brought lunch," I say with a forced cheerfulness, holding up the container I brought with me. I asked Eloise to prepare his favorite meal.

"Well... that is a *very* welcome surprise. Come here, goddess." He pushes back from his desk and pats his leg. His eyes blaze with appreciation as they sweep over my outfit—a slinky black wraparound dress, paired with high black pumps, and a tantalizing hint of pantyhose and suspenders underneath.

I perch myself on his lap, and he's quick to seize a fistful of my hair, pulling me closer. He crushes his lips to mine in a fiery kiss. Our mouths meld together in a frenzy of desire, igniting a blaze of passion that consumes us both. Even after all this time, electricity still crackles between us whenever we're together.

"Hello to you, too," I breathe against his lips when he finally releases me for air.

"Do I get to unwrap my surprise?"

"Allow me." I wink, rising from his lap. With slow deliberate movements, I untie the bow on the side of my dress, letting the material fall open. It cascades around me, revealing the lacy black garter belt, suspenders, and pantyhose underneath. His eyes devour every inch of my exposed skin, glimmering with a wicked desire that sets my pulse racing.

With a swift motion, he rises from his chair and lifts me up by the hips, effortlessly placing me on the edge of his desk. He leans me back until I'm lying flat against the polished surface, his lips and tongue tracing every curve of my body with an expert touch that's pure bliss. I lose myself completely in the sensation, forgetting why I'm here, what I need to do, as I surrender to his touch.

His office door bursts open with a bang, startling me. Tilting my head upside down, I catch sight of James rolling his eyes. It's been a week since our impromptu foursome, and the memory of that exhilarating night still brings a smile to my lips.

"When you're finished with your snack, I need you in my office," James says briskly, exiting as abruptly as he entered.

Dameon chuckles and the sound of his deep, low rumble stirs a warmth in my chest. He reaches to press a button that I suspect will lock the door, but I stop him, placing my hand on his.

"I'll never get my fill of you," he murmurs against my skin, sucking my nipple into his mouth like a hungry dog to prove his point. In a rushed exhale, I breathe out a giggle.

The sound of his belt unbuckling is like pure catnip to me. My senses become heightened, and my body responds instinctively to the sound. With each click and slide of the belt, I find myself salivating in anticipation, my desire for him growing with each passing moment. It's as if a primal instinct has been awakened within me, one that I can't control. A surge of liquid heat pools in my core, spreading through me like wildfire and intensifying the hunger I feel for him.

He thrusts inside me with a force that leaves me gasping, stretching me wide and filling me completely. I grit my teeth against the sting of being split open, but I urge him on, pushing the points of my pumps against his ass in a silent plea for more.

"Did you miss me this morning? Did you miss my cock?" he growls.

"Yesss," I hiss through the exquisite ache.

He left early this morning, before I woke. And, I'm ashamed to admit, I *did* miss his cock in my mouth. It's become a familiar craving and it grips me again now. I'm hungry for the taste of him on my tongue.

"Did my kitten miss her cream this morning?"

My eyes roll into the back of my head, his words spurring me on as a heady sensation rapidly escalates to dizzying new heights. He grips my throat and squeezes, cutting off my airway. When he finally releases his hold, my oxygen-starved body convulses, and I shatter into millions of pieces. Gasping for breath, I struggle to regain control over my body, each inhalation feeling like a lifeline as I come down from the euphoric peak. In the midst of my trembling, Dameon finds his release inside me with a rough groan.

"Fuck," he breathes, shaking his head to clear the haze. "You're perfect." I don't miss the note of awe in his voice as he gazes at me with softening eyes. He withdraws, his eyes fixated on the sight of his cum seeping out of me. With a wild, possessive look, he pushes it back in with his fingers.

"Don't clean up," he commands as he tucks himself back into his pants. "I'll be back in a sec. I need to see James." His lips brush against my forehead as he helps me up from the desk. With a seductive wink, he leaves his office, leaving me to bask in the aftermath that is Dameon.

Oof, this man kills me.

I sink into his chair, still trying to catch my breath while the reality of what I actually came here to do crashes down around me and settles heavy in my chest. Without wasting any time, I begin rifling through the minimal paperwork scattered across his desk, my heart racing. But I don't find what I'm looking for. A quick search through his desk drawers comes up similarly empty. I had naively hoped there would be something just lying on his desk for me to "accidentally" run my eye over. But nothing is ever that easy. As I reluctantly wake up his computer, a wave of guilt washes over me; what I'm about to do goes against everything I stand for. What felt like a good idea at the time now stabs at my conscience, and I just know this will become one of the worst decisions I'll ever make.

Feeling like a piece of shit, I access his hard drive and scan through the files.

How the hell am I meant to find something I can use before he comes back?

If I had a couple of hours to properly look through it, I could probably find something of value to send Mark. But time is not on my side; I have at the most another minute before he comes back. And the last thing I need is to be caught with my hand in the proverbial cookie jar. There's no way I'd be able to explain it to him.

Realizing the futility of my efforts, I exit the drive. Instead, I turn my attention to his calendar, my fingers trembling as I scroll through his upcoming meetings. Finally I find one that stands out. I take out my phone and capture a snapshot of the meeting invite, with the attached agenda and the invite list. I quickly close the calendar, return his screen to sleep mode, and throw my phone back into my purse.

Not even thirty seconds later, Dameon waltzes through the door, his dimples popping as he graces me with one of his charming smiles.

"Where were we?" He lifts me up and settles into his chair, depositing me back on his lap with ease.

Angry tears well in my eyes as a ball of conflicting emotions churns within me. I lean forward, burying my face into the comforting curve of his neck. His familiar scent envelops me, momentarily calming the storm of guilt and shame raging inside. I feel like utter scum—less than scum. The guilt claws its way up my throat like a creature trying to escape hell, but I force it back down, burying it deep within me where it belongs. A quiet sob escapes me; there's no escaping the consequences of what I've done, and the realization leaves me racked with dread.

"Hey," he murmurs softly, pulling back slightly and lifting my chin with the crook of his finger. His touch is soothing as runs his thumbs under my eyes, catching my traitorous tears. "What's wrong, goddess?"

I stutter, at a loss for words, the truth threatening to spill from my lips. But then I remember why I made that deal with Mark. For Beth. Our insurance policy. And at the end of the day, I'm a lot more scared of the consequences of refusing my stepfather's demands than Dameon's.

"I wanted to talk to you about something," I eventually manage to get out.

"Of course, what is it?" His frown deepens at my distress.

"I'm going crazy at your place, just waiting for you to come home," I admit, the words tumbling out in a rush. "I need something to do, something to occupy my time. I'm not used to having nothing to do all day." While it may be a cover, it's not a complete lie either.

"Okay, what do you want to do then?"

"I want to go back to Eden," I reply, meeting his gaze steadily. "Not working Le Jardin, just doing admin during the day... what I was doing before." Every Saturday night, Eden hosts Le Jardin, where members select a goddess to spend the evening with in private. I would never expect him to agree to that.

"Are you sure? You have the time and means to do anything your heart desires. You could go back to working in accounting, or I know for a fact that charities are always looking for help in their treasury departments. You could even go back to school and study something entirely new. The world is your oyster."

"Are you ashamed that I work at Eden?"

"No! Of course not." He shakes his head. "Did you forget I have a membership? It would be hypocritical of me to judge you for working there. What I'm saying is, you can do anything you put your mind to, and you now have the freedom and flexibility to choose. So, what is it that *you* want?"

I honestly can't remember the last time someone asked me what I want. In fact, come to think of it, I'm not even sure if anyone ever has. My eyes well up again at how kind and thoughtful he is after what I've just done. But I hold back the heavy tears of remorse.

While I don't see myself working at Eden forever, for now, it's comfortable and convenient. Having the freedom to come and go as I please is particularly important to me, especially this year while I'm working for Dameon. It's also essential for me to be able to drop everything at a moment's notice when a donor heart becomes available for Beth.

Embarking on a new career seems pointless at this moment. But who knows what the future will hold? I can't help but feel a flicker of excitement at the endless possibilities that await me after my contract with Dameon is over. I've always believed in the power of therapy—perhaps there's a way for me to support other sex workers. Being an escort wasn't exactly a childhood dream of mine, something I aspired to as a little girl. It was a temporary means to provide the best life possible for Beth and myself in a new country. I don't regret it. It is what it is. And I enjoy it. In fact, I find immense gratification in providing pleasure to my clients and fulfilling their desires.

As I think about the end of the year, my stomach flutters. On one hand, I look forward to Beth receiving her new heart and starting the next chapter of her life as she prepares for her final year in high school. It's a milestone that fills me with hope for her bright future ahead. Yet alongside this hope, there's a twinge of sadness knowing that Dameon and I will part ways. The thought of saying goodbye to him is gut-wrenching.

"For now, I just want to work at Eden," I tell him.

"Then Eden it is. They'll be lucky to have you back," he declares.

"Thank you," I murmur, touched by his encouragement.

"You're welcome, gorgeous. There's no need to cry," he reassures me softly, his lips brushing against my eyelids in a gentle kiss. I melt into a puddle on his lap. He couldn't be more perfect if he tried, and I don't deserve any of it—his kindness or thoughtfulness. I've never felt so low and conflicted as I do now.

I sigh.

I want him... and I can't have him.

Chapter Nineteen

Hailee

"Ahh, fuuuck..." I cry out, my voice echoing through the quiet office.

"Look at you, taking my cock like a good little whore." Dameon's voice fills the room as he pounds into me from behind. The sound of his hips slapping against my ass cracks in the air like a whip. "This gorgeous ass is mine, isn't it?" He spreads my cheeks apart, spitting on my puckered hole before thrusting his thumb inside to the knuckle. The sudden intrusion makes me gasp before I relax into it, enjoying the fullness. His dirty words only stoke the fire within me.

"You were made for my cock," he gasps, each thrust diving deeper. Searing pleasure rips through me, tearing me to shreds, leaving me breathless and hungry for more. With a low growl, he releases inside me, filling me up completely before pulling out, leaving a trail of cum dripping down my thighs. I make no move to clean it up, knowing he prefers me to wear his seed proudly. He adjusts my black satin gown before I sink to my knees before him, my tongue lapping him clean. When I'm finished, I tuck him back into his suit pants and rise to my feet.

"Feel better?"

"Much," he sighs.

There's something about being back at Eden that has made him feral. Maybe it's the charged atmosphere, the way the sexual tension simmers in the air, or perhaps it's as simple as seeing me in my goddess gown again. If I hadn't quickly taken control of the situation and led him back to my office, he would have succumbed to his impulses and bent me over the bar, ravishing me in front of everyone. While I wouldn't have minded, it goes against the rules. And the last thing I want is for him to be kicked out or have his membership canceled.

A knock at the door interrupts us. "Go have fun, I've got work to do," I whisper, trying to usher him out the door.

He chuckles softly. "Hold on." He bunches my gown in one hand and inserts two fingers inside me, gathering his seed. Then he presents his fingers to me, slick with our shared essence, and smears them across my lips. "Open."

I dutifully part my lips to receive his offering. As his fingers enter my mouth, I eagerly wrap my tongue around them, moaning at our combined taste.

"Don't wipe it off." His voice is low and possessive. "I want every man in this building to know that while you may be serving them, your sexy ass belongs to me." I rub my lips together to spread his essence, the scent lingering just under my nose, marking me as his and ensuring there's no chance of forgetting who owns me.

"Good girl." He slides a hand into my hair, drawing me into a burning kiss. His tongue artfully massages mine, savoring our mingled taste, before he pulls back and playfully nips at my swollen lower lip. With a wink at my dazed expression, he strides out of my office, revealing Violet waiting on the other side.

"Hey, Violet. Sorry for the wait, come on in." I gesture for her to take a seat at my desk, the same one I was just bent over. "What's going on?" I settle into my seat across from her, noticing her pale complexion and teary eyes.

"I need to leave; I can't be in Le Jardin tonight. I'm sorry to do this to you at the last minute," she sniffs.

"It's fine, but what happened?"

"I saw someone I know, and he can't see me naked on stage or know that I work here." Desperation lingers in her words. On occasion, a goddesses' real life intersects with her work at Eden when someone they know unexpectedly appears. Sometimes it's an ex-boyfriend, other times a work colleague or boss, or even a father, as was the case one time, which still makes me cringe. Regardless of who it is, it's always a shock for the goddess. It's not a pleasant experience when their two worlds collide.

"I completely understand. I'll take care of it."

"Thank you, I really appreciate it."

"No problem at all," I reassure her. While it does disrupt the numbers for Le Jardin tonight, offering a complimentary month on their membership should help smooth things over with the disappointed gentleman. The ten men booked into Le Jardin are assigned a random number when they register to indicate the order in which they will select their goddess. The women present themselves on stage, naked and in a traditional submissive pose, allowing the clients to view and make their selection. Unfortunately, it's too late to find a replacement goddess for tonight, so whoever was assigned number ten will have to be cut.

"Here," I say, retrieving a business card from my desk drawer and handing it to Violet. "This is the number of a therapist. She's excellent at what she does and she's sex worker-friendly. I recommend that every sex worker see a counselor. It's a lot to process when clients emotionally unload on you. Plus, she can help with your personal relationships." Violet nods, eyes glued to the card. "Seeing someone from your real life in a setting like this can be unsettling and having a professional to talk to will make a difference. Of course, my door is always open, but I'm not a trained therapist. I can't provide the same level of help as she can."

She offers me a small smile, tucking a piece of hair behind her ear. Any opportunity I have to suggest someone see a therapist, whether they're a sex worker or not, I take it. Everyone has demons to face and traumas to work through, regardless of their past. Some are just more complex than others.

"I'll give her a call, thank you."

"See you next week?"

"Yes, I'll be here," she breathes out. "Thank you, Hailee. I really do appreciate it."

"Don't mention it."

Violet slips out and I quickly look up unlucky number ten on my computer, the gentleman who unfortunately misses out tonight. My eyebrows shoot up when I see the name. At least it will make him easy to spot.

Heading into the main lounge, I scan the crowd for Carter Ashford, the lead singer of Pulse. The place is alive and pumping: every seat at the bar is taken and the plush red couches are occupied with well-dressed patrons. Soft lighting casts an intimate glow across the black, gold and deep red décor.

I spot Madame Sophia gracefully making her rounds, talking and flirting with the clientele. My eyes instinctively seek out Dameon and find him sitting at the bar, casually sipping his whiskey. His eyes heat when they land on mine, and I unconsciously lick my lips, the lingering taste of our encounter exploding across my tongue. A rush of desire floods my veins, causing my core to clench and the remnants of his release to slowly drip out of me. I rub my thighs together, spreading the wetness as I search for Carter amid the crowd.

Fortunately, I spot him sitting alone. I half expected him to be surrounded by his entourage, or at least his band members. On my way across the room, I pass Chloe, who's perched on a client's lap, her eyes closed and lips slightly parted. The man's hand is buried under her dress, moving slowly back and forth. Suppressing a grin, I continue on my way. One of the rules is that no sexual activity should occur in the lounge, but I'm certainly not going to stop them. He's hot, and she seems to be enjoying herself. Good for her.

As I approach Mr. Ashford, I instantly understand why women are drawn to him; he has an undeniable magnetism. Of course, being insanely good-looking doesn't hurt either. After introducing myself and explaining that one of our goddesses has gone home sick, I offer a complimentary month on his membership for the inconvenience. He takes it in his stride and graciously accepts. Given his fame, I'm a little surprised he didn't cause more of a scene. I call over Blaire, another goddess, to serve him for the evening, informing her that everything is on the house tonight. As Blaire kneels before him to serve, his eyes light up.

With the crisis averted, I check in with the operations manager and realize it's time for the announcement.

Stepping onto the stage, my gaze once again drifts to Dameon. I take hold of the microphone, ready to kick off the proceedings. "Welcome to Le Jardin, gentlemen. If you're participating tonight, you've already received your number.

We've kept you waiting long enough; it's time to commence your selection."

CHAPTER TWENTY

Hailee

Hot water rains down on me. Pressing my back against the cool tiles, the tension in my muscles begin to melt away. With a gentle roll of my head, I stretch out the knots in my neck, exhaling a sigh of relief. It's good to be back at Eden, though I've been reminded just how hectic it can be. My muscles certainly didn't forget.

Just as I start to sink into a moment of peace, the bedroom phone trills, piercing the silence and jarring me back to reality.

I quickly wrap a towel around my head and another around my body, dashing out of the bathroom to answer it before it falls silent. With wet feet, I almost lose my balance as I turn the corner but manage to catch myself just in time. The last thing I need is to earn another punishment.

"Hello," I answer breathlessly.

"Hailee dear, it's Kevin," comes the familiar and soothing voice on the other end.

"Hey Kev, what's up?"

"I have a gentleman here, Jacob Barlowe." A vague memory of Jacob at the charity ball my stepfather dragged me to floods back. An easy smile and perfect white teeth.

"Dameon's not here, unfortunately."

"He's inquiring after you, ma'am."

"Kev, how many times do I have to remind you to call me Hailee?" I tease, though my mock anger is met with a chuckle. We've done this dance many times. "Send him up."

"Yes, ma'am," he replies.

I drag the towel from my head, letting my long hair fall down my back before gathering it up into a messy bun and securing it with a claw clip. I quickly dry off my body, hanging both wet towels in the bathroom just as the elevator dings. I slip into a floor-length linen dress, its light fabric flowing effortlessly around me, and head downstairs to the foyer. As the elevator doors open, I'm greeted by the sight of Jacob with a charming smile on his face.

"Hey, nice to see you again." I smile brightly.

"Hope you don't mind me dropping by. I was in the area." He casually gestures down his body. He's wearing board shorts and a tank top, his impressive toned and tanned arms on display. He runs a hand through his wet hair, and his flip-flops are covered in sand.

"How's the swell?" I welcome him inside.

"Amazing. Do you surf?"

"No, but I'd like to learn one day. Come in," I reply as I lead the way into the living room. "Would you like some iced tea? I was making some anyway."

"Yeah, that would be great, thank you." He runs a hand through his wet hair again.

Leaving Jacob to settle on one of the couches facing the ocean, I make my way into the kitchen and grab the pitcher from the fridge. I fill two glasses with iced tea, the clinking sound of ice cubes against the glass echoing the nagging feeling in my gut. With each pour, I take deep breaths, centering myself before returning to face Jacob. *What is he doing here? He barely knows me.*

"Sorry, Dameon isn't here at the moment, but he should be back in an hour or so if you want to wait?" I say as I offer him a glass of iced tea. Our fingers brush lightly, and that nagging feeling in my gut ramps up a notch. I'm suddenly all too aware of my nakedness beneath my thin linen dress. With a forced smile plastered on my lips, I turn toward the opposite couch, but before I can retreat, Jacob's hand darts out, gripping my wrist.

"I'm actually here to talk to you, Hailee. Please, sit with me." He nods toward the spot beside him on the couch. I search his eyes for any hint of malice, but they remain frustratingly blank. His hold on my wrist remains light, and I could easily shrug him off, so I ignore my instincts and reluctantly sink down beside him. His lips curl into an unsettling smile.

"So, what did you want to talk to me about?" I ask, taking a sip of my iced tea to break free from his hold.

"Are you happy? With Dameon?"

"Yes..." I respond slowly. "What's going on, Jacob?"

"Because I can offer you a better deal. Whatever he's offering you, I'll double it." His words drip with confidence.

"Oh, um, that's very generous of you, but I'm not interested." I rub the back of my neck and fiddle with the claw clip in my hair.

"Why not? You're a hooker, the highest bidder always wins." He shrugs with arrogant certainty.

Okay, time for this asshole to leave... now.

"Listen, Jacob, I think—"

"I lost a bet because of you." His voice drops with resentment, and his sudden change in demeanor makes my heart pick up pace.

"What are you talking about?"

"I lost my penthouse in Paris. Because he cheated." He leans forward and puts his iced tea on the coffee table with a loud clank.

"I don't understand."

"And here's the thing, Hailee, I don't lose. Ever." The intent is clear in his eyes, and my gut screams at me to move, to run. I swiftly rise from the couch, but before I can make a move, his hand shoots out and grips my wrist, tighter this time. The glass slips from my hand, shattering as it crashes to the floor, iced tea splashing over our legs. In one swift move, he yanks me down onto the couch, his body looming over mine as he uses his weight to pin me underneath him. Shock and fear render me momentarily speechless. It takes a second to gather my wits, then a surge of adrenaline floods my veins.

"Get the fuck off me," I snarl, my voice trembling with anger as I push hard against his chest.

"You owe me. One fuck doesn't even come close to making up for my penthouse, but you're sure as hell gonna try." He secures my wrists above my head, pinning them together in an iron grip with one hand. His other hand grasps my jaw, his fingers digging into my skin. Panic surges through me but I can also feel a fierce determination igniting deep down, driving me to fight against him with every ounce of strength I possess.

"Time to pay up," he spits out. His eyes are narrowed into dangerous slits, like a coiled snake, deadly and ready to strike. An anger that I didn't know I possessed surges within me like a raging inferno, blazing beneath the surface, ready to explode. I buck and arch my back in a desperate attempt to free myself from his hold.

"Why are you fighting this? Take it like the whore you are." He seems perplexed by my resistance, which only fuels the flames of my fury. The audacity of his insults, the sheer contempt in his tone, it's almost too much to bear. My vision blurs with rage.

He gropes my breast before shifting his weight to free his cock from his shorts. I see my opening, and I take it. In a quick and calculated motion, I lift my knee with all the force I can muster, aiming squarely for his balls. The impact is immediate and gratifying.

His grip on me falters as pain contorts his features, his howls of agony echoing off the walls. "You fucking bitch!" he roars. I waste no time seizing the opportunity to push him off, sending him crashing to the floor amid the shards of broken glass.

I leap off the couch and make a desperate dash for the phone in the foyer. But before I can reach it, he lunges forward, grabbing me by the ankle and yanking me down with a vicious force. A sharp pain shoots through my thigh, but I don't dare look down. Instead, I focus all my energy on breaking free from his tight grip with wild kicks. I manage to connect a blow to his face and feel his nose crunch beneath my foot.

Good, I hope I broke it.

"Ahhh!" Jacob's screams pierce the air as he releases my ankle, clutching at his injured nose in agony.

"Get the fuck away from her!"

The dark timbre of Dameon's voice roars over Jacob's cries, and the room goes deadly still. I lift my head from the floor to see Dameon towering over us, like one scary motherfucker, his presence radiating pure menace. It's a side of him I've never seen before, and one I hope to never witness again. Dameon bends down, his hand wrapping around Jacob's throat like a vise. Despite Jacob's feeble attempts to stop the blood flowing from his nose, the sight of Dameon's murderous glare is enough to make his hands rise in a futile gesture of surrender. Before Jacob can utter a single word, Dameon's fist crashes into his face, a single punch landing with a sickening crunch. The sound of Jacob's screams mingles with the nauseating sound of bones breaking. When Dameon releases his grip on Jacob's throat, he collapses to the ground in a bloody and unconscious heap. His face is covered in blood, a swollen bruise already forming where the punch landed. Pushing through the pain in my thigh, I force myself to my feet.

"What the fuck do you think you're doing?" I demand, rounding on him. Dameon looks up from Jacob's unmoving body, his brow furrowing.

"What?"

"I had it under control!" I seethe, frustration flowing through me as I gesture toward Jacob's motionless form.

"Are you kidding me? I just saved you from being raped. It didn't look like you had it under control when I walked in!"

"I did! And I don't need to be saved by you or by any man! This isn't a movie; this isn't *Pretty Woman*. I can save my myself!" I shout, grasping my chest.

"Fuck's sake, Hailee, this is not the time to get on your feminist high horse." His words cut through the air like a knife, making me see red.

"What the fuck did you say to me?" I narrow my eyes. "Men like this asshole feel they have a right to my body anytime they want because of my profession. And I'm sick of it!"

"Don't lump me in the same group as this prick. You know damn well I'm not like him. And I know you can look after yourself. But let me make this clear: I will not stand back and watch while someone, whether they are male, female, old or young, is violently assaulted. And *especially* not someone I care about. In. My. Own. Fucking. Home!" Dameon bellows, his voice thundering through the room.

We fall silent, the tension between us crackling as our labored breathing fills the room. His admission lingers between us, deflating my anger like a balloon.

He cares about me?

Closing my eyes, I inhale deeply. When I reopen them, Dameon is scanning my body with concern.

"You're hurt," he observes, his voice gentle.

I follow his gaze and take stock of the damage. A large piece of glass protrudes from my thigh, blood seeping through and staining my dress. Now that the adrenaline and shock are wearing off, the pain intensifies, throbbing relentlessly. I assess myself further, noticing other scratches and cuts on my arms, yet more evidence of the struggle. It seems I fell on more glass than I initially thought.

"Can I take you to the hospital? Or would you like to drive yourself? I'm happy to sit in the passenger seat while you bleed out behind the wheel." Dameon's attempt at sarcasm makes my lips twitch.

Funny, asshole.

"Fine, let's go," I huff, my anger seeping out as a wave of exhaustion settles in.

We wait in the small cubicle at St. Vincent's Hospital for the doctor to remove the glass and stitch up my leg. Dameon paces back and forth, his focus split between my thigh and the conversation he's having on his phone.

"Thank you, Kevin. I'll call you back," he says, ending the call and slipping his phone into his pocket. He settles onto the seat next to my bed.

"Kevin's babysitting Jacob while he waits for the police to arrive. He's still unconscious. They will likely take him to hospital and arrest him there, but they will want to interview you. It's up to you whether you want to press charges."

I sigh. What's the point in pressing charges? He's powerful and wealthy and will get away with nothing more than a slap on the wrist. I have little faith that he'll face any real consequences for his actions. "What do you think I should do?"

He takes my hand in his, his thumb tracing comforting circles on my skin. "This is your decision, and yours alone. I'll support you no matter what you choose." His words are reassuring, but I can see the frustration in his eyes as he speaks. "Yes, I want to see him charged. He attacked you," he growls, anger flashing in his gaze. "But I don't think the charges will stick. He'll lawyer up, use your background against you. I'm sorry, gorgeous." His expression softens, a mixture of remorse and sympathy shadowing his features. He would know better than anyone. Men like Jacob can get away with literal murder. An attack on a sex worker in a private home will be easy to squash. I sigh heavily again.

"There is another option though…" he trails off, watching me intently.

"What option?"

"Let's just say, I'm acquainted with certain individuals who like to dole out their own brand of justice."

"Really?" His suggestion catches me off guard. The notion of vigilante justice seems like something out of a movie, not a real-life possibility. Yet, there's a flicker of temptation within me, a desire to see Jacob face the consequences of his actions, even if they're outside the bounds of conventional law. However, deep down, I know that mere retribution won't change the essence of who Jacob is.

"Would it make you feel better, if karma got him?" I ask.

"Hell yeah, it would."

"Then it's settled," I conclude with a shrug. Dameon nods in agreement. "Speaking of, what was the bet about?"

"What bet?"

"The one you made with Jacob."

"Fuck. Is that why he attacked you?"

"Yeah, he said something about you cheating?"

"I'm gonna murder that fucker." Dameon's voice drips with anger.

The curtain draws back and our conversation is interrupted by the arrival of one fine-looking doctor. Dressed in perfectly tailored green scrubs, his muscular physique is evident as he surveys the paperwork on his clipboard.

"Hailee Mann, I presume." His voice is smooth and confident. Though he looks familiar, I can't quite place where I've seen him before.

"Hey, Zac." Dameon extends his hand for a shake. "Thanks for seeing us straight away."

"No problem at all." He returns the handshake. "Hailee, how are you feeling this evening?"

"Been better, to be honest," I reply, still trying to figure out why he's so familiar.

"On a scale of one to ten, how much pain are you in at the moment?"

"About a six." Then it clicks; he's from Eden. The guy Chloe was playing with.

"Well, let's get you stitched up, and we'll give you some painkillers so you can be on your way," Zac says with a reassuring smile.

"Sounds good, thank you, Doctor."

Dameon remains by my side, holding my hand throughout the procedure. The sting of the local anesthetic was worse than the actual removal of the glass. His attentive presence provides a sense of comfort, and he diligently absorbs the doctor's instructions for aftercare and pain management. By the time I'm stitched up and ready to leave, the adrenaline has completely drained from my system, leaving me shaky and vulnerable. I can't believe I was attacked and almost raped. It's always a risk in my profession, a shadow that lurks in the back of my mind, but I never thought it would happen to me—especially not in the safety of Dameon's penthouse. The shock ripples through me, each wave bringing a fresh surge of disbelief and fear. But once the painkillers kick in, fatigue settles heavily into my bones.

Drowsy, I limp out of the cubicle. Dameon watches me intently, concern evident in his eyes. I can sense he's holding back, giving me the space to be in control. It's a gesture that tugs at my heartstrings, knowing he wants to take care of me in every possible way.

Relenting, I ask, "Can you help, please?"

"Thank fuck," he breathes out, his eyes shooting to the sky. With a gentle strength, he lifts me into his arms, holding me closely as he carries me to the car. I snuggle against his chest, finding solace in his embrace. The next thing I know, I'm lying in our bed, naked, while Dameon tenderly washes me with a warm washcloth.

"Go back to sleep, gorgeous. I've got you," he whispers, brushing a gentle kiss against my forehead.

That sounds like a mighty fine idea, so I let my heavy eyelids drop, surrendering to the tranquility of sleep.

CHAPTER TWENTY-ONE

Dameon

"Morning. How are you holding up?" I nudge the bedroom door closed with my foot and set the breakfast tray down on the edge of the bed.

Hailee blinks, rousing from her sleep, and shifts herself upright, leaning against the headboard.

"Sore," she murmurs, rubbing the remnants of sleep from her eyes. "Actually, my body hurts far worse than my leg."

Her eyes light up when they land on the array of pastries on the tray. She quickly reaches for an almond croissant, tearing off a big piece and placing it in her mouth. A soft moan escapes her lips, muffled by the mouthful, as her eyes flutter closed.

"Oh my God," she manages between bites. "Eloise has really outdone herself."

"Eloise isn't even here."

Her eyes widen. "Wait, you made these?"

"Fuck no," I say with a chuckle. "I walked down to the bakery."

I press her pain meds into her palm, and she swallows them down with a mouthful of orange juice.

When she's finished eating, I remove the tray and scooch onto the bed beside her, still holding my to-go coffee, careful to not jolt her.

"Uhh, what are you doing?"

I grab the remote and flick on the TV. "What does it look like I'm doing?"

"Shouldn't you be at work... or something?"

"Nope, I'm not leaving you."

"I'm fine Dameon, really. You don't have to babysit me. I can hang out with Beth today. Go do whatever you normally do during the day."

"No," I reply firmly. "And stop trying to boss me around. That's not how this works."

She huffs, and I bite back a smile, fighting the urge to chuckle at how adorable she looks when she's annoyed. *Tough shit.* It's my duty to take care of her. After all, she was only attacked because of me and that stupid bet.

Fucking Jacob.

I take a sip of my coffee while I watch the news. Before long I feel her gaze boring into me.

"What is it?"

"So, you're planning to spend the entire day in bed with me?" she questions, with a hint of skepticism.

"No," I reply, setting down my coffee cup on the nightstand. "After I finish catching up on the morning news, I'll help you with a bath, so you don't get your stitches wet, then I'll redress your wound. After that, we're going to watch a movie in the living room, followed by an afternoon by the pool." She continues to stare at me, her jaw slightly agape. "Does that sound all right to you, kitten?" I add, sarcastically. She promptly closes her mouth and nods. I drag my top lip over my teeth to stifle a laugh.

Two hours later we're nestled on the couch, engrossed in *Game Night* starring Rachel McAdams and Jason Bateman—one of her favorite comfort movies. Her legs are draped across my lap, and I've tucked her in snugly with a blanket, even though it's not remotely cold outside. I've surrounded her with snacks—anything to make her feel more comfortable.

My phone is blowing up in my pocket, but for once, I don't feel the usual compulsion to check it immediately. Whatever it is, it can wait. Right now, my priority is my kitten. I can't recall a time when my professional life has taken such a backseat, especially to a woman.

"Can I ask you something?" she says, breaking the comfortable silence between us.

Fuck, here we go. I've come to dread this question from her, knowing it always leads to heavy conversations rather than quick answers.

"You just did."

She smirks. "What bet did you make with Jacob?"

Well... fuck me.

The guilt I've been grappling with all day tightens its grip. Each wince or hiss of pain from her makes the ball of lead grow heavier in my gut.

I release a deep breath. "It was to see who could win you. If I succeeded, his penthouse in Paris was mine. And if I failed, my villa in Milan was his."

"Nice," she deadpans, rolling her eyes.

"I swear, it was only to ensure you didn't end up with someone like him. He's a complete fuckwit," I explain, hoping to justify my actions and avoid sounding like a total jerk.

"No shit." Her eyes widen as if she hadn't just experienced it firsthand yesterday. "Is that because you *care* about me?" She playfully bats her eyelashes at me, and I can't help but shake my head at my stupid slip-up yesterday, made in the heat of the moment. It had escaped without a thought.

"Of course I care about you," I admit. Her triumphant smile, accompanied by the dramatic gesture of tossing another chip into her mouth, tells me there's no turning back now.

"Hey, how'd you know I like Burger Rings anyway? They're like a rare treasure these days."

"I asked Beth," I reply casually. "And yes, I'm well aware of how hard they are to find."

Her face lights up with pleasure at my response and it seems I've narrowly escaped her wrath... for now. *Thank fuck.*

The house phone begins to ring, so I carefully lift up her legs and slide out from underneath them, depositing them back onto the couch with gentle precision to avoid straining her thigh. I make my way to the foyer and pick up the phone.

"Good morning, sir. I've received notification that Mr. DeMarco is trying to contact you."

"Ah, thank you, Kevin," I reply before hanging up and retrieving my phone from my pocket. Ignoring all the work calls and email notifications, I find the text I've been anticipating from Dante.

Call me back, fucker.

I dial his number, and he answers on the first ring.

"About time. You ask a favor and then disappear for twelve hours? What the fuck?"

"I know, damn it," I sigh, running a hand over my forehead. "I've been taking care of my woman."

"I'm sorry to hear what happened to her."

"Yeah, well... that's why I need this favor. He doesn't get to walk away from this unscathed."

"And he won't. I was calling to tell you that we've been doing some digging, and this isn't the first time he's done something like this. But I assure you, it'll be the last."

I glance back at Hailee on the couch, fast asleep with her hand still nestled in the chip packet. A smirk tugs at my lips. *Damn, she's fucking cute*. No one gets to cast a shadow on my ball of sunshine.

"Good. Call me when it's done," I instruct, and end the call.

Chapter Twenty-Two

Hailee

O ur driver pulls up alongside the marina, the water sparkling like diamonds in the sunshine, as if dressed up for our cruise.

"You ready?" Dameon asks, his excitement mirroring my own.

"Absolutely. Let's do this," I say, smiling. This trip has been on my mind ever since Cora mentioned it.

Dameon slides out of the car and grabs our bags from the trunk, swinging one over each shoulder. I love the way his biceps bulge through his tight white T-shirt as we make our way down the jetty.

We pass a few yachts until we reach the end, and I abruptly stop, blinking in awe at the monstrosity before me. This isn't a yacht—it's a ship.

"Holy shit. That's massive."

"That's what she said," Dameon quips with a wink as he passes me, striding up the gangplank onto the "yacht."

I may not know much about boats, but this one would have to be at least two hundred feet long. It gleams in the sunlight, practically begging for a photoshoot. There's even a helicopter pad with a full-size helicopter perched on top, and a speedboat attached to the side.

"You coming?" Dameon calls from the deck.

"Uh-huh." I follow him up and take his offered hand. I don't know why I keep forgetting he's stupidly wealthy until it hits me with moments like this. My jaw pops open as I take in the spacious and elegantly decorated main cabin, its polished wooden floors and plush furnishings in beautiful hues of cream and navy. The attention to detail is evident in every aspect of the design, from the intricate woodwork and ornate moldings to the exquisite artwork adorning the walls. Large windows frame panoramic views of the seascape, and I suck in a quiet breath, overwhelmed by its beauty. Dameon leads me out onto the expansive deck where there's plenty of room for lounging in the sun and dining alfresco.

"Yay! You finally made it!" Cora calls, waving her pinkish cocktail overhead. She's dressed in the cute red bikini we picked out on our shopping trip, the fabric barely covering her ample tits, with a sheer lace cover-up.

"You started on the cocktails early." I throw my arms around her, squeezing her tightly.

"So, I started the party while we were waiting for you guys." She shrugs and sucks loudly on the cocktail straw.

"I'm going to drop our bags into our room and let the captain know we're good to go," Dameon says from behind, his hand brushing lightly against my bare shoulder.

"Okay." Our eyes connect, and unspoken words pass between us, a promise of what's to come. The memory of his head between my thighs only an hour ago lingers. It wasn't nearly enough to satiate us. It's the reason we're running late and by the looks of it, we're the last couple to arrive upon this monstrosity.

When I came down the stairs wearing the itty-bitty bikini that I picked out with Cora, it set him off. Three orgasms later, I practically had to pry his face away from my pussy, his soft blond hair tangled in my fingers, as I insisted that I really wanted to see his "boat." Otherwise, we wouldn't have made it at all. He relented, but insisted I cover up with jean shorts and a tank top—the only time he's allowed me to wear shorts—so that the easy access wouldn't drive him wild.

"Jesus, you two. I think I just started ovulating." Cora fans her face, breaking our electric connection.

Dameon beams and gives me a peck on the lips. He grabs my ass and squeezes. "Strip for me, goddess. When I get back, I want these cute little shorts gone," he mumbles against my lips, before disappearing down a flight of stairs. Internally, I flinch at his use of "goddess." It's jarring to hear the name fall from his lips when I've become used to hearing "kitten" and "gorgeous." All it does is remind me of work.

Cora smiles and shakes her head. "Come on, let's get you a drink."

Following her lead, I make my way to the lounges on the deck. James is there, relaxed in shorts and T-shirt, a break from his usual sharp suit. He wears casual wear with the same effortless charm as Dameon. Cora perches herself on his lap, and he's instantly captivated by her. The adoration in his gaze is truly a beautiful sight to behold.

"Glad you could grace us with your presence," James drawls, earning a playful smack on the chest from Cora.

"Dameon had some business to wrap up." I bite the inside of my cheek to smother my smile.

"Hmm... Let me fix you a drink." James taps Cora on the ass as she rises from his lap. He heads over to the bar to mix me a cocktail while Cora slips out of her lace cover-up.

That reminds me.

I quickly shed my shorts and tank top, leaving them neatly folded on a nearby bench. Settling onto the lounger, I accept the fruity pink cocktail James hands me.

"I'll go check on Dameon so we can get ready to disembark." He fists Cora's hair and drags her head back so he can smash his lips to hers. The kiss is deep and filthy, and I cannot look away.

"Mmm, it's nearly time to fill you with my cum again," James murmurs, eliciting a deep blush from Cora.

"We're trying again. He's obsessed with getting me pregnant," she explains when he walks away.

"How old is Noah now?"

"Six months."

"God, time flies." I adjust the straps of my bikini in a feeble attempt to cover more than just my nipple.

"It sure does," she sighs contentedly. "Noah and Leo are having a blast with their cousins this weekend. It gives James and me some much-needed alone time."

Taking a cautious sip of my cocktail, I wince at its sweetness before asking, "So, how many kids are you planning on having?"

Cora chuckles, shaking her head. "If James has his way, I'll be pregnant for the rest of my life. There's something about my pregnant belly that drives him wild. He's insatiable... Who am I kidding, so am I. Pregnancy hormones are no joke." She widens her eyes. "Do you want kids?"

Lately I've found myself contemplating this question more than ever. Raising Beth wasn't exactly a choice I made consciously; it was more of a necessity. Nevertheless, guiding her into adulthood has been an immense honor. But if I wasn't being blackmailed, would I willingly choose to go through it all over again?

"I don't know," I admit. "Not yet... maybe one day. Right now I have my hands full with Beth."

As the boat sets off, a comfortable silence envelops us. The warmth of the sun against my skin feels amazing, and the gentle sea breeze ensures I won't overheat. Closing my eyes, I tilt my face toward the sun, soaking in its warming energy and relishing in the peaceful moment. Thoughts of Dameon and the snippets he's shared about his ex swirl through my mind. Glancing over my shoulder to ensure we're alone, I allow myself to delve deeper with Cora.

"Do you know if Dameon wants kids?" I ask. Cora frowns at me as if the question is absurd.

"Hell, no. I thought he told you about Mia?"

"He did." Although, I'm starting to think he didn't share the full story.

"Good. I'm glad he did. I think your contract with him will be good. It might help him move on and realize that he's capable of being in a relationship to some extent. It's like a practice run," she muses. My stomach drops, and her words cut me like a sharp blade slicing through my chest. But I ignore it, pushing aside the pang of hurt.

"Happy to be of service." I raise my glass in a toast to the notion.

"I couldn't believe it when James told me. I mean, who does that? Who fakes a pregnancy? It was like something from *The Bold and the Beautiful*." She rolls her eyes and I freeze at her words. Dameon conveniently left that part out of his story. I try to keep my face blank so she continues to spill the tea, but I'm not that skilled of an actress.

"He didn't tell you, did he," she says.

I sigh and shake my head. "Nope."

"I'll tell you, but you can't say anything, okay?" Her voice lowers. "I don't want to betray Dameon's trust. Or James's, for that matter."

"I promise; my lips are sealed," I assure her.

"Apparently, Mia really wanted him to propose, so she tried to trap him by getting pregnant, even though she knew Dameon didn't want kids." Cora's voice is tinged with disbelief. "When she couldn't conceive, she faked her pregnancy. And then, when she couldn't hide it any longer and came clean, he broke up with her. He was furious, as you can imagine. Learning that the person you love and trust the most could do something like that? It's messed up."

I'm utterly dumbfounded. My heart goes out to Dameon, truly, but I can't get over the audacity of Mia's behavior. How could someone even think of faking a pregnancy? That's the stupidest thing I've ever heard. It's not like she could keep up the lie forever; it's bound to unravel eventually... in nine months, to be exact.

"Wow," I mutter, shaking my head.

"I know, right? And then she has the balls to go to the media to ruin him."

"Oh, this part I know," I say. *Poor guy. That's fucked up.* No wonder he requires absolute control in a relationship.

The guys return to the deck, bringing an end to our gossip session.

"Look who we found," Dameon announces, slapping the back of none other than Carter Ashford. Carter's arm is casually draped over the shoulders of Blaire, the goddess who served him at Eden. She's positively glowing with happiness, basking in his presence.

"Hey, you're from Eden, right?" Carter addresses me.

"Sure am. We all are," I reply, nodding toward Chloe as she joins us, followed by Dr. Zac, who wraps an arm around her waist and rests his chin on top of her head.

"Well... except for Cora," I add, flashing a playful grin in her direction. "She left us for her knight in shining armor." I bat my eyelashes at her.

"Not true! I just couldn't see myself submitting to anyone else," Cora pouts, but James quickly wraps his arm around her neck, drawing her close. "Damn straight," he murmurs against her lips.

"Speaking of, I said strip, goddess... that means everything." Dameon reaches around my body and pulls the string of my bikini top until it falls away, leaving my breasts exposed. All eyes fall to my chest, and my nipples bead into hard tips, and not just from the cool breeze. Dameon dusts his thumbs over them lightly. "That's better," he says, locking eyes with me as he takes a seat beside me on the U-shaped lounge. The waters of the harbor sway and roll around us, but I'm hypnotized by the depth of his blue-green eyes.

"One for all, and all for one!" Cora interrupts our moment, her voice filled with playful mischief as she swiftly removes her bikini top. Chloe and Blair follow suit in quick succession.

"These too," James chimes in, flicking at Cora's bikini bottoms. The three of us comply, slipping out of the skimpy fabric.

"Much better." Dameon never takes his eyes off my body. The rest of the group join us on the lounge, and I've never felt more comfortable in my own skin than at this moment, surrounded by these people. It feels completely natural, as if this is exactly where I'm meant to be right now.

"How's the leg feeling?" Zac asks, indicating to my thigh. It's been two weeks since the attack, and it's healing up nicely. The stitches have dissolved, leaving behind a raw pink line that will eventually fade to white as it scars.

"Much better now, thank you. It's all healed up," I reply, offering a grateful smile. The lines around his eyes crinkle as he dips his head.

Chelsea emerges from the galley and serves each of the men a crystal tumbler filled with two fingers of amber liquid. Her presence catches me off guard, yet there's a small sense of relief in knowing she's the one serving us. She's completely unfazed by our nakedness.

My pink cocktail is long forgotten; it was way too sweet for my taste buds to endure.

"Is this the good stuff?" Carter asks, taking a sip.

"Yep, from my personal stash," James confirms.

Carter groans in satisfaction. "Fuck yeah."

"You know what would make this whiskey even better?" James turns to Cora.

"What's that?" Her teeth sink into her lower lip, but he gently pulls it away with his thumb.

"Your sweet lips wrapped around my cock." Her eyelids drop to half-mast.

"Mmm, sounds like a fantastic idea to me. On your knees, goddess," Zac instructs Chloe. She gracefully sinks to her knees between his spread legs.

"You too," Carter prompts Blaire. She still wears that look of bewilderment, as if she can't believe she's actually here with *Carter Ashford*. I suppress a snicker. It must get old for him, constantly seeing that look on women's faces. Blaire drops to her knees and I start to follow suit, but Dameon stops me with a gentle hand on my forearm.

"Not you, kitten," he whispers in my ear. "Not with your leg." He lifts me up by the hips and settles me on his lap. "Let's give them a show, something to watch while they're getting their dicks sucked." He bends my knees and parts my legs, resting them on his own spread knees, leaving me open wide. James, Carter, and Zac's eyes immediately zero in on my pussy. He lightly drags his fingers up and down my inner thighs, sending shivers dancing down my spine before parting my lower lips to give them a full view. Carter groans at the sight, and Zac tightens his grip on Chloe's hair. Meanwhile, Cora snickers around James's balls.

"Play with yourself, kitten."

I slide my hand to the apex of my thighs, gathering the wetness and spreading it around my clit. I'm dripping wet, and I can't contain the whimper that escapes my lips.

"That's it, gorgeous." His voice is a low growl in my ear. "Show them how you play with *my* pussy." I continue to circle my clit, before plunging two fingers deep inside and curling them to hit that sweet spot on my inner wall. I writhe in Dameon's lap, making him as hard as granite beneath me. His hands roam over my breasts, massaging and pinching my nipples, sending sharp jolts of pain through my body, leaving me breathless with need. Watching the girls moan in pleasure as they bob their heads on their shafts, hearing the men's grunts as they sip their whiskey, all the while never taking their eyes off my pussy being worked over by my hands, sends me careening to the edge.

"That's my girl, you can come." His praise sends me straight over the edge of the cliff, and I crash hard at the bottom, with no safety net to catch me. My back arches off Dameon's lap, and I scrunch my eyes shut, bracing for the dizzying freefall.

Dameon easily lifts me as if I weigh nothing and flips me upside down, placing my legs up the back of the couch and my head hanging off the seat. The sudden movement leaves me shaky, but when he grasps my head and nudges his cock against my lips, I regain my composure enough to open my mouth.

He thrusts inside, fucking my face with urgency. I focus on relaxing my jaw, allowing him to slide deeper down my throat in this position. Around me, I hear a chorus of moans and grunts, signaling Zac, James, and Carter coming down the girls' throats. Dameon follows shortly behind with a shout, his release erupting down my throat, spilling out of the corners of my mouth and running down my cheeks. When he pulls out, I gasp for breath, trying to recover before Dameon spins me around once again.

"That definitely improved the whiskey," James quips.

"You okay?" Dameon's voice is soft, checking in with me. Nodding my head, I smile.

"Good, because we're just getting started, kitten." Those beautiful dimples of his strike me hard in the chest.

I force the smile to stay on my lips, but Cora's words linger. *A practice run.* I push the hurt down, burying it where it won't show. I'm just doing my job. But pretending that's enough is getting harder every day.

CHAPTER TWENTY-THREE

Hailee

"**W**hat the *hell* are you wearing?" Dameon's deep voice startles me.

"What?" I'm wearing the same bikini that I wore on the yacht a few weeks ago on that epic sex-capade sea adventure. I've never been fucked so hard in my life; I left the yacht sore.

It's late afternoon, and I've just walked in the door after a refreshing dip in the cool blue waters of the beach.

"You wore *that* around Bondi?" He looks around, searching for my beach bag, I suppose. But he won't find it as I didn't bring it with me.

"I was at the beach. What's wrong with it?" I say, looking down at my bikini. Okay, so it's a little skimpy. I could have worn a cover-up... at least until I reached the beach.

"You've got other bikinis, haven't you?"

I don't bother responding; he knows I have a wardrobe full of options.

"Wear them. This one is for *my* eyes only, you got it?" he demands. "Don't act like your job, Hailee."

I suck in a breath and hold it.

Ouch.

"We're going out. There's a dress for you on the bed. Get ready; we leave in an hour."

He storms off, pulling out his phone from his pocket. "What?" he snaps into the phone. After a brief pause, he adds, "I'm going to fucking bury them when I find out who it is." He slams the door shut to his office without sparing me another glance.

I swallow hard, guilt churning in my stomach. I've fucked up, and I feel awful. I can't shake the feeling that call was about what I did, and I'd wager all the tea in China on it. I'm torn. If I confess and come clean, I risk shattering everything that's growing between us—plus, Beth still hasn't had her surgery.

With a heavy heart, I retreat upstairs to our bedroom. There, laid out on the bed, is an exquisite blood-red ball gown. The fabric is soft as silk, and I run my fingers over it absentmindedly, lost in thought. Raising the gown to my chin, I hold it against my body and gaze at my reflection in the mirror. The gown's strapless sweetheart neckline and mermaid silhouette is beautiful. But all I see reflected back at me is a woman consumed by remorse.

An hour later, I'm dressed and ready to go with ten minutes to spare. Given his current mood, I'm erring on the side of caution.

"You are a vision in that dress. Like Aphrodite herself." Dameon pulls me close, planting a gentle kiss to my temple. "Stunning."

My eyes flutter closed, and I try to conceal the sparks that work through my body at the touch of his soft lips. His scent, the warmth of his breath and his protective aura are intoxicating. Despite being pissed at him for his words earlier, I'm overcome with the need to capture this moment, to imprint it on my brain, so I'll never forget what it feels like to have the devotion and care of a man like Dameon. The realization that I won't always have his lips at my disposal makes my heart ache. I can no longer lie to myself that I don't want his soft, intimate kisses for the rest of my life.

We arrive at a charity ball, not too dissimilar to the one we attended in New York—the night my entire life changed when he placed that small black card in my hand. The ballroom is dripping with ostentatious opulence as Sydney's elite arrive to dispense with a small fraction of their fortunes for the underprivileged, all in the name of good appearances.

"Let's get this over with. That dress is coming off the moment we get out of here. And I'm going to smack that ass the same shade of red for making me walk around half-mast." Dameon discreetly adjusts himself, making me smirk.

He threads his fingers with mine, leading me around the ballroom until we spot James and Cora.

"I didn't know you would be here," I remark, kissing Cora's cheek and embracing James.

"I hate these things. I'm here under duress," she complains, shooting James a pointed look. He responds with a raised eyebrow, a silent warning that causes her face to flush pink.

"Hello, gentlemen. Don't you both look dashing." An older woman joins our group, extending her hand to Dameon and James. Her gown is elegant, understated yet beautiful, and her white hair is pulled back into a sophisticated chignon.

"Evelyn, this is Cora, my wife," James says, a tender expression playing on his face. "She's also Hayes & Hayward Media's PR manager, and we would be lost without her." Cora leans into James' body, her face mirroring his affection. It's clear they share a deep love for each other.

"It's a pleasure to meet you," Cora says warmly as she shakes her hand.

"And this is Hailee," Dameon says, introducing me. Sensing an opportunity for a little payback, I bite my lip to hide my smile and the rush of excitement. His meltdown earlier over my bikini had nothing to do with my outfit. Deep down, I know he doesn't really give a shit what I wear—especially since I know he enjoys showing me off. I'm consumed by guilt over causing him stress, but I refuse to be a punching bag. He doesn't get to talk to me like that. The thought of giving him a taste of his own medicine has me feeling almost giddy.

I grab Evelyn's hand and give it a rough shake, her smile straining at my forwardness. Dameon frowns at my sudden assertiveness. He has no clue what it really means to act like a whore, but he's about to find out.

"And what do you do, dear? I imagine being a newlywed keeps you very busy," Evelyn inquires with a polite smile.

"Oh, we're not newlyweds," I respond with a small, fake laugh and a flick of my wrist. "I actually suck dick for a living." I hear Cora snort into her champagne. The shock on Evelyn's face is priceless. I almost wish there was one of those caricature street artists nearby to capture her expression for me. I would treasure that drawing. Forever.

"Men pay me a *ridiculous* amount of money to get on my knees for them. But I'm also an entrepreneur. I'm an OnlyFans model when I'm not bleeding wealthy men like your husband dry," I say, casually eyeing the large diamond on her finger. "I mostly sell pictures of my feet these days, though, oh, and I play with myself on camera. You know how it is. Life is tough in this economy, and bills don't pay themselves," I add with a shrug, smiling at our group.

Cora struggles to suppress her laughter, attempting to hide it behind her champagne glass, and James wears a massive shit-eating grin on his face, clearing enjoying the spectacle. I chance a look at Dameon. His expression is nothing short of murderous. If looks could kill, I'd be splayed out on this floor, hemorrhaging like a gutted pig.

"Well, that's very interesting, dear..." If she were wearing pearls, Evelyn would be clutching them.

"Would you please excuse us for a moment?" Dameon grits through clenched teeth, his grip firm on my upper arm as he drags me away from our friends and the bewildered Evelyn.

"What the fuck are you doing?" he seethes under his breath as he corners me in a quiet spot of the ballroom. I rip my arm away from his hold, meeting his powerful gaze head on.

"What am I doing? I'm just acting like my job. I can't seem to help it!"

His jaw twitches, and his eyes blaze with fury. After a few moments of intense staring in a silent standoff, he closes his eyes and breathes out heavily through his nose. When he reopens them, regret flickers across his features.

"I'm sorry for implying"—I narrow my eyes at his attempt at an apology—"for *calling* you a whore in anger. I didn't mean it. But if you wear that bikini in public again, I'm burning it."

I smile in victory. "For your eyes only, I promise." Standing up on my tiptoes, I give him a peck on the lips. He responds by deepening the kiss, and by the time he pulls away, I'm panting. A smear of red lipstick adorns his lips. I wipe it off with my thumb, although I'm tempted to leave it—a mark of my ownership, a sign that says "Back off, bitches, he's mine."

He pinches my chin between his thumb and forefinger, tilting my head up so our eyes lock. "If you ever pull a stunt like that again, you won't orgasm for the rest of the year."

Remembering the way he tortured my poor pussy and kept me on edge during my last punishment is enough for me to heed his warning. Not coming for the rest of the year? No, thank you.

"I understand, sir."

"Good girl. Go wait for me on the balcony; I'll get us some drinks." He taps me on the ass, heading toward the bar with one hand in his pocket, looking very debonair.

I take a moment to freshen up in the bathroom, twisting the end of my lipstick and coating my pout in a deep shade of red. As I refine the edges with a touch of my finger, the door swings open, revealing a tall, curvy brunette in a sublime off-the-shoulder black ball gown. Our eyes meet in the reflection, and a sense of recognition claws at my consciousness.

I know her.

She settles beside me, placing her clutch on the counter and fussing with her hair, though not a strand seems out of place. It's an act, something to occupy her hands, much like brushing off an invisible piece of lint. Our eyes meet in the mirror, and she offers a cool smile. Suddenly, it clicks, like the few remaining pieces of a jigsaw puzzle sliding into place to form the whole picture.

"Do I know you from somewhere?" I ask politely, but what I really want to ask is, *Why the hell are you following me?*

"I'm Rachael." She extends her hand with a subtle air of superiority. The back of her hand faces upward, and I hesitate before grasping it in a weird, dainty handshake. If she expects me to kiss it, she can fuck right off. "I'm Dameon's fiancée." I drop her hand like a lead weight, my eyes widening.

"Oh, I take it he didn't tell you?" she taunts, a cruel smile playing at her lips as a wave of dread washes over me.

What. The. Fuck.

With practiced ease, she retrieves her lipstick from her clutch and applies it, her gaze never leaving mine in the mirror.

"I know who you are, Hailee. And I know what you're doing with my fiancée." I stand, frozen, as she dabs gloss over her lips with her finger.

"And once your contract is through, he'll be done with you, and we can move on with our lives. You're just a temporary distraction. He promised me a future, and I can wait while he has his fun."

There's something off about this woman. The more she talks, the more her words feel hollow. Coming out of my stupor, my eyes narrow at her in the mirror.

"I don't believe you. Dameon would have told me."

Finished with her preening, Rachael turns to face me, her clutch tucked under her arm.

"We dated eighteen months ago, and there were no contracts and no NDAs. He trusts me. Can you say the same?"

Ouch.

Her words sting and I swallow hard, the magnitude of her implications hitting home just as she intended.

"You don't belong with him. If you think you can sink your claws into him, you're severely mistaken. You're nothing but a two-bit whore who sucks like a Hoover," she says, eyeing me up and down.

My spine stiffens. "More like a Dyson," I quip, the corners of my lips tugging up. She flushes red, and I swear steam almost comes out of her ears. But beneath the surface of her anger, I sense a simmering instability. My shock and dread have quickly morphed into amusement. For a moment, I thought Dameon had lied to me. But it's becoming obvious this woman is delusional.

"When he's done with you"—her voice drips with malice—"and mark my words, he *will* be done with you, I'll be there waiting. And if you try to interfere, you'll regret it." She pushes past me, making me stumble in my heels and leaving me shaking my head in disbelief.

Did she just threaten me?

I wade through the crowd and spot Cora looking rather bored, while James appears to give a seminar to the group of men surrounding him. When we make eye contact, I tilt my head toward the balcony. She excuses herself, kissing James on the cheek, and meets me halfway.

"Oh my God, did you see Evelyn's face? That was absolutely hilarious!" Cora exclaims, and we burst out laughing. I can't believe I did that. I just hope she wasn't anyone important to Dameon.

We step out onto the balcony, where I'm hoping we'll find a reprieve from the humidity, but the stifling night air doesn't bring the expected relief.

"Gosh. I'm sweating my tits off." Cora grabs a tissue from her clutch and dabs between her cleavage.

I look out over the manicured gardens lit up by spotlights. It's unbelievably beautiful here, a reminder of the kind of life people like Dameon and my mother take for granted.

"You wouldn't believe who I ran into in the bathroom just now."

"Who?"

"That woman from the restaurant who was staring at me. I've just remembered, I saw her with Dameon in New York as well. She claims to be his fiancée."

"Are you serious? He's not engaged," Cora snorts.

"That's what I thought," I say, fanning my face with my hand in an attempt to cool down.

I need a drink.

Glancing at the bar, I spot Dameon conversing with a leggy blonde. Her back is turned toward me, so I can't get a glimpse of her face, but I can see that her bright pink dress has thigh-high slits on both sides, revealing long, toned legs. She throws her head back in laughter and playfully swats his chest, flicking her hair around as if she's got a bee stuck in it. Dameon doesn't seem to be laughing along with her, but he also doesn't remove her hand from his chest.

First, Rachael, now this woman. Move it, bitch.

The woman slithers up close to his chest, her body pressing against his, and I'm done watching.

"I'll be back in a sec," I tell Cora, and storm toward them. *What am I going to say?* I've already caused one scene tonight; I really don't want to cause another. Just as I approach them, the woman turns around, and it stops me in my tracks.

"Oh, hello, darling, have you met Dameon Hayward?" my mother says with a charming smile that only I can tell is pure cunning.

Her face is meticulously made up, like a doll. Despite her mature years, she looks unnaturally young, her features enhanced by surgery and fillers. Her tight dress rivals the white gown I wore to the New York charity function for indecency, and her massive fake tits spill out of the plunging neckline.

"Mother," I say tersely. "What are you doing here?" Dameon's eyebrows rise slightly, indicating he didn't know who this woman was. I mean, why would she introduce herself as my mother? It's not like she's earned the title.

"I've missed you, darling. Thought I would drop by to see how you're doing," she says sweetly.

What a load of crap.

She hasn't reached out to me or Beth once in the ten years since we left her crazy ass behind. She doesn't care how we're doing, and she certainly didn't miss us. She's here to fuck things up for me.

"Would you please excuse us for a moment? It's been so long, I'd love to chat with my mother alone," I say to Dameon. His expression remains blank, revealing nothing, as he nods and departs.

When he's out of hearing range, I drop all pretenses. "Cut the shit. What are you doing here?"

"I was invited to this event. The charity is doing such good work, and it's a cause I'm immensely passionate about," she responds innocently.

"For fuck's sake, Liz. I mean here in Sydney. Why are you even here? What do you want?" I press.

"Well, I thought I would stop by to make certain you follow through on your promise to Mark." There's no covering her sinister smile with charm this time.

Ah, there we go.

"I gave him what he wanted. And I told him, I'm done. I'm not sending him anything else."

"Oh, dear daughter, you really need to learn a thing or two when you make a deal with the devil," she says, tsking. "Mark won't let you off the hook that easily. He *will* make you pay. And I *will* gladly watch him destroy your life and everything you care about, piece by piece."

"What the *hell* is wrong with you? Why do you hate me so much?!" I whisper-shout, my voice cracking with emotion. The question slips out without thought, and I regret it immediately. It makes me appear weak, as if I still care what she thinks of me.

I loathe that she can get under my skin so easily. She's like a tick, burrowing deep, and no matter how much I scratch, I can't get rid of her.

Her painted pink lips curl into a vicious smile. "You act so high and mighty, as if taking Beth from me earns you some kind of Mother Theresa award, but it doesn't. You're no different to me. You can call yourself a high-class escort or companion or whatever the hell you want to dress it up as, but at the end of the day, you're just a *dirty* whore. And when you get older, and your pussy becomes loose, and you can no longer rely on that beautiful face of yours, all you'll be is a *dried-up, dirty* whore. You despise me because I use men for their money and power. Well, darling, you are no different. You are *not* better than me." She jabs her long fingernail into my shoulder, punctuating her words.

"I will *never* be like you," I hiss. "I see through the vile poison that you spew; your words no longer affect me. I'm not so easily manipulated anymore. I'm done with you, and I'm done with Mark. I gave him what he wanted; I've honored the deal we made. I'm not doing it again. Stay away from me and Beth. Another ten years is too soon, so let's make it twenty this time... Or how about never?"

She narrows her eyes, her lips thinning in annoyance as she realizes she hasn't gotten the reaction she wanted.

"Take care, *Mother*." I turn on my heel and leave her and her toxic energy behind. I'm proud that I didn't stoop to her level. I could have, and I wanted to. Desperately. But all that therapy would have been for nothing. I can't change who she is, nor her behavior, resentment, or hatred toward me. But what I can change is my response to her and how I let it affect me. I choose my own reactions, and, in this moment, I choose *not* to react. I search for Dameon in the crowd, eager to get the hell out of here. I'm done with this night.

Chapter Twenty-Four

Hailee

"Two whiskeys, neat."

"Coming right up." I pour our top-shelf whiskey into two glass tumblers, place them on the server's tray and take a moment to survey the crowded lounge. It's still as packed as it was an hour ago, even though it's a Wednesday night. I'm covering a shift at Eden because one of the goddesses called in sick, and my body is already protesting the decision. My back twinges, my feet are killing me, and sweat is beading on my forehead. I grab a cocktail napkin and discreetly wipe it around my face.

"Mmm, I like seeing you sweat," Dameon says with a smirk.

It's sweet that he wanted to join me tonight. He could have been at home, chilling out, but he chose to keep me company instead.

Gross, I mouth at him, wrinkling my nose. He gets that look in his eye, and I realize I've unknowingly issued a challenge. I bet he'll be licking me clean and making me scream by the end of the night.

"All of your bodily fluids are delicious, like a fine wine meant to be savored."

I roll my eyes, but there's no time to respond. I have to prepare another drink order. Harriet has been working her ass off, and I don't want to leave her to carry my weight because I'm distracted by my sexy master sitting at the bar.

Dameon watches me intently over his whiskey all night, and I feel the heat of his gaze on my skin with every move I make. Frantically pouring drinks in this sizzling environment is challenging enough without adding his overwhelming gaze to the mix. I'm practically ready to combust.

Two hours later, the crowd has thinned out, and the bar is now manageable with just one person.

"Night, Harriet," I call out, slipping on my jacket and grabbing my bag. She smiles and waves me off, already attending to the next server.

"Ready to go home, gorgeous?" Dameon murmurs. I love it when he calls me that, but I love it more when he calls his place "home," like it's ours. It's probably a slip of the tongue, but it's nice to hear, regardless.

"Let's go."

"You okay?"

"Mmhmm... just tired," I mumble, stifling a yawn. The gentle sway of the car is lulling me into a hazy state, somewhere between sleep and wakefulness.

"Here, give me your foot." I shift in my seat, placing my back against the car door, and swing my feet into his lap. He slips off my ballet flats and digs his thumb into my arch, and I groan at the relief. My body isn't used to standing behind a bar for hours anymore.

"Ah, that feels good," I say as he expertly massages my foot with firm strokes, then moves on to the other one. "I've died and gone to heaven," I moan. "Like, dead as a door nail."

His chuckle is like catnip, and combined with his scorching stare all night, and his strong fingers kneading the tension from my feet and calves, I'm teetering on the edge already.

I exhale a sigh and squirm in my seat. "A little bit—"

"I know what you need, kitten," he interrupts. "Let me take care of you."

His hand snakes under my denim skirt, finding me bare and wet, primed for him. A low growl escapes his chest.

"Have I mentioned how much I fucking adore your pussy?" he rasps, his voice thick with lust. "Always so wet and eager for me. You're absolutely perfect." I preen at his words, relishing his praise.

As his thumb circles my sensitive nub, his other hand continues its soothing massage on my foot. Then, he leans down, trailing his tongue along the arch of my foot before sucking my big toe into his mouth.

A surge of pleasure courses through me, and I come so hard and so fast it scares me. "Oh my fucking God," I gasp, my whole body tensing into a tightly coiled ball before releasing, squirting my juices all over his hand.

I collapse against the seat, my limbs like jelly after such an explosive release. When I open my eyes, Dameon is licking up my juices from his fingers, savoring my taste like a fine wine, just as he promised.

This man will be the death of me.

Exhaustion pulls me under, but my phone's shrill ringtone cuts through the car's quiet before I fully drift off. With a sigh, I grab my handbag from the floor and fish it out.

"Hello, Hailee speaking."

"Good evening, Ms. Mann, I'm Dr. Sanchez from St. Vincent's Hospital. I've got great news. We've found a compatible match for Beth, and we need you to come to admissions as soon as possible so we can start preparations." The doctor's words hit me like a bolt of lightning, and for a moment, I'm speechless. Then, a rush of emotion floods through me—relief, hope, and overwhelming gratitude.

"Oh my God! Thank you, Doctor," I choke out. "We'll be there right away."

I've been waiting for this phone call for months, but its arrival still catches me by surprise. Excitement surges through me, tinged with nerves. Until this moment, it never felt real. But it's definitely real now. It's finally happening—Beth has a chance at a new lease on life.

I end the call and turn to Dameon, my eyes shining with tears. "It's Beth," I explain, my voice breaking. "There's a match."

"I heard." His dazzling smile and those gorgeous dimples momentarily steal my breath away. Or perhaps it's the overwhelming moment. Everything is happening so fast. He gently takes my trembling hands in his and brings them to his lips.

"Let's go get your little sister."

Chapter Twenty-Five

Hailee

"What's wrong?" Beth frowns as she looks between us. It's one in the morning—no wonder she's alarmed to find me pounding on her door like a madwoman.

"You're getting a new heart," I announce. It takes a second for the gravity of it to sink in, but when it does, her face lights up with a radiant smile that could rival the sun.

"Hell, yeah! About time!" She pumps her fist in the air.

Twenty minutes later, we arrive at the hospital—Beth's bag has long been packed in preparation for this moment. A flurry of activity begins as soon as we step through the doors. We're whisked from one specialist to another—the cardiologist, the surgeon, the anesthesiologist—each one briefing us on their role in the procedure ahead. The nurses bustle around us, preparing Beth for surgery with quiet efficiency. Everything moves so quickly that I don't get a chance to fully process the enormity of what's happening. Or check in with Beth.

Dameon's steady presence by my side is a relief as we navigate the flood of information. True to his word, everything outlined in the contract has transpired seamlessly. The team of professionals he has arranged for Beth's surgery are nothing short of exceptional, and I know she's in safe hands.

Before they wheel her away, I'm granted a quiet moment alone with my sister.

"How are you feeling, Betty Boo?" I gently sweep back a stand of hair from her forehead.

"You know I hate that name," she grumbles.

"Alright, alright, poo brain, chill out," I tease, holding my palms up. "But seriously, how are you feeling?"

"I'm good. I'm ready." She nods with determination, her gaze steady.

"Are you sure? It's okay to feel scared or nervous."

"No, seriously, I'm good. We've been waiting forever for this, and now that it's finally here, I'm just... relieved." She blows out a deep breath.

"You're in good hands. And you'll come out of this bigger, better, faster, and stronger," I assure her.

"I don't want to be bigger," she retorts, frowning.

"Okay, wrong choice of words. Not bigger. Better, faster, and stronger, though. You know what I mean."

"I do." She squeezes my arm, a small smile playing on her lips.

"I love you very much, and I'll see you on the other side."

"What?!" she splutters.

My eyes widen. "The other side of surgery! Not the other side of the tunnel. Just don't go toward the light," I add hastily.

"God, you suck at pep talks," she laughs, shaking her head.

"I know, I'm sorry. I'm doing my best!" I say, wincing.

A nurse pops her head around the door. "We're ready for you now, Beth," she announces softly.

"Let's do this," Beth says, her voice clear and sure.

The nurse fusses around the bed, preparing to wheel Beth to the operating room. Before she goes, I lean down and place a tender kiss on her forehead, silently conveying all the love and support I can muster into the press of my lips. I follow them out of the room and join Dameon in the corridor. He wishes Beth luck with a wink before she disappears behind the double doors of the operating theater.

With a heavy heart, I stare at the doors for a beat longer. All I can do now is trust the skilled hands of the medical team, knowing they will bring her back to me. They have to.

The one constant in life, the bedrock upon which everything else rests, is time. It moves forward steadily, indifferent to our desires or fears. Every second passes without fail, an unyielding march toward an unknown future. We know and accept that time moves forward, and there's nothing anyone can do to stop it, reverse it, or change it. Each tick of the clock repeats at the same pulse forever.

Yet, despite its unwavering nature, time has a peculiar way of bending and warping depending on the circumstances. On vacation, having the time of your life? It slips through your fingers like grains of sand, each day blending seamlessly into the next.

But in the sterile confines of a hospital, waiting for news that could alter the course of your life? It slows to a crawl; the second hand of the clock drags around the face. Each passing moment stretches out into an eternity of anticipation and anxiety. I'm convinced time doesn't just stand still here; it goes backward. I would know, as I've been staring at the clock relentlessly, willing it to go faster. And I could have sworn at one point that I saw the second hand hesitate, faltering in its forward momentum before flickering backward. I've even entertained the notion that the clock itself might be faulty. I'm on the verge of lodging a complaint with the nurse. But I know it's just my mind playing tricks on me. Time will do that to you. Maybe I simply need another cup of coffee to jolt me back to reality.

It's been six hours, thirty-eight minutes, and twenty-two seconds. No, twenty-three seconds. But it feels like it's been days.

"I'm going to get a coffee. Want one?" I announce, springing up from the uncomfortable plastic chair and shooting a silent *fuck you* at the clock.

"I'll get it," Dameon offers, pocketing his phone.

I wave him off. "I could do with a walk. If I don't focus on something else, I'm going to murder that clock."

He arches his eyebrows, silently questioning my sanity.

Don't worry, so am I.

I've annoyed everyone at the nurses' station by repeatedly asking for updates. Dameon eventually intervened, threatening to restrain me to the chair with the bondage rope he keeps in the car if I asked again. And I know it wasn't an idle threat. He would do it. So I bypass the nurses' station without pausing to study their expressions for any hint of what's happening. Why it's taking so long.

I will my feet to keep moving until I spot Dr. Sanchez emerging through those double doors. His head swivels, searching for me amid the oppressive silence of the waiting room. His expression is stoic, and I can't get a read. Without hesitation, I jog up to him, unwilling to wait another second.

"Any news? Is she okay?" I blurt out.

"Beth is doing really well." His calm voice is a welcome relief. "The surgery was a success; it was a routine procedure, and we didn't encounter any complications."

"Oh, thank God!" I exclaim, my hand flying to my chest. The relief and tension drain from my body, leaving me feeling nothing but exhaustion. I'm too spent to even muster up excitement or happiness for Beth. Dameon appears behind me and enfolds me into his chest. His arms support my frame just as my knees threaten to collapse beneath me.

"She will be moved into ICU for a few days before transitioning back to her room in the ward for a couple of weeks to recover," Dr. Sanchez explains. "She'll feel brand-new in six months. But as you know, the risk of organ rejection is high during the first year, so we'll need to monitor her closely. But Beth's a fighter." He squeezes my shoulder, offering a kind smile.

"Thank you, Doctor," I manage to say before he makes his way toward the nurses' station. Dameon gently turns me around in his arms and cradles my head, his comforting presence a balm to my frazzled nerves.

"Look at me. Beth is going to be fine. Just breathe... I've got you," he soothes. "In this moment, nothing else matters."

He's right. Beth's health is paramount right now. But his acknowledgment of that fact, and his willingness to put his own needs aside for the time being, means the world. Dameon's been nothing but kind, attentive, and supportive. Every touch, every caress, feels intimate. He presses his lips to mine, and in that simple act, I find solace.

I'm fucked.

Every fiber of my being is screaming that this is real. There's no aspect that feels transactional anymore. I can no longer mask this feeling as ignorant bliss. It's unlike anything I've ever experienced, neither in a relationship nor with a client. Our connection runs soul deep.

I'm so *fucked.*

"Hailee, Beth is settled in ICU if you want to see her now?" One of the nurses interrupts my inner freak-out.

"Go, I'll wait for you out here," Dameon says.

"Thank you," I reply softly, pulling away from his embrace and following the nurse into the ICU. As I walk away, the weight of everything hits me like a ton of bricks.

I'm beyond fucked.

"Gin," I declare, tossing my cards onto the bed.

"God, you suck! How do you keep on winning?"

"No, you suck. That's how."

"Whatever." Beth rolls her eyes.

"Don't hate the player, hate the game." I shrug.

"Please don't ever say that again," she says flatly, and we both burst into laughter.

Beth throws her cards on the bed and I gather them up, shuffling. I glance at the time. It feels like we've been playing cards for hours, but it's only been forty minutes. The clock and

I are now mortal enemies, locked in a battle of wills over the passage of time.

"How long is this going to take?" she whines.

"Patience, Beth. We've been here for four weeks; another hour isn't going to make a difference."

Beth is being discharged today, and we're waiting on the doctor for final sign-off. Every time someone walks past our door, our heads snap up in hope that it's Dr. Sanchez.

We're itching to get out of here. What was supposed to be a two-week recovery ended up stretching to four weeks after she became seriously ill with a nasty infection, thanks to her compromised immune system. It was terrifying to watch her weakened body struggle to combat the infection. At one point they were even considering moving her back into ICU, but she made a turn for the better just in time.

I've stayed by her side the whole time, only leaving to shower, change, and bring back more of her things. My back is completely messed up from sleeping on the pull-out bed. The mattress is so thin, the springs poked through. But it was a small price to pay to stay with her. After I spent the first night awkwardly sleeping on the visitor's chair, Dameon demanded the hospital provide a bed for me. I wasn't going to complain about the lousy trundle bed; if I had, he would have arranged for a proper bed with a full-size mattress to be brought in and installed.

Dameon has been incredible throughout Beth's recovery. He visits us every day, even though he's swamped with work, and spends hours by our side. He brings us food, despite the fact we're easily able to order Uber Eats ourselves when the hospital meals don't cut it. He's been my backbone, my rock. And with each passing day, I find myself falling a little bit harder. There's no stopping it now; it's a runaway train.

With all this time on my hands, I've had ample opportunity to scrutinize my feelings for him. My days have revolved around Beth, assisting her with everything from showers to walks to boosting her spirits with Big Macs when she turns her nose up at the hospital stew. We've passed the time playing cards, watching TV, and reading books together. But during the quiet moments, especially at night when the loud noises of the ward kept me awake, my mind would wonder, and my thoughts would inevitably drift to Dameon.

What would have happened if we hadn't met at Eden, but under different circumstances? What would our life be like if we had crossed paths in a random café instead? I've wrestled with the question of whether to tell him how I feel and if so, when to do it. Should I speak up now, or wait until our contract is over? And then there's the nagging doubt—does he feel the same way? Though I'm fairly sure he does, there's always that lingering uncertainty. Would he even want to date me for real, knowing my profession? Or has he been too scarred by his past relationship to open himself up to vulnerability again?

And then there's Mark, the inevitable shadow looming over everything. How on earth am I going to explain what I've done? It's a conversation I know I need to have, and I don't intend to keep it hidden forever. Once Beth is fully recovered, at the six-month mark, I'll tell him everything. Including my feelings. By then there won't be much of the contract left, and I can only hope I haven't waited too long and missed my opportunity.

"What's taking sooo long?!" Beth groans.

"Let's play another game. Poker this time," I suggest, trying to placate her. I shuffle the cards and deal them out.

A few moments later, Dr. Sanchez waltzes through the door, and both Beth and I throw our hands up in the air, cheering. The cards fall down around us like autumn leaves, and his cheeks tint pink at our dramatic response to this entrance.

"I hear you ladies want to get out of here." He smiles.

"Damn straight, a month here is a month too long." Beth's already grabbing her bag, ready to make a run for it.

"I totally understand. Please remember everything we've told you and take it easy, as your body is still recovering. I'll schedule a follow-up for you in a couple of weeks," he adds, handing me the discharge paperwork. We thank the doctor, and with the paperwork in hand, we're ready to leave this place behind for good.

Dameon is waiting for us at the entrance with his Porsche SUV. He insisted on driving himself to pick us up. Leaning against the car, he looks devastatingly handsome in his dark suit, his legs crossed at the ankles and his hands in his pockets. When he spots us, his dimples appear, and my heart skips a beat.

"Hi, gorgeous." Dameon greets me with a peck on the lips. His endearment is cute but I feel far from gorgeous. In fact, I feel more like a grotesque troll with matted, oily hair, frumpy clothes, and the stench of hospital clinging to my pores—a lovely combination of bleach and death.

"Welcome home, Beth," he says, helping her into the backseat of the car.

"Let's get this show on the road. I want my own bed, and I want my own space. This one has been up my ass for weeks." She jerks her chin at me.

He chuckles, and that sound does delicious things to my neglected core.

"Didn't I tell you?" I tease as I slide into the front passenger seat while Dameon takes the wheel. "I'm coming to stay in your apartment to help look after you." Dameon visibly stiffens.

"What?" Beth gasps. "Hell, no!"

"Relax, I'm joking," I assure them both, laughing. I squeeze Dameon's thigh and shoot him a playful wink.

Chapter Twenty-Six

Dameon

Navigating the packed bar, I catch sight of the guys in one of the VIP booths. After the day I've had, I'd prefer a quiet drink on my own than to deal with the crowded chaos of Ivy. My mood is as dark as the lighting, and I'd rather be anywhere else. We should have opted for Eden instead; it's more relaxed, and we'd have plenty of pleasant distractions to enjoy. Although, I do have a pleasant distraction of my own waiting for me. I should have just gone home and worked out my frustrations on her ass instead of hitting the gym.

Another merger fell through today, snatched up at the last minute by none other than Mark Strickland. This is the second time it's happened, with deals that were solid suddenly crumbling, only to be acquired by Strickland's company. I can't say I'm surprised; it's most likely payback for interfering in his plans for his stepdaughter. Once could be chalked up to luck, but twice feels like foul play. It's niggling at me. I was considering skipping drinks with the guys tonight, but James convinced me to come since we haven't caught up since the cruise.

"Well, look who decided to show up," James quips when he spots me.

Zac, James, and Carter are already three drinks in, judging by the empty glasses scattered across the table.

"Why, did you miss me?" I slide into the empty seat and signal to a passing waitress for a whiskey and another round for the boys.

"You know you look ridiculous, right?" I say to Carter. He's wearing a baseball cap pulled low over his face and dark sunglasses. We're tucked away in a back corner of the VIP section where no one is going to see him, let alone recognize him.

"I can't be fucked taking photos with fans tonight," he responds with a casual shrug.

As the guys get back to talking shop, I tune them out and nurse my drink. My mind is consumed with figuring out how Strickland is sabotaging my mergers.

"What's eating you?" Carter asks.

"Nothing." I swallow the last mouthful of my whiskey.

"Two of our recent acquisitions have gone south," James supplies. They talk around in circles for a while, dissecting the mergers, but I zone out. I don't need to rehash it—I was there.

"How's it going with Hailee? You popped the question yet?" Zac snickers, pulling me out of my thoughts.

"What? What are you talking about?" I look around the group, confused.

"Come on, man. It's obvious you're crazy about her. Every time you look at her, you've got hearts in your eyes," Zac teases. My gaze drifts from one friend to the next, noting expressions ranging from amusement to pity.

What the fuck is going on?

I shake my head. "You've got it all wrong. It's not like that with us. It's strictly business. She's my sub for the year," I say, though they already know this.

"Riiight…" Carter smirks.

"What's that supposed to mean?" God, I sound like a woman, but they're really starting to piss me off.

"When was the last time she kneeled for you?" James asks.

It was every night until that asshole attacked her, leaving her with a stab wound in her thigh. I can't expect her to kneel with her leg in that state.

My silence apparently speaks louder than words.

"Exactly. When was the last time she sucked your dick?"

She used to wake me up every morning with her hot little mouth wrapped around my cock. But since Beth had her heart transplant, our routine has been disrupted, and we haven't fallen back into it. I've been getting up early to go to the gym, and I haven't wanted to wake her.

"When did you last tie her up and dole out a punishment?" James continues.

"What about the last time she addressed you properly?" Zac adds.

Come to think of it, she hasn't called me "sir" in a long time. A very long time. And I can't even recall the last punishment I gave her, although she's broken every rule I've set more than once. Lately, she's been sporting leggings more often than not. But I haven't said a thing. A lot has happened, and we've been so focused on Beth's recovery that I haven't pushed her for more than what she was able to give.

My eyebrows knit together. I'm having trouble grasping the fact that I didn't even notice the signs. I've been content. Happy, even. Things have felt complete; nothing seemed lacking. I haven't felt the need for her complete submission all the time to maintain control. Even in those moments when she was only partially submissive, I still felt a sense of control. I always thought that's what I needed to be with a woman again after Mia. But that belief is crumbling before my eyes. If it were true, I would have craved for it from Hailee while she was focused on Beth. But I didn't.

Hailee brings me a sense of happiness and peace I've never experienced before. Her analytic mind impresses me, she's drop-dead gorgeous, and she's the perfect balance of assertive and submissive. Ever the optimist, her smile lights me up from the inside out like the ball of sunshine that she is. And the fact that she can put away as much food as I can is the icing on the cake. *God, no, it can't be...*

"I'm not in love with her," I say quickly. The guys have been observing my silent meltdown, and I can't stand the pity in their eyes. "I'm not!"

"For fuck's sake, get your shit together," James says. "It doesn't matter if you're in love with her. She's an amazing woman, and you know it. You would be lucky to call her yours. But you can't date her if you're still her client. And that's exactly what you're doing. You two act like lovebirds, lost in your own little world, nothing like a dom–sub transactional relationship. You're blurring the lines, and it's not healthy. Make up your mind; either end the contract or enforce it."

Fuck, he's right.

I rake a hand through my hair, pulling at the roots.

"I warned you, man. One day, some woman would come along and turn your world upside down. And look where we are." He grins. "And I'm absolutely loving it."

The guys chuckle, and I punch him in the shoulder... hard.

Fucker.

Chapter Twenty-Seven

Hailee

A loud crash startles me awake, and I'm instantly alert, scanning the darkness of our room. My heart races, and I struggle to calm my fight or flight response with deep breaths. My hand reaches out instinctively for Dameon, but his side of the bed is cold and empty. Another loud noise, followed by a muffled curse, echoes from downstairs.

A glance at my phone tells me it's three in the morning. I pull on my dressing gown and head downstairs to a sight I've never seen before. Dameon is beyond plastered, swaying and struggling to focus as he leans over the microwave. He's squinting at the buttons, attempting to work them. It's kind of cute, and I pull my lips over my teeth to stop the laugh from bubbling out.

"Let me help you with that." My voice startles him, but when he realizes it's me, a sloppy smile spreads across his face.

"Hey, gorgeous, did I wake you?" he slurs.

"That's okay. Let me heat you up some food." I quickly check the microwave to ensure there's no foil inside, then set it for two minutes.

"Big night?" I inquire.

"Mmhmm." His eyes roam over my body, their depths darkening into swirling sea storms. He toys with the lapel of my dressing gown.

"Did I say you could wear clothes inside the house?" His question catches me off guard.

"No…" I respond slowly. "But I wasn't—"

"Take it off," he interrupts, his tone commanding. I was about to explain that I didn't want to be naked while investigating a loud noise in the middle of the night. What if it wasn't Dameon? What if Jacob was back?

"Right now!" he bellows in my face, causing me to jump. I swiftly shed my robe, letting it fall into a puddle at my feet.

"Get on your knees and unzip me."

I sink to my knees on the unforgiving kitchen tiles. I have no idea what the fuck is happening right now. With trembling hands, I unzip his slacks, and he unveils his thickening cock. Despite the gleam of desire in his eyes, there's a hint of confusion, too. Perhaps from the alcohol? I don't know. As he traces the outline of my lips with the head of his cock, smearing precum in its wake, tension crackles in the air.

"You know what to do."

"Dameon, what's going—"

"Do *not* call me by my name. It's sir or master to you." He sways on his feet, and I instinctively reach out to steady him by gripping his thighs. "In fact, from now on, you'll address me as master. And you'll be punished every time you forget." I meet his troubled gaze, searching for answers or some explanation for his sudden change in behavior.

"Now, do your fucking job for once and suck my dick. This is what I'm paying you for, isn't?"

Oh.

I stare up at him, stunned. Does he think I haven't been fulfilling my duties? He's been so accommodating and understanding; maybe I've taken advantage of his kindness for too long. But he never showed signs of being unhappy. Clearly I've misjudged the situation. Perhaps I've misjudged a lot of things.

Fed up with waiting, he grabs my hair and thrusts his dick into my mouth, catching me off guard once again, and causing me to gag in surprise. I quickly adjust my position on my knees and set to work, sucking him deep into my mouth and swirling my tongue around his head. Using both fists, he grips my hair firmly, maintaining control by keeping me on a tight leash. I suck him hard and fast in the hope he'll blow as quickly as possible so I can retreat to bed and fume over my foolish assumption that our feelings were mutual. His deep, guttural moans reverberate through the kitchen.

Come on and blow already.

He better not have whiskey dick because I don't plan on being on my knees all night. Luckily, within moments, his cock twitches in my mouth and he comes hard, sending hot spurts cascading across my tongue and down my throat. I dutifully swallow every drop, like the good little sub I'm being paid to be. Once he's spent, I finish him off by licking him clean, leaving no trace of his release behind.

"Thank you, master," I murmur, unable to meet his eyes. The microwave dings, and he tucks himself back into his trousers and stumbles over to retrieve his food. I rise from my knees and scurry out of the kitchen, eager to escape the awkward tension that lingers in the air. As I reach the threshold, his commanding voice stops me in my tracks.

"I haven't dismissed you. Get back here on your knees," he orders, taking a seat at the kitchen table and pointing to his feet with his fork. With my head lowered, I slowly pad back toward him and drop to my knees at his feet. I wait silently, head bowed, while he eats his dinner, each passing moment a struggle to contain my emotions. I'm flushed with anger, and I want nothing more than to hide in bed. I'm hurt, I'm sad, and I'm embarrassed. Being with Dameon has never felt like a job, not even during our time at Eden. I've always desired him, never felt obligated—until now. I've always been proud of who I am, but in the last few minutes, I felt ashamed. And I hate it. I hate the way his words and actions have made me doubt myself.

But above all, I'm angry with myself for allowing him to affect me so deeply. I'm angry that I fell in love with a client, for losing sight of my boundaries. And I'm angry that I succumbed to the same trap I vowed so vehemently to avoid.

CHAPTER TWENTY-EIGHT

Hailee

I toss and turn, punching my pillow as if it's the source of all my frustrations. Closing my eyes, I count to thirty before they snap open again.

For fuck's sake.

Sleep eludes me for the fourth night in a row. No matter how exhausted I am, how I desperately crave its embrace, it slips through my fingers, leaving me at the mercy of my looping thoughts and churning emotions.

I can't take it anymore. I'm on the verge of a mental breakdown.

I'm not the praying type, but *God, if you're up there, grant me sleep, and I promise I'll do a good deed. Not just a "helping an old lady cross the road" good deed, but something substantial. I don't know what yet, but I'll think of something... after sleep... when my brain isn't fried.*

After our encounter in the kitchen four nights ago, Dameon stumbled into bed and promptly passed out, leaving me to stew all night as I listened to the symphony of his snores. As dawn broke, I faced the harsh reality: I had fucked up. I allowed myself to lower my walls and entertain the idea of something more with him. Ultimately, it's my responsibility. I'm the professional who should have maintained boundaries, not him. I got swept up in his soft words and sweet kisses. I can't blame him for misleading me. That's why I woke him up the next morning with my mouth attached to his dick and greeted him with a fake smile and a sweet "Good morning, master." When I wished him a lovely day at work, he looked at me oddly, confusion clouding his hungover eyes.

The last few days have been exactly the same. I've been the perfect sub for him, per the contract. I never forget to refer to him as master. I kneel by the door when he returns home, serve him dinner, and kneel at his feet when he eats. I don't do anything without his implicit instructions.

We haven't talked about what happened; he seems keen to ignore it, and I'm more than okay with that. He made his desires clear, and it's my duty to fulfill them. In fact, we haven't spoken much at all, other than him barking orders and my immediate "yes, master" in response. He hasn't fucked me once or touched me intimately in any way. And I'm relieved, because I'm not sure I could maintain my defenses. There's every chance they would crumble with just one gentle caress.

Even though I've rebuilt my walls and firmly closed the door to my heart, I'm still hurting. I dared to hope he was different, that there was something deeper between us. But I was wrong.

Now, he's just like every other client. Which I hate, because despite it all, I miss him. Maybe I should pop a sleeping pill to silence the incessant chatter in my brain. I don't just need sleep, I crave it. I feel like a junkie, desperate for my next hit of sweet relief.

The bedroom door opens and Dameon steps inside, flicking on his bedside lamp. Though I'm facing away from him, he can tell I'm still awake. I hear him undress and prepare for bed.

"Tomorrow night we're going out," he says stiffly. "A package will arrive for you in the afternoon. You are to wear everything it contains."

"Yes, master," I intone without turning around.

"Be ready by seven. Get some sleep."

"Yes, master."

I would if I could.

"You look like shit," Maddy declares.

Dark circles plague my eyes, and I swear I've seen a few new wrinkles appear over the last week. Sleep eluded me again last night. So, she's not entirely wrong, but still... rude.

"Don't you have some cleaning to do rather than prancing around in that get-up you call a uniform? Dameon's not going to fuck you, you know." I don't really know that; I'm just guessing that they used to sleep together. In fact, I don't think he likes her all that much, given some of their recent interactions I've witnessed. Then again, what do I know? I thought he felt something for me.

What a joke.

I'm surprised at my cattiness. The fatigue is really bringing out my inner bitch.

"You'll be gone soon enough, and then he'll be back," she replies.

I have no doubt.

I turn my back and leave before another bitchy remark slips out. I refuse to stoop to her level, even if I am sleep-deprived.

"A package arrived. It's in his bedroom," she calls out as I walk away. I ignore her and make my way to our room to see what he's left for me to wear. A medium-sized box rests on the bed. But for some reason, I was expecting a much larger package, like a garment bag, perhaps holding a ball gown or something similar. I'm perplexed yet intrigued. Popping open the box, my eyebrows hit my hairline.

Where exactly are we going tonight?

I pull out a black bandage dress that looks like a series of straps, along with lube, a large anal plug, nipple clamps, and a small butterfly clit stimulator with ties.

What on earth does he have planned?

Under normal circumstances, I would be squealing with excitement, dripping wet at the prospect. And, honestly, I kind of am. But there's a weirdness now, a formality, which takes the fun out of it. The shine has worn off; everything feels subdued. I spread out all the items on the bed and begin the process of getting ready.

It's late afternoon, granting me ample time to prepare, and I've got nothing better to do. I've spent the entire day with Beth, as I've done every day since we returned from the hospital. I'm immensely proud of her; she's approached her recovery with determination, diligently following all the necessary steps and always maintaining a positive attitude. Not once has she grumbled that it's too hard or dropped a "Why me?"

I draw a bath, intent on taking my time scrubbing every inch of my body, making it soft and smooth. I've got my work cut out for me, considering I resemble the walking dead.

After two hours of primping and preening, I've indulged in every beauty treatment available, determined to bring myself back to life. I fasten the magnetic silver clamps onto my nipples, enjoying their sharp bite. They're snug but not overly tight, offering a steady stream of stimulation. Glancing at the sizable butt plug, I wince. It's an elegant stainless-steel piece, cold and impeccably smooth, crowned with a glittering, deep red ruby at the top.

Surely it can't be real, can it?

Knowing Dameon, it probably is. It's also larger than anything I've ever dared to try before. Covering it with a generous coating of lube, I tentatively insert the tip.

Oh God, it's not going to fit.

I continue to push, biting my lower lip at the sensation of being spread wide open. Sweat beads on my forehead and I pant heavily with each thrust, gradually easing it deeper. After what feels like an eternity and a lot of *fucks* escaping my lips, it's all the way in, snug to the hilt. Bending over I catch sight of the sparkling red ruby nestled between my cheeks in the mirror. It's mesmerizing, but I feel so full I could burst. The butterfly clit stimulator is a dream to put on after that. The final item is the collection of straps masquerading as a dress. I search for shoes in the box, but find none; evidently, he intends for me to go barefoot.

It takes a while but I eventually decipher how to put on the dress—it would have been helpful if it came with instructions. A long band runs down my torso, wrapping around my neck like a choker and cinching at my hips. Four straps extend from the central band, barely covering any skin. One crosses over my chest, concealing the nipple clamps while leaving the curve of my breasts exposed at the top and bottom. Two straps encircle my abdomen, while the last one barely covers my crotch. The tiniest shift will expose my pussy and ass to the world. Glancing at myself in the mirror, I can't help but burst into laughter. It's my first genuine laugh in over a week, and it feels good.

The outfit is utterly absurd. I'm aware of his penchant for showing me off—he's a voyeur through and through—but I can only hope we're headed somewhere where this type of attire is appropriate. I doubt he'd deliberately subject me to humiliation; he wouldn't be that cruel. But then again, I've been wrong before. My amusement quickly fades, replaced by a swarm of angry butterflies in my stomach. The thought of potentially being humiliated in front of high society makes my palms sweat.

My phone lights up on the bed, its glow catching my attention in the mirror's reflection. It wouldn't shock me if it's the master himself, issuing more commands. I audibly groan when I see the sender's name.

Mark

> This is your final warning, Hailee. Send me what I want, what YOU promised. Or I'll destroy your life. Last chance.

Fuck!

How many times do I have to tell him no? He can try to intimidate me, he can even involve my mother, but it won't sway me. I gave him what he wanted, I kept my word, and I followed through. I won't do it again. It was wrong from the start, and I feel terrible about it.

Me

> I already told you no. I gave you what you wanted, and you used it o your full advantage. I'm not sending you anything else. Stop texting me. Our deal is done.

I can't make myself any clearer. Should I be worried about his threat? Yes. Should I take it seriously? Absolutely. Mark didn't become the ruthless businessman he is without following through on threats. But right now, I just can't find it in me to care. Beth has a new heart; he can't take that away from us. And I've earned a significant amount of money from this contract. I have more than enough to support us for a very long time. How could he possibly ruin me?

"Hailee, you ready?" Dameon's booming voice carries upstairs. *Damn.* I glance at the clock: it's already five past seven. I completely lost track of time. I was supposed to be on my knees waiting for him.

Shit.

It's my first slip-up since I've been the perfect little sub for him. He didn't include a purse for me, so I plug my phone into the charger and rush downstairs, my bare feet thudding against the carpet.

He's waiting near the elevator, hands in pockets, legs spread wide. When he sees me in the outfit he sent, his eyes ignite, his face transforming into something resembling a wild animal.

"I'm so sorry, master. It won't happen again," I apologize, stumbling over my own feet in my haste to reach him. His eyes widen momentarily as he reaches out to steady me, and for a fleeting moment, I catch a glimpse of my old Dameon. But just as quickly the moment passes, his arms dropping back to his sides, and the spark fades.

I sink to my knees before him, bowing my head. "I accept whatever punishment you see fit."

"You'll receive a punishment whether you accept it or not," he chuckles darkly. "Stand."

I rise to my feet, readjusting the straps of the dress that shifted during my near-face-plant. Once I'm finished, he moves around me, his gaze assessing me as if I were a rare piece of art. Squatting in front of me, he retrieves a box that I hadn't noticed in the commotion. Flipping it open, he takes out a pair of patent black, six-inch Louboutin stilettos.

"Raise your foot." I lift one foot as he slips the stiletto on, then repeats the process with the other. They're higher than what I'm used to, but I think I can manage. I'll probably be on my knees most of the night anyway.

"Present yourself."

I spin around, straightening my legs, and bend over slightly. Honestly, I don't need to bend over at all; the black band barely covers my ass, and from his position on the floor, he can clearly see the sparkly butt plug. He taps it twice before standing up, and I grit back a moan at how full I feel. He intertwines his fingers with mine, and a pang shoots through my chest, pushing through my walls, reminding me of how much I've missed him. How much I've missed the feel of his hand in mine.

"Let's go." With a simple command, he leads the way, pulling me into the unknown.

CHAPTER TWENTY-NINE

Hailee

D ameon graciously opens the car door, shielding me from the prying eyes of his driver. Stepping out into a dimly lit alley, we approach what appears to be a discreet back entrance to a venue. The door swings open, revealing a burly security guard who nods in recognition at Dameon before allowing us entry. His blank gaze passes over me; I might as well be invisible.

Dameon guides me through a labyrinth hallway and into a bustling kitchen, where the culinary staff move with efficiency. No one spares me a glance or acknowledges my existence. I'm little more than a shadow passing through their world. Given my outfit, I'm surprised I'm not garnering at least a few curious looks.

We push through double doors into a stylish restaurant, causing me to dig in my six-inch heels.

Oh.

He's brought me to a classy restaurant.

Dameon stops and looks back at me. The horror on my face must clue him into my thoughts, because he leans down and whispers into my ear, "Stop. Whatever you're thinking, stop. Look at the people. What do you see?"

The tightness in my chest eases slightly, allowing me to take a deep breath and steady my racing heart. I glance around, taking note of the patrons for the first time. The restaurant is full, every table occupied by couples, with a few tables hosting small groups, like double dates. Only one table stands out, with four men and one woman. Everyone is dressed impeccably, but as I stare, the subtle details that I hadn't noticed initially become apparent.

One woman's dress is completely transparent, while another is writhing in her seat, seemingly teetering on the brink of orgasm. At a different table, a gentleman is hand-feeding his companion, and she sensually licks his fingers clean after every bite.

Suddenly I'm enveloped by it—the overwhelming sexual tension that chokes the room. It's a level of intensity I've never experienced before, not even at Eden. The heat of it almost suffocates me. I suck in a quiet breath, my eyes widening as I take in the scene before me, trying to absorb every detail.

"You'll fit right in. Trust me," he assures me, pulling me through the restaurant by my hand. This time, everyone takes notice; the women offer friendly smiles, while the men's eyes openly appreciate my scantily clad body. I hold my head high and follow Dameon, proud to be on his arm. As we reach our booth, he gestures for me to slide in first before joining me. The shift of the plug inside me serves as a reminder that I'm stuffed to the brim. Or rim, in this case.

A waiter approaches and begins detailing the menu options and specials. His attention is solely on Dameon, so I tune him out, observing the couples around us. I do a double-take when I catch sight of a woman kneeling under a table. With the red soles of her stilettos peeking out from beneath the tablecloth and the unmistakable expression of pleasure dancing across her partner's face, there's no denying what's happening. I burst into giggles, drawing Dameon's attention.

"What would you like to eat?"

"Whatever you would like me to eat," I reply automatically, ignoring the frown that creases his brow. Too bad. If he wants a traditional submissive, that's exactly what he'll get. I wasn't paying attention to the waiter anyway. Dameon orders for us both before dismissing the waiter. As he stretches his arm across the back of the booth and leans in close, his delicious scent surrounds me, tempting me to close my eyes and breathe him in.

He grips my jaw firmly and locks eyes with mine. "You look beautiful tonight," he murmurs. "Every man in this restaurant wants you. I saw the way they looked at you, wanting to possess you, stuff you full of their cum. But they can't, can they? Because you belong to me, don't you, kitten?"

"Yes, master," I reply breathlessly, but his frown deepens.

"Perhaps I should give them a taste, show them what they're missing," he muses. My breath catches at his suggestion. "Your oral skills are unmatched. They'd be envious once they experience what you can do with that tongue of yours." His fingers squeeze my cheeks together, and he nibbles on my lower lip that juts out. I'm dripping wet from his words. I don't want to be, but I can't help the way my body is wired. The idea of pleasuring others for him is exhilarating, but the reality is not that enticing. I don't want to be passed around, not like this.

"If that's what my master desires." I attempt to mask my unease, but he pulls back in disbelief. I peer into his angry eyes and can't, for the life of me, work him out. I'm giving him exactly what he wants. Why is he reacting this way?

The waiter approaches with our entrées, and Dameon retrieves a remote from his pocket and activates it. The butterfly vibrator nestled against my clit hums to life at a low intensity, sending ripples of pleasure through my body. I bite back a moan, knowing he has every intention of torturing me tonight. With a sinful smirk, Dameon begins to feed me my meal by hand, his fingers lingering in my mouth as I suck and lick them eagerly, like the kitten he wants me to be.

"How do these feel?" He lightly traces circles around my nipple through the tight band that holds my tits in place. A whimper slips from my lips this time, as the pressure of the nipple clamps heightens every sensation. The slightest touch will make me come.

"Sensitive, master," I manage to gasp out, my voice barely above a whisper.

"Good," he murmurs. He pulls the band down, exposing my tits to his hungry gaze, and ravenously sucks a clamped nipple into his mouth. My body instantly convulses in my seat as the climax hits me head on. I throw my head back with a silent scream, and I can do nothing but surrender to the sensation, letting it consume me.

"Stunning. You come so prettily," he whispers, his words a soothing balm as my orgasm ebbs.

"Thank you, master," I utter breathlessly, mentally pulling myself together. Not daring to adjust the band without his command, my hands remain by my side, leaving my chest exposed.

Suddenly, a piercing wail disrupts the atmosphere, and we turn toward the source—the table occupied by the group of men. Their companion lies naked upon the table, serving as a surface for their dessert as they dine off her. She's in absolute heaven, her body trembling in the aftermath of an intense orgasm.

"Looks like they're having a feast. Although, that's a lot of dick for only three holes." He locks eyes with me, a wicked glint dancing in this gaze.

"Get on your hands and knees and crawl over to them. Offer them the use of this pretty little mouth of yours," he commands, his eyes dropping to my lips. "If they decline, move onto the next table until you've serviced four men in this restaurant. I want you to swallow every drop they offer you."

What. The. Fuck.

I stare into his beautiful sea-green eyes, desperately hoping he's not serious. But his face is etched into stone... He's deadly serious. This must be a test. A test of my obedience to determine whether I can fulfill my role as his perfect submissive. The word "red" lingers on the tip of my tongue, but I hold it back. Sharing, subject to his discretion, was a clause in the contract that I willingly signed. My hesitation hangs heavy in the air between us.

"Well? What are you waiting for?"

That's the thing—I don't mind being shared. In fact, I love it. I enjoy the feeling of being watched, desired, wanted. If it were my old Dameon asking, and this was just a fun, kinky date we were on, I would do it in a heartbeat. But it's not. He's pushing me to say no so he can use it against me, to remind me that I'm not doing my job. There's a part of me that's tempted to say "yes, master" just to gauge his reaction. But my dignity is worth more than that.

I look deep into his tumultuous eyes and murmur, "Red." The word escapes in a whisper, so faint I'm not even sure he caught it. He remains stoic, but then, in a sudden shift, he closes his eyes and exhales a relieved, "Thank fuck." Running his hands down his face, he slumps back into the chair, the tension draining from his features like water gushing from a broken dam. He looks utterly spent. I'm baffled, trying to make sense of it all.

"Wait a minute, you didn't really want me to do it?" I ask.

"No! Of course not!" He turns toward me, grasping my hands in his and planting a tender kiss on the back of them. It's the first time his face has softened since that night in the kitchen.

"I don't understand." I shake my head.

"I've been pushing you all week, hoping you'd push back. You've been on autopilot ever since that night I got wasted. If I have to hear another "yes, master" from your lips, I swear I'm going to lose it." He tugs on his hair in exasperation.

"Hang on, I'm just giving *you* what *you* want." I narrow my eyes at him, jabbing my finger into his chest. "You said that night that I was to do my 'fucking job,' because that's what you're paying me for. Have I not been the perfect sub for you all week?" I ask incredulously.

"Yes, you have, gorgeous, but I don't want a slave," he responds, his tone softening. "Why do you think I haven't touched you? I don't fuck mindless robots. You're cold and closed off. I just want things to go back to the way they were," he pleads, his eyes searching mine.

I close my eyes, anger bubbling beneath the surface. "The only reason I've been a mindless robot is because of *you!*"

"I know. I'm sorry, kitten." He takes a deep breath. "I'm sorry for my behavior that night and the things I said. I had an eye-opening realization that night that sent me spiraling. I lashed out at you, hoping to regain some semblance of control. I'm not trying to excuse my actions because I know I can't."

His admission surprises me; it's not something he would typically say.

"I've done a lot of thinking this past week. I even saw a therapist," he adds. Suddenly, it all clicks into place. "I know how much therapy has helped you over the years, so I thought it wouldn't hurt to give it a try."

"And did it help?" I sigh, my anger deflating.

"It did, but I'm still working stuff out." He lifts his shoulder. "I'm sorry I hurt you."

His openness and willingness to seek help makes me smile. I'm glad I've influenced him in some small positive way. "I know," I say, pressing my lips to his. He responds by deepening the kiss, his tongue melding against mine in a sensual dance. His kiss is tender and loving, brimming with so much feeling that I draw back, gathering the courage to voice what has been weighing on my mind all week. "But, Dameon, we can't go back to the way it was before."

"What? Why not?" His expression falls.

"Because..." I pause, grappling with my own emotions. It's a leap of faith to admit this, risking my emotions, the walls I've built to protect myself. But it's all or nothing at this point. "I've fallen for you," I confess.

The smile that spreads across his face lights my soul on fire, reigniting the spark of hope that I snuffed out this past week. And boy, have I missed those dimples.

He starts to speak, but I gently press my finger against his lips. "Let me finish, please. I've fallen for you, and that's why we can't go back," I say firmly. He shakes his head slightly. "As much as I want to return to the way things were, we can't. We were behaving like a loved-up couple, and while it was incredible and it made me fall even harder for you, I can't go down that path again while under contract."

I pause, gathering my thoughts. "You're paying me to do a job, to be your submissive and cater to your every desire. I'm more than happy to abide by the terms of our agreement, but we need clear boundaries, and emotions can't be a part of it. We have to maintain the professionalism we've had this past week. It's my responsibility to uphold these boundaries, and to enforce them. And it's my fault that things escalated, and the lines got blurred. If that's not what you want, I understand, but I can't offer you more than that while you're still my client." I drop my head, hoping he hears the sincerity in the voice and understands my perspective. I've put my thoughts, feelings, and emotions in his hands.

"What are you suggesting, that we terminate the contract?"

"Well, we can either maintain the professional boundaries we've established over the past week, or... we can end the contract and try dating for real," I propose, holding my breath as I await his response. His silence stretches, and I can sense the freak-out racing through his mind. Disappointment digs its claws into me.

He doesn't want me.

"Here's the thing," he says at last. "I like you, Hailee. I like you a lot. That was the realization I had the other night. In fact, I more than just like you. And it's taken me this whole week to come to terms with that. I don't want a 24/7 dom–sub relationship anymore. I only want you, every part of you. But I'm still grappling with the idea of a relationship without a contract. Edward seems to think I've been using it as my safety net to ensure that I won't be betrayed again."

"Wait. Who's Edward?" I ask, puzzled.

"Dr. Edward Avery, my therapist."

"I think Edward might be onto something," I say, biting the inside of my cheek to stop the smile threatening to spill across my face. "Why don't we keep things professional until you're ready to let go of the contract? I'm a patient woman, I can wait."

He blows out a strained breath as if I've just suggested that he bend over so I can conduct a prostate exam. I can't help but laugh at his pained expression. He narrows his eyes playfully and flashes that panty-dropping smile.

"Okay, deal," he agrees, crashing his lips to mine and kissing me deeply.

"Deal," I sigh when he eventually lets me up for air.

Who would have thought I'd profess my love and have a mature heart-to-heart conversation with my master about our relationship, with my tits hanging out and a plug the size of an eggplant up my ass, in the middle of a kinky restaurant?

Certainly not me.

Chapter Thirty

Hailee

One week. Seven days.

That's all it took of maintaining a professional facade before Dameon reached his breaking point. He stormed into our bedroom with the contract in hand, making a dramatic show of ripping it up. Frustration poured off him as he paced back and forth, his hands linked behind his head, declaring that he couldn't go on like this. He wanted me, all of me, mind, body, and soul, and above all, my heart.

I may have laid it on extra thick with the perfect little sub routine—perhaps a bit too much. But it worked like a charm.

And I'm relieved he broke first. Because that week was a struggle. Reconstructing my walls and locking my heart away for safekeeping again was one of the hardest things I've ever had to do. Opening up to him, baring my feelings, only to face his hesitation at the idea of a real relationship, was agonizing. I hovered on the brink of surrender, unsure how much longer I could hold out. Despite reassuring him of my patience and willingness to wait until he was ready, the uncertainty was grating on me by the seventh day. How long would I have had to wait? A month? A year? He might never have been ready.

The realization that love alone might not have been enough to bring us together was tortuous. Despite knowing his feelings for me, the fear of getting hurt again loomed larger. Yet, after just one week, he made another breakthrough, and I couldn't be prouder of my man for taking a leap of faith.

Now, as I lounge by the infinity pool with Beth, I smile as I replay the magic moment he confessed his love in my mind.

"This is heaven," Beth says, stretching on the sun lounger. Her scar peeks out above the neckline of her swimsuit.

"Mmhmm," I agree, tilting my face toward the sun, soaking in the vitamin D. "Don't forget to cover that scar with sunscreen. It can't be exposed to the sun."

"Yes, Mom," she drawls.

Her happiness is another reason to be satisfied. I knew Beth would love it out here.

"I'm gonna miss this place when the contract is over," she sighs.

Three weeks have passed since Dameon dramatically tore up the contract. That same night was also my first experience in making love. For the first time in my life, I learned the difference between being railed and lovemaking. Don't get me wrong, I love being bent over and fucked raw, and I certainly don't favor one over the other. However, I now appreciate the depth and intimacy it brings to the equation when you look deep into your man's eyes while he tenderly thrusts inside you.

These three weeks have been bliss, like floating on a cloud. We've effortlessly slipped back into our old rhythm, sharing jokes, deep conversations, and just having fun. I love bringing him pleasure and seeing him happy. Dameon's been absolutely amazing, fully embracing our relationship with no reservations, jumping in with both feet.

However, I haven't told Beth that we're officially dating now and that the contract is done and dusted. I'm not sure what's holding me back. Maybe it's my guilty conscience, that nagging voice in the back of my mind that won't let me forget the compromises I've made, the lines I've crossed. The awareness of the gray area of our relationship, the moments where right and wrong blurred into one another, leave me questioning my own moral compass.

Or perhaps it's how it all started, the shadow of our unconventional beginning casting doubt on the legitimacy of what we now share. One of the risks of being involved with a former client is the lingering fear of being taken advantage of, used for free sex. It's not like that with Dameon; I trust him. Still, there's a part of me holding back, waiting to see where this relationship will lead.

I'm head over heels in love with him, utterly swept off my feet by his affection and attention. But at the same time, there's a tiny reservation that maybe he rushed into this too quickly and he's going to do a one-eighty on me. Healing from trauma is a journey that takes time and effort, and it can rear its ugly head when you least expect it if not properly addressed. Noticing the signs is half the battle. My only hope is that I can help him through it when the time comes, and that it doesn't tear us apart.

"There's only three months left," Beth says now. "Where are we going to go? We moving back home or somewhere else?"

"Don't know, I haven't thought that far ahead yet. There's still time," I reply. I look out to the ocean, sparkling like a sapphire, and enjoy the fiery kiss of the sun on my skin, tempered by the soft sea breeze. Surfers bob up and down with the swell, and I'm reminded of Fuck-Face, also known as Jacob. I silently hope that whatever Dameon organized with his "acquaintances" brought him the karma he deserved, and then some.

Massaging sunscreen into my skin, I take care to cover every inch, before adjusting my bikini straps. My modest pink polka dot suit covers much more skin than the one Dameon prefers. I've kept my promise, wearing it only for him. That bikini holds a special place in my heart, filled with many cherished memories. From the day I picked it out with Cora, to our adventures on the cruise, and the charity gala where I shocked poor Evelyn.

"What are you smiling about?"

"Nothing... just thinking," I reply, unable to wipe the smile off my face.

"Something dirty?" she teases.

I shake my head, laughing.

The balcony doors explode open with a deafening crash. Beth and I whip our heads around in shock, to see Dameon storming out toward us. His face is twisted in animalistic fury, and I inhale sharply.

Something's wrong.

His cold eyes glint as they lock onto mine, sending a shiver down my spine. I jump up, discarding my hat and sunglasses, and meet him halfway. Beth does the same, standing beside me.

"What's going on?" My heart hammers in my throat.

"Get the fuck out of my house," he snarls.

One hour earlier

"Sir, Mr. Strickland is here to see you."

"Thank you, Portia. Send him through." I hang up the phone and recline in my chair.

Well, isn't this just delightful.

What brings the ruthless prick to Sydney? If he's here to gloat about stealing the last two mergers from us, he can fuck right off. The frosted glass door of my office swings open, and in strides the man who once attempted to seize control of my company. I've always hated the way he carries himself with an air of superiority.

"Well, this is quite the setup," he remarks, surveying my office as he approaches the floor-to-ceiling windows overlooking the Sydney Harbour Bridge and the Opera House. "This would have made a perfect office for my secretary. She loves a good view when she's bent over," he adds with a creepy smile. I roll my eyes. This asshole does absolutely no favors for the male population.

"I'm sure she would have loved it, but then, anything beats staring at your ugly mug while she counts the seconds." I smirk. "It's a shame you overplayed your hand with the takeover. Underestimating us was a mistake, one I'm sure still stings." There's no missing the clench of his jaw at that.

"What brings you here, Mark?" I snap. I'm done playing games.

He casually unbuttons his suit jacket and settles into the chair opposite my desk. "Feel free to make yourself comfortable," I say sarcastically, gesturing toward the chair.

"I came to see how my stepdaughter is treating you," he begins, a sneer plastered on his lips.

"Our relationship is none of your concern."

"But it is, you see," he continues, his tone dripping with arrogance. "Hailee has been diligently feeding me information on your mergers for months. How did you think I knew when to pounce at the last minute?"

My heart drops like a stone, and I go deathly still.

It can't be true. Can it?

For months now, I've been trying to figure out how he was getting hold of our confidential information. What he's saying is logical, but not possible. She wouldn't betray me like that. Not Hailee. She hates her stepfather, and the idea of her spying on me for him feels far-fetched. I'm fighting the urge to wipe that look off his face with my fist.

"You're lying."

"Am I?" His eyebrow pitches, and we lock eyes, staring each other down for a tense moment. And I just know, by the look in his eye, he's not lying. My world drops out from under my feet as the realization sinks in. The denial lingers on my tongue, ready to fall, but I swallow it back at the last second.

He nods, tries to look sympathetic. "Ah, your silence says it all. Deep down, you know I'm telling the truth."

Fury unlike anything I've ever felt boils through my veins, scorching my heart and turning it to ash but I maintain my stoic expression, refusing to give him the satisfaction of seeing the pain her betrayal has caused me.

This can't be happening again.

Mark chuckles and gets up to go, his point served. "Oh, and congratulations, by the way," he says, holding the door to my office open. "I hear you're going to be a father. Hailee's very excited. I look forward to joining our empires together in the future... Welcome to the family." His grin is triumphant as he strides out of my office.

Panic grips my chest, constricting my lungs. The world blurs and spins around me, and I grip the desk to steady myself, but it doesn't stop the spiraling motion flashing before my eyes. I push my chair back and bend over, putting my head between my knees.

Each inhale feels like a battle against suffocation, my lungs starved of oxygen, my chest threatening to burst under the pressure. Slowly my breathing regulates, and the black spots dancing on the edge of my vision fade away. As I calm down, I chuckle bitterly at the irony that only Hailee could bring me to my knees like this.

With that thought, my anger returns full force and kicks my ass into gear. I slam my laptop shut, shoving it into my bag along with my keys, phone, and wallet. Bursting out of my office, I bark orders at Portia to have my driver ready. I descend in the elevator with my heart clenching tight in my chest. I can't even think; my mind is a whirlwind. Betrayal tastes bitter on my tongue, making it difficult to swallow, while fury and pain intertwine like a volatile cocktail urging me forward. The entire car ride, the only thought that runs through my mind is: *This cannot be happening again.*

At home, the sight of Hailee and Beth laughing by the pool sends me into a wild rage. I storm upstairs to the bathroom, searching frantically for Hailee's contraceptives. It was a stipulation of the contract that she take birth control provided by my doctor. I can't even remember when she last had her period. *Fuck!*

I empty the contents of her cabinet, sending makeup, lotions, and aspirin crashing to the floor in a chaotic mess, but I couldn't give a fuck. When I don't find anything, I slam my hands down on the sink and glare at my reflection in the mirror. Pain is etched into my features, and the sight of it only adds to my fury.

I grab the closest bottle of perfume and hurl it against the shower door, the glass exploding into a million tiny pieces. As the liquid drips down the screen, my eyes land on the bin beside the shower. I reach for it in two steps, wrenching it open and upending it, scattering its contents across the floor. My heart pounds as I sift through the debris with the tip of my shoe, freezing when I spot the small plastic stick with two tell-tale lines. Clutching it tightly in my fist, I storm downstairs and burst through the balcony doors.

Dameon's face is red and his eyes wild. My heart thrashes against my rib cage as if desperately trying to break free.

"Dameon, what's going on?" I repeat.

"You tell me," he booms, flinging something hard at my chest. It hits me with a thud and clatters to the tiled floor. I squint at the object, trying to make out what it is before squatting down to pick it up. My face drops when I realize what I'm holding.

"Where did you find this?" I whisper.

"In our bathroom, Hailee. Don't you dare play dumb with me right now!"

"I don't understand," I say, shaking my head. "This isn't mine."

"Don't lie to me!" He's shaking with fury, and his eyes bleed so many emotions it's hard to pinpoint one.

"I'm not lying," I mumble, confusion clouding my brain. Glancing at Beth, I see she's white as a sheet. She's picking at her nails, making the cuticle on her thumb bead with a drop of blood. A nervous tic she's had since childhood. The sight of her anxiety manifesting physically again only adds to the heavy ball of dread forming in the pit my stomach. Then it hits me: Beth used my bathroom earlier to change into her swimsuit.

"I-I can explain," I stammer, shifting my gaze back onto the furious man in front of me.

His eyes bore into mine, demanding answers. "You can explain? Sure, why don't you start with how you've been spying on me and secretly feeding your stepfather confidential business information."

I stop breathing, and my jaw drops open. I know I need to explain myself, but I can't find the words. It's as if my brain has decided to abandon ship, leaving me to sort out this mess alone.

"I trusted you. We started this relationship weeks ago. *That* was the time to come clean and tell me everything." His voice is heavy with disappointment, and he shakes his head. "You're just like your mother."

"I'm nothing like *her*!" I snap, his insult jolting my mouth into action.

"Why didn't you tell me sooner then, huh? Because if you did, you knew I would have kicked you and Beth out. And without the contract in place, she would have gone without the rehab, training, nurses, and all the support I've provided. You're a user... just like her."

I blink back tears, my vision blurring with each fresh new wave.

"Do you have any idea what you've done? You've caused two major mergers to fall through, costing me billions. Worse, you made me look like a complete idiot."

"I only took one photo..." I sniff.

"I don't want to hear it! You lied to me and manipulated me. After everything I went through with Mia, I can't believe you would betray me like this. Did you ever give a shit about me at all?"

"Of course I do! I love you!"

"This is fucking bullshit," he mutters under his breath, running a hand through his hair. He looks back at me, hands on his hips, and shakes his head. "No pussy is worth billions."

I suck in a sharp breath. All I can do is stare at him in utter disbelief. His words pierce me like poison-tipped arrows and I'm numb, speechless. Beth shuffles on her feet beside me, drawing me out of my head.

"Get the fuck out of my house," he says again, defeated, refusing to spare us another glance as he strides back inside. I watch him retreat, taking a piece of my broken heart and the other half of my soul with him. But now isn't the time to confront him and untangle this mess. Beth needs me, and she's my number one priority.

"Come on, Beth, let's get out of here," I murmur. We gather our beach bags and make our way to the elevator, descending to Beth's apartment one floor below. Inside, we slump on the couch, enveloped in a heavy silence. After a few moments, I glance at Beth. She's still pale as a ghost, her breaths heavy and her body trembling.

"Here," I say softly, rising from the couch to grab a throw pillow. "Lie down, Beth." I guide her gently, helping her settle her head on the pillow. Grabbing a blanket from the armchair, I cover her before heading to her room to find something we can both change into. Thankfully, Beth and I are similar in size. I slip into a pair of sweats and pull a T-shirt over my bikini and grab a set for Beth as well. As I'm about to head back into the living room, the doorbell rings and a surge of hope spikes in my chest.

"Put these on." I thrust the clothes into her hands and dash to the door. I swing it open it in a flurry, and my heart sinks to see Kev standing there, his expression unreadable. It was stupid to hope Dameon would be on my doorstep.

"Dameon wanted you to have your purse and your personal items," Kev says, handing over my handbag and an overnight bag.

"Kev, I don't know what he's told you, but I'll explain everything when I work out what's going on. I'll make it up to Dameon," I promise.

"It's not my place to get involved, ma'am," he responds, avoiding my gaze.

Ma'am.

Tears well up in my eyes at the thought of disappointing Kev and Martha. They've been like parents to us during our time here. Beth and I have grown close to them, and it hurts my heart to know they're hurting as well.

What have I done?

"The rest of your belongings will be delivered tomorrow," he adds. "Dameon would like you to vacate the apartment by the end of the week." Finally, he meets my eyes, and I see sympathy shining back at me. I could cry at the kindness I find there.

"Can you deliver a message for me? There's been a huge misunderstanding," I plead.

"I can't, I'm sorry, love. He won't listen to me anyway."

"Okay, thanks, Kev." I squeeze his arm and shut the door. I drop my forehead against it, closing my eyes to hold back the tears. I don't even know where to begin.

First things first: Beth. I turn around to find she's changed and back under the blanket on the couch. Making my way to her kitchen, I grab a soda. She needs sugar to pull her out of whatever shock she's in. I sit on the edge of the couch and hand her the can. She cracks it open and takes small sips.

How on earth did she end up in this situation? Was I so consumed by Dameon that I overlooked the possibility of her sneaking off with someone? If that's the case, then Dameon was right. I'm no better than my mother. I've failed her, and I've failed myself. I'm a terrible substitute for a mother. Closing my eyes, I exhale deeply, making a promise to myself that I won't let her down again. I'll support her no matter what and help her through this. Is it even safe for her to fall pregnant so soon after major surgery?

"Are you feeling better now?" The color in Beth's cheeks is gradually returning.

"Yeah, I'm okay. Just felt a bit dizzy." She sits up, places the soda on the coffee table and wraps the blanket around her shoulders. "Sheesh, that was intense."

"You can say that again."

"I didn't know you two were in a relationship. When did that start?"

"Only a few weeks ago. But it doesn't matter now," I sigh.

"Why didn't you tell me?" she asks, hurt evident in her tone.

"I honestly don't know..." I trail off, rubbing my forehead. Any excuse I can think of would sound pitiful. "Like I said, it doesn't really matter. We've got bigger things to deal with at the moment." I give her a weighted look, which she promptly ignores.

"Is what he said true? Did you really send Mark stuff about Dameon's business?"

"It's complicated, Beth."

"What's complicated about it? You either did or you didn't!"

I shake my head, exasperated, and flop back onto the couch.

"I'm not a kid anymore, Hailee. You can tell me what's going on."

"No shit, especially when you're out having sex and getting pregnant. Safe to say the chapter of your childhood is now firmly closed."

"What are you talking about?!" she shrieks, dropping the blanket from around her shoulders and turning to face me. "I'm not pregnant! I thought *you* must be!"

"What?! Are you serious? I need you to be a hundred percent honest with me." I look her dead in the eye. "Are you pregnant? Because, Beth, this is not the time to joke around."

"I'm. Not. Pregnant." She punctuates each word with a pause, and I take in the confusion on her face. "When the hell have I had time to go out and meet someone, anyway? I've been focused on my rehab. And unlike you, I would tell you if I met someone," she adds, giving me a dirty look that hits its mark. I drop my head into my hands, feeling like shit.

"Wait a minute, if you're not pregnant"—she eyes me warily, and I shoot her a "what do you think" look—"then who does the pregnancy test belong to?"

"Fucked if I know," I mumble, dropping my head back into my hands.

Chapter Thirty-Three

Dameon

Ignoring the buzzing of my phone, I flip it over, face down, on the bar.

"Are you going to answer that?" James asks.

"Nope." My chin is resting on my linked hands on the sticky bar as I stare blankly at a TV playing AFL rematches. A nearly empty bottle of cheap whiskey sits beside me on the bar.

He blows out a breath. "Are you coming into the office today?"

"Nope."

"Well, you need to do something. Starting with a shower, 'cause you fuckin' reek."

He's right. I've been here since yesterday afternoon, rooted in the same spot at the bar, only moving when I need to take a piss. The bartenders have left me alone to wallow in my misery, and for that kindness, they're going to receive a hefty tip. James joined me around midnight, and we've been shooting the shit all night, getting wasted.

He picks up my phone and shoves it in my face. "Answer your damn phone."

I ignore him and return my focus to the TV. James checks his Rolex and sighs. "We've got a meeting with New York this morning, I assume you're not coming?"

"Nope."

"Alright, I'll handle it. I gotta go and shower, then," he says, standing up and stretching out his back. "You should do the same," he adds pointedly. "Seriously, Dameon..." He waits until I turn my head to look at him. "Go home, shower, sleep it off. I know you're fucking pissed. I would be too. But you need to speak to her. Don't make the same mistake I did."

"Mmm," I grunt, still fixated on the TV.

"If I remember correctly, you once told me not to be a fucking idiot. Now I'm returning the favor. But this time, actually listen to me, and don't repeat my mistakes."

"I'm not that stupid." The corner of my lips tilts up.

James slaps me on the back. "Good, I'm outta here." He throws a couple of notes on the bar before leaving.

He's right; I should go home and sleep this off. I'm too drunk to think about it anymore. I scrub a hand down my face, feeling crushed by exhaustion. Picking up my phone, I open the unread messages, scrolling through a series of texts from Hailee. They range from *We need to talk* to *Please, don't do this* and *Dameon, call me back.*

The latest text that just came through is longer than the others:

Hailee

Since you're being a stubborn jerk and won't talk to me, you've left me no other choice. I. AM. NOT. PREGNANT. I don't know why that pregnancy test was in our bathroom or who it belongs to, but it's not mine. I'm telling the truth. I'm NOT Mia. I would never try to trap you or manipulate you like that. You know ME.

I type back my response.

Me

I thought I did. But I also thought I knew Mia. How do I know you're telling the truth? That this isn't just another lie?

The text bubbles instantly pop up:

Hailee

It's the truth. If I have to pee on a stick in front of you and take a blood test, I will.

Me

Water sports and needle play ain't my kinks.

I exit our chat and mute our conversation. Then I dial the number of the only person who I know can help me through this.

"Good morning. It's Dameon Hayward and I need to see Dr. Edward Avery today. It's urgent."

Chapter Thirty-Four

Hailee

"Where does this go?" Cora asks, balancing a sizable box in her arms. I glance at the label on the side and point her in the direction of my bedroom. Cora has been an absolute saint this past week, helping us with packing and moving.

As instructed, we moved out of Beth's apartment to a charming two-bedroom unit in Bronte, a few beaches down from Bondi. Having lived near the water for several months, we wanted to stay close by. We also decided to end the lease on our house, both of us adamant that we didn't want to return. Going back there would have felt like taking a step back, and we're both eager to push ahead into new beginnings.

"This is the last box," Beth declares, striding into the apartment and kicking the door shut behind her. Our new home, while nowhere near as lavish as Dameon's, has its own charm. Nothing will ever compare to that level of luxury, but this cute, bohemian beach shack is more than enough for us.

I check my phone once more: still no text from Dameon. After his stupid "kink" text, I responded with *Don't be a dick*. Which was followed by twenty-four hours of silence until finally, a more serious message: *I need time and space*. His mature response brought a wave of relief, giving me hope that we might eventually be able to have a proper conversation about what went down with Mark.

So, time and space are what I'm giving him, even though it's tearing me apart. I've lost count of how many times I've begun composing a message, only to swiftly delete it before hitting Send. My phone has become my constant companion; I check it a thousand times a day in anticipation of a message announcing he's ready to talk.

Sliding my phone back into my pocket, I work on easing the knots in my neck.

"Okay, where do you want to start?" Cora says, emerging from my bedroom.

"My room. I've got a ton of homework to finish this afternoon," Beth responds.

Four hours later, after setting up the two bedrooms, bathroom, and living room, Cora and I find ourselves sitting on the floor of the kitchen, quietly unpacking a box of pots and pans.

"You doing okay?" Cora asks, studying me.

"Yeah, I'm fine, I suppose. I just really want to clear the air with Dameon. I miss him," I admit.

"Give him the space he's asked for; he'll come around."

"I know, I'm trying to. It's so hard though," I reply, placing my hand on my stomach to settle my nerves. This past week I've been so anxious that I've made myself physically sick. Remembering how furious he was, the pain and betrayal radiating from his eyes, makes my stomach churn.

I hate that I've hurt him like this.

I bolt upright with a gasp, my heart hammering against my ribs like a trapped bird. My hands reach for my throat, clawing at an invisible belt tightening around my neck, restricting my airway. As my eyes fly open, I'm momentarily disoriented, my mind struggling to piece together the fragments of reality. Gradually the unfamiliar room comes into focus, and I realize that I'm alone in my new bedroom. With a heavy sigh, I sink back onto the mattress.

Grief is a sneaky ninja, creeping into every nook and cranny of your life when you least expect it. It doesn't just mess with your feelings; it messes with your body and mind, too. Whether you're mourning the loss of a loved one or saying goodbye to a relationship, grief remains a constant, always lurking around.

It's something that everyone will experience at least once in their lifetime, but it hits each of us in its own unique way.

During that first brutal week after Dameon threw us out, anguish racked my body like a storm, leaving me drained and defeated. Anxiety and the raw ache of loss combined, making it impossible for me to hold anything down. Nausea became my unwanted sidekick. As the days wore on, the anxiety started to ease, but the weight of sadness and the longing of missing Dameon hung over me like a dark cloud, a constant reminder of the hole he left in my life.

Night after night, sleep slips through my fingers, chased away by relentless nightmares. They're like twisted reruns of that fateful scene by the pool, playing out in my mind with eerie precision. I'm trapped in a macabre loop, watching different versions of the same horror show unfold before me, each one more unsettling than the last.

In one, I'm reaching out to Dameon, pouring my heart out, and seeking comfort in his arms. But in another, he's wielding that fucking pregnancy test like a dagger, stabbing me with it right in the heart. My subconscious has become my worst enemy, a twisted playground for all the emotions swirling inside me, crafting vivid and sometimes downright disturbing scenes of my grief and longing. It's a constant tango of agony and despair, every night a new battlefield where I wrestle with the beautiful memories of our time together and the uncertainty of our future.

Going back to sleep is impossible at this point, so I reach for my phone, the dim glow of the screen illuminating the dark room. My heart skips a beat when I see a text from Dameon waiting for me. With a surge of adrenaline, I sit up, brushing aside the stray strands of hair clinging to my forehead.

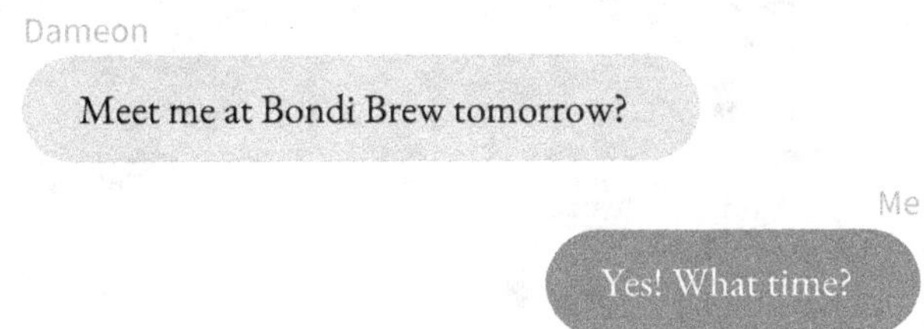

His response comes almost instantly, and I glance at the time. It's two in the morning. Obviously, he's not sleeping either.

Clutching the phone to my chest, I release a sigh of relief. It's been two weeks. Two weeks of relentless torment, each day dragging on with agonizing slowness as I've patiently waited for this moment—the chance to speak with him face to face. I only hope it will bring an end to the nightmares and provide me with some semblance of peace. Dameon's absence has left a gaping hole in my heart so wide, I fear nothing could bring the pieces back together again.

Chapter Thirty-Five

Dameon

"Double shot latte," the waitress announces, placing the steaming cup in front of me. I flick the sugar stick, tear it open, and pour it into my coffee.

"Thank you," I say curtly, dismissing her.

"Is there anything else I can get you?" She bats her overly long, fake lashes. Her thick, painted-on black eyebrows and splotchy fake tan make her look like she could use a good scrub in the shower. When will women learn that most men prefer natural beauty?

"I'm good, thanks," I say.

"Well, if you change your mind..." She winks and saunters back behind the cash register.

I sip my coffee and focus on what I'm going to say. I've being doing a lot of soul-searching these past few weeks. It's killed me to have no contact with Hailee. Going cold turkey and cutting her out of my life was a lot harder than I thought it would be. I'm glad she respected my wishes and didn't contact me, but it stung at the same time. I was craving a fix of my human ball of sunshine. Dr. Avery said that I needed time and distance to calm down and look at things rationally. So, I took his advice. But damn, did I miss her. Badly.

"Hey." Hailee slides into the chair opposite me, looking beautiful as always, her face fresh and the tips of her blonde hair still wet from the shower. Her sundress is short and cute, just like her.

"Morning."

She smiles, but there's a hint of sadness in her eyes, which are shadowed by dark circles that suggest sleepless nights. *Welcome to the club.*

"How are you doing?" I ask.

"Been better." She shrugs.

Being in her presence is bittersweet. It hurts, yet at the same, I crave more.

"Don't I know it," I say. I feel sorry for her, but at the same time, she brought this upon herself. She did this to us. "You wanted to talk, so here I am. What is it that you wanted to say, Hailee?"

She takes a deep breath and places her palms on the table. "I am *not* pregnant. You believe me, right?"

She looks into my eyes with such sincerity, how can I not believe her?

"Your stepfather was *overjoyed* about the news," I tell her.

"Wait, Mark told you that?" she asks.

"He came to see me that afternoon to share the *wonderful* news of your pregnancy, and to fill me in on how the two of you have been scheming behind my back. I thought he was lying at first, just trying to get under my skin. But when I found that pregnancy test, well..."

"Oh my God. I can't believe him!" She looks ready to murder someone. "I have no clue how that pregnancy test ended up there, but it's definitely not mine, or Beth's."

"Okay... I believe you."

She sighs and mumbles "thank fuck" under her breath, which makes my lips twitch.

"Can I get you anything?" the waitress interrupts, glaring at Hailee.

"I'll have a green tea, please."

"Hold on, can you bring her a breakfast burger too?" I add.

Hailee pitches an eyebrow.

"You look like you need it," I explain.

When the waitress returns with her pot of tea and breakfast, she inhales it like a seagull, and my lips twist to the side to smother my smile. I'll always care for her, no matter what. But that pregnancy test is niggling at me. If it's not Hailee's, someone inside my home was setting her up.

"Let me explain about that slimy bastard, Mark," Hailee says, wiping her mouth. "There has only ever been one piece of communication between us. And I can assure you, if I ever was pregnant, he'd be the last person on earth to know. I can't stand that prick," she adds. "But I did betray your trust, Dameon. And I'm so, so sorry. If I could take it back, I would. All I sent him was a photo of your calendar, outlining one of your meetings. There was no scheming behind your back, no spying, no grand plan to ruin you, certainly not on my part."

"And what did you think he would do with that information?" I ask incredulously. Mark wasn't going to sit idly on that intel and not use it to his advantage. She must have known that.

"I don't know! But I didn't think it could be used to bring down two mergers. It was just one photo!"

"Show me the photo."

"What?"

"Show me what you sent him."

She reaches for her phone in her handbag, scrolling through the messages before handing it over. I look through their conversation as she scrambles to explain.

"When you offered me the position, I made a deal with Mark, as backup. It was stupid, I know that now, but I agreed to send him any information I could find about your company, just in case our deal didn't work out. I didn't know you then, not like I do now. The thought of you going back on your word is preposterous. But back then, I didn't know that. And I had to put Beth first."

It's clear from their texts that their relationship isn't what Mark made it out to be. It's more like restrained animosity at best. I reach the photo of my calendar, spanning a two-week period from a few months back. It shows the first company merger meeting, but not the others. It's not enough intel to sabotage two mergers, barely even one. There's no detail about our offer, just the company name and our intention to take over. Mark would need a lot more to derail our mergers, which means he must have another source. This isn't anywhere near as bad as I had imagined... but still. I skim through the rest of the conversation and see he was pushing for more info, which she refused.

"He threatened you," I state after I finish reading the last text message he sent her. "Why didn't you tell me? I would have handled him."

"I don't know," she says with a small shake of her head. "I guess I didn't think I had anything to lose, now that Beth has her heart. But I was wrong, so very wrong. I ended up losing the trust of the most amazing man I've ever met." Her eyes fill with tears and she tries to blink them away. "Can you forgive me for being so stupid?"

When she looks at me like that, I can't deny her anything. I love her. Was what she did stupid? Absolutely. But she didn't cost us billions like I thought, and she wasn't acting out of spite or running some grand scheme or manipulation. She wasn't sleeping with me for information. She was used by a powerful and conniving man, and she did what she thought was necessary for Beth. I can't blame her for that.

"Of course I forgive you," I murmur with a sad smile. Tears roll down her cheeks, and I fight the urge to lean over and wipe them away. The relief that pours off her is palpable.

"Thank you." She scrunches her eyes shut. "When he said he would ruin me, and that I would regret it, I didn't know this is what he had in mind." She chuckles through a choked sob and reaches for a napkin to wipe her nose.

"It's never what you expect," I offer in consolation. I should know.

"So, where do we go from here?" she asks softly.

I close my eyes briefly, then meet her hopeful stare.

"I don't know, Hailee. I forgive you; I really do. But this whole situation has hit me hard. It brought back all the crap I went through with Mia. I felt like I was back at square one, spiraling out of control. I can't go through that again. I need some time to process everything and move on. It wouldn't be fair to you if we just jumped back into things if I'm still holding on to what happened. I don't want to resent you or hold a grudge. That's not how I want us to be. I care about you too much for that. I love you, but if I can't get past this, then I need to let you go."

Her gasp lands like a punch to the gut, and the hurt written all over her face is clear to see. It's like watching her heart shatter into a million pieces right before my eyes. And my heart feels just as ruined, ripped from my chest and bleeding out in her hand.

"Give me time. Can you do that for me?"

She nods. "I'll wait as long as it takes for you to find your way back to me." More tears spill from her eyes. Unable to resist this time, I lean over and gently cradle her head in the palm of my hands, wiping away her tears with my thumbs.

"I'll do my best to come back to you," I say. "I promise."

CHAPTER THIRTY-SIX

I miss you.

Three simple words, yet they possess the power to breathe life back into my soul. For an entire month, I've waited for this, waited for any sign that he still cares.

Staring at Dameon's text message, I feel more alive than I have in a long time. A smile creeps across my face, shattering the numbness that has accompanied me for weeks.

I have no one to blame but myself. I played with fire, and I ended up singed beyond recognition. Each day blends into the next, and I move through them mechanically. I shower, I eat, I work, but I'm only half present. I'm alive, but I'm not truly living.

Even though the nightmares still haunt me, they're not as frequent as before. I don't wake up in a nightly cold sweat; now, it's only a weekly occurrence when my soul reaches out and yearns for its missing half.

As I stare at those three words illuminated on my screen, my heart races with excitement, a spark of joy pushing through the suffocating fog of depression at last.

All this from three little words.

I spend far too long contemplating what to write back. I draft several responses, but in the end, I delete them all and settle on something simple, leaving the conversation in his hands.

Me

I miss you too.

His reply is swift.

Dameon

I have an offer for you. One you'll find hard to refuse. And no, not in a "dead horse head in your bed" kind of way. Interested?

Cute, Mr. Hayward. Okay, I'll bite.

Me

What's your proposition?

Dameon

Meet me at Eden for Le Jardin tonight.

Not what I was expecting, but I don't really care where we meet as long as I get to see him.

Me

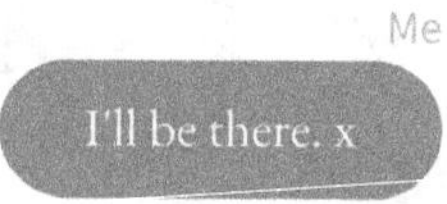

I slide my phone back into my desk drawer, my shoulders bunching in excitement. Little does he know, I'm already at Eden, sorting through a backlog of applications. Curious, I pull up the member list for Le Jardin tonight and find Dameon's name on it. *When did he get added?* He wasn't on the list this morning when I checked the schedule. I browse through the goddesses' names and am surprised to find my own name listed there as well.

The office door swings open, and in walks Madame Sophia, her long red hair pulled back into a tight ponytail that sways behind her.

"Oh, good, you're here already." She looks me over, and her red lips curl up in a satisfied smile. "Well, well, well. Welcome back, Ms. Mann. Nice to see you've rejoined the land of the living."

I roll my eyes and playfully stick out my tongue at her. Childish, I know, but I'm feeling almost giddy.

"Did you add me to Le Jardin tonight?" I ask.

She nods. "I did. Dameon called in a favor this morning, asking for both of you to be added to the list. You know I don't make changes to the schedule once it gets locked in, but I can't stand to see you walking around with the weight of the world on your shoulders any longer." She perches on the corner of my desk and crosses her legs. "You're totally killing the vibe around here."

"Sorry to be a bummer," I drawl.

"Just get back together already and save everyone from witnessing your bleeding heart. It's depressing as fuck."

I burst out laughing. I didn't realize I was such a buzzkill.

"I've made sure he's first up tonight. The last thing we need is for you to be chosen by another client." Her eyes practically hit the ceiling as she shakes her head.

"Thank you, Sophia. You have no idea what this means to me."

"Of course I do. Why do you think I did it?" She smiles warmly and saunters out of my office with a sway of her hips. I glance at the clock: Two hours until we open, four hours until Le Jardin. I blow out a nervous breath. Waiting is all I seem to be doing lately, and I'm over it. Time has made me her bitch once again. But it ends tonight.

Bring it on.

I kneel naked, my spine straight, knees spread, and head lowered. A position of complete submission, just like the other goddesses on stage with me. It's been well over a year since I took part in Le Jardin. When I first started here, I was eager to participate every week. The pay was good, and it satisfied my needs better than random hook-ups that always left me wanting more. But after a while, the novelty wore off, and I lost interest. I only participated when I knew Dameon was on the list, as he would always choose me. Over time, I preferred to take on an administrative role and help to guide new goddesses in this industry.

That break from the spotlight must be why my heart is hammering now. Nervous anticipation swirls around me, enveloping the entire stage. It's an addictive sensation. Knowing that Dameon is in the crowd, watching me, adds to the excitement. I hear Madame Sophia stepping onto the stage to take over my role and make the introductions. A few moments later, when she announces the commencement, Dameon's polished black shoe appears in my line of sight.

"Let's go, kitten." The rumble of his voice hits me hard, and it takes everything I have not to burst into tears. It's been so long since I've heard the rough timbre of his voice. How I've yearned to hear those words whispered in my ear. He holds out his hand, and I rise from my knees. He links his hand with mine, and we walk off stage together. All I want to do is raise my head and look into his eyes, to search them, to see whether he missed me just as much as I've missed him.

We enter our suite, and he leads me over to the large bed in the middle of the room. I start to relax; I've always felt safe in here with the mood lighting, plush black, red, and gold furnishings, and the little chill-out area with a TV and couches.

Dameon drops my hand and lifts my chin with the crook of his finger. "Look at me, kitten."

Raising my head, I'm blown away by the emotion swimming in his sea-green eyes.

"Sir, I—"

He scrunches his eyes shut as if it hurts to hear my voice and presses his lips to mine in a desperate kiss, silencing me. All thoughts melt away, and I fall into his embrace, consumed by him once again. I struggle for breath as our tongues battle and meld together. It's intoxicating; if I could, I'd happily lose myself in this man's kiss for the rest of my life.

Dameon abruptly pulls away, his eyes still tightly shut. He spins me around and bends me over the foot of the bed, pushing my knee onto the mattress to open me up. The sound of his belt buckle clinking fills the room, and I arch my back, searching for friction. I'm so wet that when he runs a finger from my clit down my slit, he hisses.

"Fuuuck..." I moan loudly.

"Shh, no talking, kitten." He spanks my left cheek with force, causing me to jolt forward, and pins me to the bed by the back of my neck. Relief floods through me when the head of his cock rubs back and forth over my slit, gathering wetness. But this time, when he slowly pushes in, it feels different.

God, I'm so full.

I whimper, my body trembling to accommodate his size. It's been too long since he's sunk himself into me.

"You can take it, kitten. A few more inches to go."

Trying to relax my muscles, I arch my back further, allowing his cock to slide deeper. It feels never-ending, like he'll end up in my throat.

"That's it. Good girl," he praises.

When he's seated to the hilt, the head of his cock reaches a spot deep inside me that causes me to climax instantly. He doesn't move, and doesn't allow me to either, keeping me pinned beneath him. The feel of his suit against my sensitive skin adds to the sensation, and my core repeatedly clenches around his cock, milking his length. The orgasm is so powerful that tears form in my eyes.

"Look at you, kitten. Soaking my cock like my good little whore. And I haven't even fucked you yet."

I gasp, trying to catch my breath, but he doesn't allow me any time to recover before he roughly pounds into me, making me tighten up from the force.

"Relax," he whispers in my ear, still holding me down by the back of my neck. When he feels my muscles loosen, he lets go, holding nothing back, and punishes my pussy with full force. I bite my tongue to hold back my scream and take everything that he gives me. I can't move to meet his thrusts; I just brace and focus on keeping my body as relaxed as possible. He doesn't last long at this pace. He explodes with a roar, and I remain still, letting him pulse inside me. But when he pulls out, the usual rush of cum doesn't arrive. I roll onto my side to face him and find him bent over, panting hard, his eyes shut. I look down at his cock peeking out of his suit pants; he's wearing a condom.

Oh.

When his eyes eventually find mine, remorse twisting his face, my stomach drops.

No. No. No. Don't do this.

"I'm sorry."

His apology crashes around me, and I almost collapse in disbelief. I shake my head. Denial tightens its grip, robbing me of my voice.

He kisses me gently on the forehead, his eyes scrunched shut. Then he tucks himself back into his pants, condom still on, and heads for the door.

"Please, don't do this," I choke out, tears streaming down my cheeks.

He swallows roughly, shakes his head and closes the door behind him.

CHAPTER THIRTY-SEVEN

Dameon

The whiskey burns its way down my throat, the familiar warmth settling in my stomach. I'll need all the help I can get tonight. Because tonight marks the end, the final nail in our coffin.

I'm constantly drawn to this place, like a moth to a flame, all because of *her*. Hoping for just a glimpse as she moves about the bar, mingling with patrons, serving drinks. It's starting to feel like a cruel ritual, and I'm beginning to resent it. But tonight, it's over. It has to be.

I had thought our final fuck at Le Jardin last month would be enough to get her out of my system, but it only made it worse. It's as though she's carved out a spot in my heart. Dr. Avery would be furious with me if he knew what I'd done. The devastation on Hailee's face as I walked away will haunt me forever. I'll replay the sight of her broken expression in my mind for the rest of my life.

I had hoped time would ease the fear of betrayal embedded deep in my bones. But it hasn't. It lingers, a constant presence.

I want to trust her, I do. She holds my heart, my body, my soul. Yet, that niggling doubt that sits in my gut like a tapeworm, burrowing deeper, refuses to let me have what I want: *her*. Rebuilding trust isn't as simple as I thought. Despite confronting the pain in my past, I'm unable to move forward. I have no idea if I'll ever trust Hailee, or any woman, again.

It wouldn't be fair to keep her hanging, clinging to false hope. She deserves the chance to move forward too. Even though I walked out on her at Le Jardin, she hasn't let go—Cora keeps me informed. It's time for both of us to move on.

Hailee glides into the lounge, effortlessly commanding attention as she steps onto the stage to begin the introductions. Her black gown does little to hide the swell of her tits and the faint outline of her nipples. I down the last of my whiskey, swishing it around my mouth and swallowing it in one smooth gulp.

"Good evening, gentlemen…" I let her familiar introduction fade into the background, focusing instead on absorbing every detail. This will be my last visit to Eden, and I'm determined to imprint her image on my memory. Her lips, naturally pouty and soft; her long white-blonde hair, glittering like snow under the subdued lighting; and those radiant emerald eyes, sparkling brightly.

"It's time to commence your selection." Hailee's soft voice pulls me from my thoughts. The token in my hand is marked with the number eight—almost last in line. One by one, men walk onto the stage, each choosing a goddess.

When it's my turn, I stroll to the front of the room with a hand in my pocket, in no rush for this moment to end. Each step brings us closer, yet it's also a step closer to the expiration of *us*. When our eyes meet, what shines back at me nearly brings me to my knees: understanding, compassion, regret. She knew I'd be in Le Jardin tonight; my name would've been on the register. I smile, hoping to convey how I wished things were different. Her expression, filled with love, only makes this moment that much harder.

I tear my eyes away and gesture to the nearest goddess—it doesn't matter who I choose, they're all the same if it's not my kitten. Without looking back, I lead the goddess to suite eight. *It's time to move on.*

Shutting the door behind us, I lean against it and blow out a deep breath. In front of me is a beautiful brunette, naked and kneeling in the middle of the bed, waiting for me. But she's not the one I want. Not even my dick is on board. I stare at her, ready and willing to serve me, but there's no movement whatsoever. Zilch. My cock knows it's not Hailee and it's punishing me. It only wants that leggy blonde, my bubbly ball of sunshine. *I get it dude, I get it.*

Closing my eyes, I sigh and tilt my head to the ceiling. *What the fuck am I doing?*

The words tumble out before I can stop them. "Listen," I hear myself say, "this isn't going to work. Sorry."

Chapter Thirty-Eight

Hailee

What are you doing? I type.

I need a distraction. After seeing Dameon choose another goddess and leave with her, I'm desperate to drown my sorrows. Thoughts of him kissing her, touching her, loop through my mind, making my stomach churn. I get why he did it; I'm not angry, just really fucking sad. When did love stop being enough? It's utter bullshit.

Even though he shattered me last month when he chose me and walked away, my stupid little heart still clung to hope. Living in this perpetual state of limbo can't be healthy for me. I'm driving myself crazy. It's time to let go.

My phone dings.

Cora

What do you think I'm doing? It's 11 p.m. I've got a kid attached to my tit.

I "heart" her message and toss my phone into the locker, strip off my dress and pull on a pair of shorts and a tank top, along with my trusty flip-flops. Clients would be shocked to see the state we arrive and leave in—usually in our most comfortable, ugliest sweats, hair bundled up in a messy bun. Grabbing my handbag, I head home, ready to wallow in misery for the last time.

A gentle knock sounds at the front door, and I open it to see Cora holding a bottle of Fireball and two tubs of my favorite cookie dough ice cream.

"Did I wake Beth?" she whispers.

"Nah, you're good. Come in."

We cozy up on the couch with a blanket, the whiskey, two glasses, and spoons, the familiar comfort of *Seinfeld* reruns playing in the background.

"So. What happened?" Cora asks, forcing the lid off her ice cream tub.

"Dameon was in Le Jardin tonight. And he picked Michelle," I say in one breath, and shove a spoonful of cookie goodness into my mouth, followed by a shot of Fireball. Mixing cinnamon whiskey with dairy might not be the wisest idea, but I honestly don't give a shit right now. That's tomorrow's problem.

"You're joking!" Her jaw drops open, her spoon paused halfway to her mouth.

"Nope." I pour two shots and pass her one. "I want to make a toast. Tonight is the last night I'll cry, bitch, and moan over Dameon Hayward." I hold up my glass and clink it against Cora's.

"Damn right!" she exclaims.

The whiskey goes down smoothly before the heat inevitably travels back up my esophagus. I wince and wipe the back of my hand over my mouth.

"I need to move on. I can't be stuck here, pining over his ass forever, when he's out fucking other women. He's not ready to let go of his past, and he may never be."

"I really thought he would get his shit together," Cora says, shaking her head.

"Me too," I reply.

"Come here." She scoots closer, wrapping her arm around me, and I lean my head on her shoulder. "I've told you this before, but I'll tell you again. You're a smart, hella sexy woman who's not only compassionate but has the kindest heart I know. And, word is, you can suck dick like no other," she adds, and we burst out laughing. "Seriously though, Dameon is dealing with his own demons; it's no reflection on you. You deserve someone who's willing to go to hell and beat down their demons for you. And who won't come back up until the job is done."

I chuckle at her analogy and wipe the few tears that have escaped from the corner of my eyes. She's right. I deserve better.

"I know you love him. But your emotions are not a light switch that you can easily turn on and off. So, if you do think about him after tonight and mourn the loss of him, don't be so hard on yourself. Give yourself time."

Her words sink in, and I understand where she's coming from. I do love him. And I still have feelings for him; I always will. But as I sit here with Cora by my side, I silently vow to myself that after tonight, I'm back, baby. No more being a shell of who I was, no more waiting with my heart in my throat for him to come back to me or desperately checking my phone for his call or text.

I'm done.

CHAPTER THIRTY-NINE

Hailee

"**I**'m here to meet Dr. Aiden McKamey," I say, greeting the hostess with a confident smile.

Today, I'm feeling unstoppable. I'm rocking a sleek black power suit, with bold red lips that match the soles of my stilettos. I'm ready to take on the world.

"Right this way, your guest has arrived." Grabbing two menus, she leads me to a table where the esteemed Dr. McKamey is waiting for me. I suppress the urge to squeal with excitement. I want him to take me seriously, therefore fangirling over him is not going to cut it.

"It's an honor to meet you, Dr. McKamey," I say, eagerly shaking his hand. "Thank you so much for taking the time to meet with me; I'm very grateful. I have to admit, I'm a bit starstruck." A nervous chuckle slips out.

The doctor's smile crinkles the corners of his eyes. With his rounded stomach, white hair, and beard, he resembles a charming, teddy bear version of Santa.

"It's wonderful to meet you, Hailee. Please, call me Aiden."

I reluctantly release his hand and settle into the booth across from him. The five-star restaurant is bustling with entrepreneurs and corporate types engaged in lunch meetings and negotiations. It's the new hot spot of the city, the place to see and be seen. *Dameon probably comes here all the time.* And that thought can fuck right off.

"When Sophia called and mentioned she had someone dying to meet me, I was intrigued. It's not every day a young, beautiful woman like yourself wants to hang out with someone like me," he says with a laugh.

"Are you kidding? I've read all your books and dissertations. I've been a huge fan for years. I'm really grateful to Sophia for setting this up. She's been looking out for me and my sister since we arrived in Australia."

"She's a good woman, and I could never say no to her. She's been a close friend of my wife's for years."

"Thank you. I'm incredibly appreciative of your time."

I take a deep breath. Dr. McKamey is a luminary in the field of psychology, revered for his sharp intellect and contributions to the community. I've avidly followed his work for years and of course, I've stalked his social media. While he's gained influencer status with a substantial following, he never takes it for granted—he utilizes his platform to empower people to become better versions of themselves. He's also a professor at the University of Sydney, overseeing its highly regarded psychology degree. And that's why I'm here.

"What can I help you with, Hailee?"

In this moment, everything feels perfectly aligned, as if I'm exactly where I'm meant to be. It's the start of a new chapter in my life—as long as I don't blow it.

"I've been reflecting a lot lately, trying to figure out the path I want to carve for myself," I begin. "Your work has been incredibly helpful to me. I've seen several psychologists and therapists over the years, and I still value regular check-ins—ongoing maintenance, if you will." He nods, encouraging me to continue. "I owe much of my progress to the support I received. Your work has been a huge inspiration to me as well. I want to pay it forward and help people confront their traumas, empowering them to thrive no matter what may have happened to them in the past. We all have trauma to varying degrees, and it takes time and effort to acknowledge it and not let it affect our present or future. My dream is to study psychology so I can help others heal."

"That's wonderful, Hailee. I can tell you're passionate about this, and coupled with your empathy, and what Sophia tells me is a formidable intellect, you're destined for great things in this field. If you harness the full force of your brain, there's no limit to what you can achieve." He pauses. "I'd be happy to be your mentor if you're open to it?"

"Really?" I squeal, my palms pressed together. I had hoped to pick his brains for guidance on navigating this industry and charting the best way forward. But what he's suggesting is beyond my wildest dreams. A mentorship with him is like winning the lottery. I'm certain thousands of students must compete for the opportunity to have him as their mentor.

"Yes, I'd be delighted to help. If you're serious about study, I'll arrange a meeting with the university's entrance board. Our psychology course is considered the best in Australia. You'll need to come prepared with any previous university transcripts, a résumé, and a letter of recommendation. It wouldn't hurt if you've done community service work as well."

"Oh my goodness. Thank you so much!" I shake my head, placing my hands on my cheeks to cool them down. I'm flushed—I never get flushed.

His phone begins to ring and he pulls it out of his jacket pocket, lighting up when he sees the caller's name. "I'm sorry, I need to take this," he says. "My daughter is pregnant, and it's almost her due date. Do you mind?"

"No, not all. Please, go ahead."

He nods his thanks and steps away.

I take the opportunity to compose myself, still barely able to believe my luck. I had an undeniable feeling of being in the right place at the right time when I arrived here today. It's all coming together: I'm finally doing something for myself. Not for Beth, not for my clients. For me.

Being a psychologist is probably similar to being an escort, I muse. I'll still be providing emotional support and connection—except I'll be keeping my clothes on. Fanning my flushed face, I glance around the restaurant looking for Aiden. A loud cackle of women laughing draws my attention to their table.

My eyes go wide, and I slowly lower my hands to the table, freezing in place. Every muscle in my body goes still as my brain struggles to comprehend what I'm seeing.

The three women at the table are beautifully made up, their plumped faces animated in conversation. As one finishes her story, the others cheer and clink their champagne flutes together. It looks like a regular ladies' lunch—except that these women, who shouldn't know each other, are laughing like lifelong friends.

The world around me blurs, and my vision goes black around the edges as I narrow in on the table. The only thing I can hear is the steady thud of my heartbeat in my ears. As the pieces of the puzzle fall into place, I release a rush of breath, followed by a sharp intake of oxygen.

Suddenly Aiden appears in my line of sight, cutting off my view of the table.

"Are you okay, Hailee?" he asks, his bushy white eyebrows pinched together.

"Yes, I'm fine. Sorry, did you say something?" I manage to recover, swallowing roughly.

"I was just saying that I've got to head off; my daughter is in labor." He's still holding his phone in his hand, and his smile is infectious at the prospect of being a grandfather.

"Oh, congratulations!" I force a smile, though I doubt I'm fooling anyone, especially someone as perceptive as Dr. McKamey.

"Are you sure you're okay?"

"Not really, but I will be." I blow out a breath and nod.

"Alright, then. I am sorry I can't stay, but I'll call you soon with the meeting details."

"Thank you again for your support; you have no idea what this means to me," I garble, my mind firmly planted on the women across the restaurant.

"Take care, Hailee. I'll be in touch." We shake hands, and he disappears out of the restaurant.

Should I leave? Should I stay? Or should I go over there and confront them? A server interrupts my musings. "Would you still like to order, ma'am?"

For fuck's sake. I need a minute of uninterrupted silence to wrap my mind around this.

"Yes, thank you." I open the menu and frantically scan the first page, selecting a dish at random. I don't care what it is, as long as she pisses off and leaves me alone. In a way, she's made my decision for me. I can't simply leave without ordering something, it would be rude, especially in a five-star restaurant. And sitting here like a weirdo without eating or drinking is out of the question.

"And to drink?" the server asks.

Kill me now.

"Coke, please." I smile politely and hand over the menu, reminding myself she's only doing her job.

As soon as she leaves my head snaps back to the women's table. Their entrées have arrived, but they've barely touched them—they're too busy chatting.

What the fuck is happening?

A fourth woman appears and sits down, and it's then that I realize there was an unoccupied seat with a half-drunk champagne and a napkin neatly folded on the table. She must have been in the bathroom. Though I don't recognize this woman, there's a nagging sense of familiarity about her. While I know the other three women well, there's something about this newcomer that I can't quite put my finger on. I discreetly take out my phone and snap a quick picture of the table and send it to Cora.

Me

Do you know this woman in red?

I tap my fingers on the pristine white tablecloth as I await her response. Minutes pass, and she still hasn't even seen the message, leaving me on Unread. *Come on!*

Me

THIS IS AN EMERGENCY!

Cora

Okay, relax. I'm not attached to my phone like you are. What's going on? Another rando stalking you?

Me

DO YOU KNOW HER?

Cora

Can't see shit, it's too blurry. Get a better shot of her face.

I roll my eyes.

Me

I can't exactly shove my phone in her face. Hang on...

A plan forms and I turn around in the booth seat with my back toward their table, pretending to take a selfie but aiming the camera at their table. I hold the position, trying to appear casual, but the longer I wait, the more I look like a complete poser. Finally, the woman turns her head, offering me a clear shot. *Gotcha!*

Me

This better?

Cora

Yes, I do know her! That's Piper. She works in finance at Hayes & Hayward. Why? What's happening?

Heat shoots up my neck. I'm so furious that I'm surprised steam isn't billowing from my nostrils like a raging bull. Every fiber of my being trembles with rage.

Me

> I'll explain later. Do you know where Dameon is at the moment?

Cora

> I assume he's with James - they're sealing a deal on a merger today. Let me check with Portia where it's taking place. I'll let you know.

God, I wish I knew what the women were saying. I'd give anything to be a fly on their champagne bucket. My heart pounds, and I close my eyes, willing myself to calm down. Now that the pieces have fallen into place, I'm seething with anger at myself for not figuring it out sooner—for not questioning things earlier. While I wait for Cora's response, I pull up Kev's number on my phone and begin typing out a message.

Me

> Hey Kev, it's Hailee. Did my mother ever come visit while I was living with Dameon? This is super important - it could affect Dameon.

I add that last part knowing how loyal Kev and Martha are. They'd never do anything to betray his trust or hurt him. They practically raised him.

While I wait for his response, my meal arrives. I don't remember ordering the pasta, but whatever. I dig in, and after a few bites I realize I must look absolutely ridiculous. If this weren't so serious, I would laugh at myself—shoveling spaghetti into my mouth, hunched over my plate, eyes narrowed on a table across the restaurant. I've officially hit psycho status.

My phone pings, and I snatch it up.

Cora

> They're at their office. Merger taking place at 2 p.m. I also sent Portia the photo, she confirmed it's Piper. She mentioned her sister works for Dameon?? What the hell is going on? I'm freaking out!

Fucking Maddy!

That's why she looked familiar. They both have that whole "high-class hooker" look going on, even though hookers don't actually dress like that.

A notification from Kev pops up on the screen, but I flick it away so I can respond to Cora.

Me

> Can't talk right now, I'll explain later.

Now, what's Kev got for me.

Kevin

> Yes, ma'am. Your mother came over, and Maddy confirmed you approved her access.

What a bunch of bitches. The voice of Lonny, the Uber driver from *Office Christmas Party*, sounds in my mind. I don't know why my brain conjures up movie quotes at the weirdest times—it's gotta be a stress response.

I have to hand it to her: my mother is a force to be reckoned with. She's certainly resourceful. Slipping my phone back into my purse, I consider my options.

The temptation to confront them is strong, and the scene in *Mean Girls* where Cady goes primal and attacks Regina in the cafeteria flits through my mind. I'm tempted... but it's not my style. Just moments ago, I was speaking with my idol about how much therapy has helped me become a better version of myself. Attacking a group of women in a five-star restaurant would hardly prove my point.

Taking a few deep breaths, I toss some cash on the table and stand, pushing my shoulders back and tilting my chin. I refuse to give them the satisfaction of seeing me defeated. With each step I summon a confidence and swagger I didn't know I possessed. Exaggerating the sway of my hips and wearing a bright, beaming smile, I approach the women with an air of nonchalance, as if I don't have a care in the world—as if they didn't conspire to ruin Dameon and me.

"Hello, ladies, fancy seeing you all here!" I greet them with my sweetest smile, relishing the shock that crosses their faces. "Enjoy your meal, because you never know… There might not be too many more fancy lunches in your future," I add casually, with a flirty wink directed at my mother, Maddy, Piper, and Rachael. With my head held high and their stares burning into my back, I walk out of the restaurant.

God, that felt good!

I wish I had the time to gloat but I need to reach Dameon as fast as possible. Outside, I hail a taxi and breathe a sigh of relief when one pulls over immediately. Sliding into the back seat, I instruct the driver to take me to the Hayes & Hayward Media building. It's only a few blocks away, so it should take no time at all, but just in case I don't make it, I pull out my phone and dial Dameon's number. The call goes to voicemail. I hang up and silently will the taxi to move faster. They can't walk into that merger unprepared—they're about to be blindsided again.

We're one block away when the traffic slows to a standstill. I quickly pay the driver and jump out of the car, immediately regretting my choice of heels for the day. The skirt of my power suit restricts my stride, but I push forward, determined to reach Dameon before it's too late.

I realize this won't change anything between us, but he needs to know what happened, and he needs to know *now*. With each step, urgency builds within me. He needs to postpone the merger and come up with a different strategy. I refuse to be the reason for him losing another company and potentially billions of dollars. The building looms ahead of me and I search for the nearest crossing. It's about a quarter of a mile behind me, which means I'll have to double back.

Fuck that.

I look left, I look right. And I dash across the road, looking up at the skyscraper that the man I loved and lost owns. I'm nearly on the other side when my left heel snags in the gutter grate. Panic shoots through me as I try to yank it free, but the heel remains stubbornly stuck. I look up just in time to see a car hurtling around the corner toward me.

Fear paralyzes me; somehow, the car seems to speed up. I tug harder but my heel remains firmly stuck. Realizing there's no sense in dying over a shoe, even if it is a Louboutin, I pull my foot free from the stiletto and fling myself onto the safety of the sidewalk.

The passage of time once again distorts. My senses sharpen and every detail plays out in high definition. I see the car rushing toward me, its driver wide-eyed in panic. I see the shimmer of sweat on his brow. I see his pupils dilate, swallowing up the color that surrounds them. I see the car inexplicably mount the curb before me.

In that split second, my body tenses, bracing for impact, and my mind races with succinct thoughts—it's not my life flashing before my eyes, but rather the stark realization that this is it. I'm going to be hit.

A sharp pain shoots through my leg, and I swear I hear Dameon call out my name. My eyes flutter shut and my mind conjures up his smile and his beautiful dimples. With that vision lingering in my mind, one last thought filters through a haze of unconsciousness.

I always knew my laziness would get me killed one day... I just didn't think it would be today.

Chapter Forty

Dameon

Sharp nails rake through my hair, scratching my skull in a strangely comforting rhythm. It feels amazing, almost hypnotic, and when it abruptly stops, I groan in protest. Then it hits me like a bolt of lightning, and I jolt upright. Blinking away the fog of sleep, I wipe the drool from my lips with the back of my hand and find myself staring into a pair of bright emerald eyes—the eyes that belong to other half of my soul.

"Hey, sleepyhead." Her cheeky smile strikes me right in the chest.

"You're awake!" I exclaim. "How long have you been awake for?"

"Not long... You looked so peaceful sleeping."

"You should have woken me." I haven't left her side since that bastard hit her with his car. I was on my way back from lunch with James and our senior management team when I saw Hailee—and then the car. I roared her name so loudly that the entire street froze, but it didn't stop the car from plowing into her. I ran to her as fast as I could, the fastest I've ever moved in my life. My heart stopped, and as I fell to my knees beside her, fear unlike anything I've ever experienced had me in a chokehold—the fear of losing the love of my life.

Someone had the presence of mind to call an ambulance, and I suspect it was James because I remember seeing his mouth moving, but I couldn't hear a word of it. My mind had deserted me, hiding from the *what ifs* that threatened to overwhelm me—*what if I hadn't been a coward, what if I didn't let her go, what if she... dies.*

She looked peaceful with her eyes closed, as if she were simply asleep. I wanted to cradle her head in my lap, but I was too afraid to touch her, terrified of making her injuries worse. I haven't left her side since they lifted her into the ambulance.

I must have nodded off while waiting for her to regain consciousness. "How do you feel?"

"Like I've been hit by a bus and not by a Ford," she replies with a chuckle.

"You're incredibly lucky. Other than a broken leg and a concussion, you're relatively unscathed. I saw the whole thing; you have no idea how close you came to dying." My voice trembles slightly as I recall the terrifying moment.

She looks down at her leg in the cast. "That's all, a broken leg?" she asks.

"And a concussion," I add.

"I feel a hell of a lot worse than that."

"Your body's been battered and bruised. It'll take time for you to heal."

"What on earth happened? Why did he try to run me over?"

I rub my hand over my mouth and chin and exhale heavily. "He didn't. The man driving was having a heart attack."

"For fuck's sake," she mutters, closing her eyes briefly then instantly opening them again. "Is he okay? Did he survive?"

I shake my head.

"Shit." She winces. Her eyes suddenly widen. "Oh my God, I totally forgot what I was doing there. I was on my way to see you!"

"Me?"

"Yes! That's right... I was on my way to warn you that your merger was going to fall through, because I found your mole. It's Piper!"

"How do *you* know that?"

"Wait, you knew already?"

"Yeah, we figured out she was being paid by Mark. We were going to trap her at the merger. How the hell did you know?"

"I saw her having lunch with my mother, Rachael, and her sister—Maddy. My bitch of a mother must have been behind the whole thing, including the pregnancy test."

Un-fucking-believable. I shake my head.

"To be honest, I hadn't fully realized how unstable Rachael was," I admit. "She came to me with a marriage proposal, suggesting that we make it a business arrangement, and offered her father's company as collateral. I refused, of course. Then she sweetened the deal by offering up the mole in my company. So I played dumb and pretended to accept, and she gave up Piper just like that." I snap my fingers.

"Oh my God," she murmurs.

We lapse into a comfortable silence, both lost in our own thoughts as we process everything. But I don't want to waste any more time.

"I missed you, gorgeous," I whisper, picking up her hand and pressing my lips to her skin, lingering for a moment to breathe in her scent. "Watching you get hit by that car, I was petrified I had lost you before I even had the chance to have you. I've tried to move on, I really have. But I couldn't. The thought of being with anyone else made my skin crawl. I've wasted a lot of time running from my past, and I don't want to waste another second. I'm done running. And I'm done pushing you away." My voice breaks. "If you'll still have me, and I'm not too late."

Her eyes well with tears, but she graces me with one of her heart-stopping smiles.

"You're not too late. I've been waiting for you."

CHAPTER FORTY-ONE

Hailee

There's something surreal about being back where we started almost two years ago. Instead of pouring rain, we watch white, fluffy snow fall delicately onto the sidewalk from our position near the restaurant window.

It's January, and Dameon has whisked me away on his private jet to celebrate Christmas and New Year's Eve in New York. I hadn't experienced a white Christmas since Beth and I moved to Australia, and I didn't realize how much I'd missed it. My memories didn't do it justice; it's magical. All I can remember from my youth is murky white sludge. But this... this is something else. The pure white crystals blanket the ground, and I can barely tear my gaze away from it.

"Beautiful, isn't it?" I say, mesmerized.

"It sure is," Dameon agrees, his gaze searing into me.

I smile, recalling the time on his penthouse balcony when we watched the sun set over the ocean, and he said those exact words. I remember secretly hoping that he was referring to me.

Despite telling myself *this is just a job,* I knew right from the start that his sweet words would be my undoing.

"Who would have thought we'd be back here together, years later," I muse, shaking my head as I take in the décor of the Madison Avenue restaurant.

"In fact, I think I was sitting at this very table," Dameon says, looking around, trying to gauge the layout of the restaurant.

"Yeah, with your fiancée Rachael," I mutter dryly.

He chuckles and runs a hand down his face. "What a psycho."

"You can say that again." I nod in agreement, although I feel a pang of sympathy for the woman. After she gave up Piper, Dameon immediately backed out of their marriage agreement. He had no intentions of following through with it, and when she eventually realized he would never return her feelings, she broke down. She needed help, which, ironically, I could have provided her. I'm halfway through my psychology degree with the best mentor in Australia, and I'm incredibly lucky. I only wish Rachael had sought the help she desperately needed; it could have saved her a lot of unnecessary pain.

Unfortunately, we couldn't tie my mother or Mark to paying off Piper, so they walked away unscathed. I'm still working on forgiving them—for myself. I'm a firm believer in practicing what you preach. But Dameon has made it very clear that he would neither forgive nor forget. And honestly, I can't blame him.

Maddy and her sister, Piper, were promptly fired, and Dameon sued them both for breach of contract. He wanted to go after them further, including my mother and Mark, and was tempted to reach out to his "acquaintances" again. But I managed to convince him otherwise. Revenge might be sweet but I knew deep down it wouldn't bring us any peace.

Last I heard, Jacob was behind bars after being charged with the rape of a minor. I don't know how Dameon's "acquaintances" did it, and to be honest, I don't want to know, but there was no sweeping it under the rug when it was splashed all over media outlets. It made huge international news that the wealthy oil heir was behind bars. And from what Dameon has mentioned, it didn't take long for Jacob's fellow inmates to dole out their own brand of justice.

"And I was sitting right over there"—I stifle a yawn as I gesture toward the table on the opposite side of the restaurant—"the first night our paths crossed outside of Eden... And I'm glad they did."

It was also the night that marked the beginning of a new chapter for Beth. She's now at university, living the full life she always deserved. She's eighteen and an adult, and I'm confident I've raised her to navigate this sometimes complicated and hard life. That doesn't mean I'll ever stop worrying about her—she's my Betty Boo—but my job is done, and I'm proud of her, and me.

"Me too." Dameon leans over and presses his lips to mine, his tongue teasing me. His kisses have always been able to make me lose my head and forget where I am.

The clink of plates interrupts us, but the rich aroma of the black truffle tagliatelle I ordered turns my stomach and I suck in my breath.

"What's wrong?"

I wrinkle my nose. "Wanna swap?" I suggest, eyeing his rare wagyu beef.

"Sure." We exchange plates, and I'm glad to get the smell out from under my nose.

"You okay?" Dameon asks.

"Yeah, just tired, I think." Our New York getaway has been exhilarating, filled with Dameon's thoughtful surprises, and I've loved every minute. But sometimes, he forgets we're not teenagers backpacking through the US. My energy levels are not the same as they once were.

"Don't worry, I'll take it easy on you tonight." His flirtatious wink sends a spark straight to my core, making me squirm in my seat.

My back crashes against the window of our bedroom overlooking Central Park. Dameon cradles my head in the palm of his hands, sucking my lower lip into his mouth and pulling.

"Wait," I mumble, pushing at his chest. He's like a hungry animal, and if I don't pry him away from me, he'll devour me whole. When he releases me, I run my tongue over my swollen lip, savoring his taste. His eyes are a deep shade of stormy sea green. My favorite. "Can you get me some painkillers first? I've got a massive headache."

"Of course, gorgeous." He kisses me on the temple and heads into the bathroom.

A moment later he returns, his eyes narrowed, breathing heavily. "Are you pregnant?"

His words hit me like a thunderbolt, triggering a surge of pure panic, throwing me back to that fateful day by his pool.

"No! I would've told you if I were," I retort, trying to steady my racing pulse.

Are we really doing this again?

His features smooth out and he graces me with one of his dirty smirks, complete with those gorgeous dimples.

"The thought of a little piece of me growing inside you? It's got me harder than steel, kitten." He grabs his length through his slacks and palms it.

My jaw practically hits the floor. "Seriously? You want children? Since when?" I'm caught totally off guard.

"Since I realized they'd be yours." His expression doesn't change as he closes the distance between us, slowly stalking toward me like the king of the jungle. "Come here, kitten." The smooth timbre of his voice promises exquisite pleasure in the next few hours. Without a doubt, I'll be full of his cum before dawn breaks.

And I'm here for it.

Want to read more? Sign up to Jade's newsletter to receive a super-HOT additional scene from the yacht. Simply scan the QR code below.

About the Author

Jade May is an international bestselling author of angst-filled, high-heat romances laced with kink—where the tension runs deep, the chemistry runs hot, and happily ever after is always guaranteed.

Jade is also an advocate for people with disabilities and those suffering from chronic illnesses. She has been featured in several major Australian media outlets speaking about the power of romance fiction to help people with disabilities awaken their sexuality and cope with chronic pain. Inspiring others to embrace their desires and live their best lives through her fiction is a dream come true for Jade.

Jade lives in sunny Sydney with her two favourite humans: her husband and son.

Connect with Jade

Sign up to Jade's newsletter for the latest news on releases, giveaways and previews of covers and exclusive book art!

www.authorjademay.com

@authorjademay